"Goddamn, somebody's embalming technique needs work."

Whirling, Kane saw the lid of a sarcophagus slowly rising, pushed up from within. The stench of purification increased almost exponentially, and even as he watched, his autorifle raised, gnarled brown fingers curled around the edge of the lid.

Flesh crawling with revulsion and a mounting horror, Kane felt rooted in the mire of a nightmare. The ripping sound of Decard's Sin Eater on full auto broke the spell of terror threatening to engulf Kane's mind. He whipped his head around, as Decard fired a steady burst at the approaching figure. By the strobing flame licking from the pistol's bore, Kane saw a withered, wizened shape with dried, dark limbs like dead wood, showing through moldering, ragged bandages.

The figure shambling from the burial chamber was a mummy, and Kane's reason recoiled from the sight, his breath seizing in his lungs. The fusillade tore strips from the animated cadaver's body, the impacts turning it this way and that, but still it shuffled forward.

Other titles in this series:

James Axler
Outlanders

MASK OF
THE
SPHINX

A GOLD EAGLE BOOK FROM
WORLDWIDE®

TORONTO • NEW YORK • LONDON
AMSTERDAM • PARIS • SYDNEY • HAMBURG
STOCKHOLM • ATHENS • TOKYO • MILAN
MADRID • WARSAW • BUDAPEST • AUCKLAND

First edition August 2004

ISBN 0-373-63843-4

MASK OF THE SPHINX

Special thanks to Mark Ellis for his contribution to the Outlanders concept, developed for Gold Eagle.

And did you talk with Thoth, and did you hear
The moon-horned Io weep?
And know the painted kings who sleep beneath
The wedge-shaped Pyramid?

Lift up your large black satin eyes which are
Like cushions where one sinks!
Fawn at my feet, fantastic Sphinx! And sing me
All your memories!

—Oscar Wilde

The Road to Outlands—
From Secret Government Files to the Future

Almost two hundred years after the global holocaust, Kane, a former Magistrate of Cobaltville, often thought the world had been lucky to survive at all after a nuclear device detonated in the Russian embassy in Washington, D.C. The aftermath—forever known as skydark—reshaped continents and turned civilization into ashes.

Nearly depopulated, America became the Deathlands—poisoned by radiation, home to chaos and mutated life forms. Feudal rule reappeared in the form of baronies, while remote outposts clung to a brutish existence.

What eventually helped shape this wasteland were the redoubts, the secret preholocaust military installations with stores of weapons, and the home of gateways, the locational matter-transfer facilities. Some of the redoubts hid clues that had once fed wild theories of government cover-ups and alien visitations.

Rearmed from redoubt stockpiles, the barons consolidated their power and reclaimed technology for the villes. Their power, supported by some invisible authority, extended beyond their fortified walls to what was now called the Outlands. It was here that the rootstock of humanity survived, living with hellzones and chemical storms, hounded by Magistrates.

In the villes, rigid laws were enforced—to atone for the sins of the past and prepare the way for a better future. That was the barons' public credo and their right-to-rule.

Kane, along with friend and fellow Magistrate Grant, had upheld that claim until a fateful Outlands expedition. A displaced piece of technology...a question to a keeper of the archives...a vague clue about alien masters—and their world shifted radically. Suddenly, Brigid Baptiste, the archivist, faced summary execution, and Grant a quick termination. For Kane there was forgiveness if he pledged his unquestioning allegiance to Baron Cobalt and his unknown masters and abandoned his friends.

But that allegiance would make him support a mysterious and alien power and deny loyalty and friends. Then what else was there?

Kane had been brought up solely to serve the ville. Brigid's only link with her family was her mother's red-gold hair, green eyes and supple form. Grant's clues to his lineage were his ebony skin and powerful physique. But Domi, she of the white hair, was an Outlander pressed into sexual servitude in Cobaltville. She at least knew her roots and was a reminder to the exiles that the outcasts belonged in the human family.

Parents, friends, community—the very rootedness of humanity was denied. With no continuity, there was no forward momentum to the future. And that was the crux—when Kane began to wonder if there *was* a future.

For Kane, it wouldn't do. So the only way was out—way, way out.

After their escape, they found shelter at the forgotten Cerberus redoubt headed by Lakesh, a scientist, Cobaltville's head archivist, and secret opponent of the barons.

With their past turned into a lie, their future threatened, only one thing was left to give meaning to the outcasts. The hunger for freedom, the will to resist the hostile influences. And perhaps, by opposing, end them.

Chapter 1

The Archuleta Mesa, New Mexico

Decard didn't know whether he was still alive through sheer happenstance, divine intervention or simply a judicious management of time. At the age of seventeen, with the new badge of the Magistrate Division still gleaming brightly on the molded left pectoral of his body armor, it was easy to believe in the latter.

But even if one of the factors he attributed to keeping him alive had been absent during the near total destruction of the Archuleta Mesa facility almost two months before, he knew he would have either been buried under tons of rubble or reduced to a handful of ash.

In the minutes preceding the devastation, Decard's commanding officer, Crowe, had dispatched him to the far side of the installation, on what the young Mag had initially considered a grunt's errand—to help unload a shipment of food. On one hand, he had resented being given such a menial job, but on the other, he eagerly awaited the chance to eat something other than the MREs he and the other new badges had subsisted on. The ration packs were nutritious, but their taste was vile beyond description. Therefore, he didn't dawdle on his way.

Decard had just reached the entrance to the storage facility, a cave cut into the base of the mesa, when the roof fell in—literally. The world turned into a carousel of searing heat, and a torrent of falling stone gave him a concussion that bowled him off his feet. When his senses returned, he saw how the passageway he had just strode through was clogged with tons of debris. Death had missed him by inches.

Even now, two months after the disaster, Decard wasn't altogether certain of its cause. Opinions offered by survivors of the Mag security force varied, but the consensus seemed to be that the installation's power source had suffered a catastrophic failure. Regardless, no one disputed that a wave of smashing, scorching force had swept through the facility. If not for a series of vanadium alloy blast shields, the entire mesa could have been obliterated.

Decard wasn't satisfied by the explanation, but he knew better than to ask Crowe or any of his fellow Mags for further information. Duty at the Archuleta Mesa was of the highest priority; therefore, so was the keeping of its secrets. Early on, Decard realized he had to know in advance what questions to ask and when, and of whom, to ask them. The people he definitely knew not to question were the small, delicate-featured personnel who were the permanent residents of the installation.

He had no idea who or even what they were. None of the security force dealt with the strange people directly. The Mags were segregated from them, although each of the four sec squads had a designated intermediary who conveyed their orders.

Before the destruction of the facility, Decard had only caught glimpses of the strange people. All of them possessed slender, almost childish builds, large domed heads and huge, slanting eyes staring out of faces that seemed all brow ridges and cheekbones. He had seen a couple of the males walking around with plastic tube-shaped holsters strapped to their thighs. At least he assumed they were males—it was hard to differentiate the sexes at first glance, since both the men and women wore one-piece unisex garments of a dark, metallic weave.

Only in the days following the disaster did Decard learn the people were called hybrids, and that they were linked in some mysterious, but very important way with the nine barons. He also learned most of the hybrids had perished in the explosion that ravaged the installation.

After the catastrophe, the relationship between the human personnel and the few surviving hybrids became, out of necessity, much less segregated, but still coldly formal, one of superior and subordinate. Crowe cautioned Decard that as far as he was concerned, there were no differences between the hybrids and Baron Samarium himself.

Among the many casualties the hybrids suffered were their children, and it became part of his daily duty to care for the tiny, helpless creatures.

His black, polycarbonate helmet tucked under an arm, Decard strode down a dimly lit corridor toward the makeshift nursery. Although electricity had recently been restored to this particular section of the facility, complete rebuilding would require years. He had heard rumors that rather than try to repair the extensive damage, the installation would be salvaged of anything useful and transferred to a new location.

Decard hoped he wouldn't be among those transferred. Profoundly shaken by the impact of his own mortality, he wondered obsessively about how long he would survive, before death finally closed the few inches by which it had missed him the first time.

As Decard turned a corner, he saw a female hybrid digging through a tangle of coaxial cable and a scattering of electronic components. Her compact form was encased in a silvery-gray skintight bodysuit. He immediately recognized her fall of silky, blond-white hair and huge, upslanting eyes of a crystal blue.

"Where are you going, Magistrate Decard?" Quavell asked. Her tone, though crisp, held an undercurrent of a soul-deep weariness.

He ducked his head deferentially. "On my way for the daily patrol. I thought I'd stop by the nursery first and see if I could offer any help."

"No," she replied flatly. "Your help is not needed this day. Continue to your assigned duty."

Decard felt a jolt of anger at her autocratic manner, but also experienced a twinge of admiration for Quavell, too. At five foot ten, he towered a full head and shoulders above her and in his body armor he probably outweighed her by a hundred pounds. He ran a hand over his close-cropped sandy-blond hair, and his brown eyes met her direct gaze without blinking.

She displayed not the slightest fear of him. Her face, although all angles and curves, held an unearthly beauty slightly off center from the human standard. But Decard sensed Quavell's differences from human women went far deeper than looks.

He started to move on down the passageway. "If it's all the same to you, I'll stop by and see for myself."

Quavell said curtly, "No. You must leave this area immediately."

"Why?" he asked.

She drew herself up, tilting her head back at a haughty, arrogant angle. "Do not question me. Do as you are told, Magistrate Decard."

He opened his mouth to protest, but she declared sharply, "I forbid you to visit the nursery."

Surprised by her vehemence, he averted his gaze. "Very well."

The young Magistrate continued on his way, seething with resentment. At a corner, he paused, then backtracked a dozen yards before entering an ancillary corridor. It required only a few more minutes for him to reach the nursery by that route. Before he entered, he glanced back in Quavell's direction and said in a whisper, sneering, "Go fuck yourself. Nobody else will."

The huge room was filled with transparent plastic boxlike cribs. The cribs had no lids. Within the transparent cubes lay hybrid babies, ranging in age from newborn to four months old. All were naked and lying listlessly on excrement-stained foam pads. Red, naked bulbs hanging from extension cords shed an eerie illumination in the chamber. He saw no attendants, either human or hybrid. Normally such a lack of personnel would have struck him as odd, but he had already seen the perfunctory kind of care given to the children.

Since his first day pulling nursery duty, Decard found it unconscionable how no one attempted to give the sickly youngsters any sort of special care or attention. He removed a bottle half-filled with formula from a warmer and moved silently between the rows of cribs until he reached a particular one.

A tiny naked girl child stared back up at him with her huge golden eyes. The child's stomach was bloated from malnutrition, and her ribs pushed against the thin skin covering them. Somehow she found the strength to lift her small arms toward him.

Decard murmured, "Hello, little Gem. How are we today?"

He picked up the baby, feeling shock as he always did at how frail she felt in his hands. He held the youngster as if she were made of porcelain. The infant leaned into his armor-plated chest and sucked weakly on the bottle he was holding. Not once did her eyes leave his face as she fed.

For a reason Decard couldn't fathom, he had established a special bond with this particular baby. She never cried and her expression was always characteristically inscrutable, but he sensed a rapport with the child, so much so he had christened her Gem, but he never spoke her name when anyone else was present.

The bottle empty, Decard placed the youngster back inside the crib and started to turn away. To his surprise she held on to his hand, wrapping her small fingers around his thumb, refusing to let go.

"Sorry, little Gem," he said quietly, "but I have patrol duty to pull."

Gently he pulled her fingers from his thumb. The infant stared up at him and Decard forced himself to turn away from her, feeling his throat constrict. He took two steps toward the door when he heard the murmur of voices from the passageway beyond.

For a couple of seconds he considered marching out as if he had every right to be there, but when he recalled Quavell's words, he cut diagonally across the nursery and slid into a storage closet, closing the door behind him. He waited for a minute, not even breathing, then he carefully opened the door a half an inch.

Peering out through the crack, he glimpsed two male figures wearing identical bell-sleeved robes of gold brocade. One of them wore a tall, conical headpiece with a back-curving crest and the brim ringed by nine rows of tiny pearls. Both men were so similar in appearance they might have been twins. Their builds were the slender, gracile type of the hybrid, but they were several inches taller than most Decard had seen, perhaps five and a half feet tall. Both of their faces were sharply planed, with finely textured skin drawn tight over prominent cheekbones.

Both men shared the same close-cropped, wispy blond hair. Only eye color differentiated the two faces. The man wearing the headpiece had eyes like damp pieces of obsidian, while the other man's held the milky-blue color of mountain meltwater.

Decard realized instantly the reason behind Quavell's insistence that he not visit the nursery. She knew in advance of the visit of the two barons. Icy hands seemed to grip his limbs, holding him immobile. Cold terror stole over him, and he clenched his teeth to keep them from chattering. Sweat sprang to his forehead.

Decard had never dreamed he would see a baron. He understood that personal audiences with barons were exceedingly rare and conducted with great ceremony and secrecy. Part of his mind knew that maintaining a baron's mystique was contrived, an intimidation strategy, and an old psychological gambit. But still, the baronial oligarchy ruling the nine villes was more than the governing body of postnukecaust America—they were god-kings, serving as a bridge between predark and postdark man, the avatars of a new order.

The two barons spoke quietly. The one wearing the headpiece went from crib to crib, touching the infants as he did so. Decard leaned against the door and tried to listen in on what was being said.

"—suffering from malnutrition and vitamin deficiencies," one of the barons said in a musical, lilting voice.

As they moved farther into the nursery, the words spoken by the barons became fainter and fainter. Decard couldn't make out what they were saying and he opened the door a few inches more.

Suddenly the baron in the headpiece swept his arm in a wild wave around the room and the small cribs. "They have not seen this!" he cried angrily. "We of the hybrid dynasty are doomed if we do not seek outside aid. And it doesn't appear as if any will be forthcoming from the Archon Directorate. If necessary, we must circumvent the oligarchy and find other allies."

The baron's obvious anguish drove Decard back into the closet, pulling the door shut. He knew if his presence was discovered, if it was even suspected he had overheard the baron's private conversation, his life was forfeit.

"Inconceivable as it may seem," the angry baron continued, "the humans who caused this tragedy are now the only ones who can save us from it."

Decard held his breath and waited to hear more. He strained his ears, but no sound reached him. After a minute, he nudged open the door. The nursery was empty except for the cribs and the infants. The barons were gone.

Moving swiftly and quietly, he left the nursery. He didn't encounter anyone in the corridor, and he was glad of that. He didn't want anyone to see the turmoil and confusion the barons' words had awakened in him.

Reaching an L junction in the passageway, he saw Crowe pacing back and forth impatiently.

By way of a greeting, Crowe demanded, "Where the hell you been, kid? We've got reports of a perimeter breach on the southern quadrant. Outlanders, most likely. Dregs, probably."

Crowe was a tall man with a burly, bearlike physique, a craggy and weathered face and dark blue eyes. His black hair showed streaks of gray. A senior hard-contact Magistrate of Ragnarville, he claimed to have been a friend of Decard's father. Although Decard's father had served in the Division, he wasn't sure of Crowe's claims of friendship. Still, the older man had taken a paternal interest in him since his assignment to the mesa.

Falling into step beside Crowe, Decard said, "I hope this report turns out to be something substantial, for once. I'm damn tired of chasing what turns out to be jackrabbits or horny toads."

Crowe smiled bleakly. "We're all tired, Decard. But

getting this station back up and running is our top priority. When we're transferred back to the ville, we can get all the rest we need there."

The corridor opened up into the main garage. Vid spy eyes affixed to brackets on the ceiling recorded every move, every entrance and exit, or Decard assumed they did. He wondered if the interior security network really was up and running.

Parked in the cavernous chamber were several vehicles, including a hover tank, Land Rovers and several armored Sandcats. The garage was illuminated poorly by overhead naked lightbulbs that cast a feeble glow over worktables, tools, chain vises, band saws and drill presses.

Crowe led the way to a Sandcat with its gull-wing doors open and the engine purring quietly. The Sandcat's low-slung, blocky chassis was supported by a pair of flat, retractable tracks. The gun turret, concealed within an armored bubble topside, held a pair of USMG-73 heavy machine guns. The hull's armor was composed of a ceramic-armaglass bond.

Crowe climbed in behind the wheel, securing the safety harness around his polycarbonate-encased torso. Decard took the seat beside him and Crowe engaged the gears, gunning the engine. The Sandcat picked up speed as they approached the double vanadium doors. Decard glanced nervously at the Magistrate behind the wheel and then back at the rapidly approaching doors.

Crowe cast a sidelong glance at the younger Magistrate and chuckled. Just when Decard thought that they were going to crash, the huge multiton doors began to slide into recessed slots. The entrance to the facility was carefully camouflaged, using the natural terrain. The wag sped through the doorway and onto the desert floor of New Mexico.

Decard couldn't resist glancing back. The Archuleta Mesa loomed sheer above the harsh, dry sands, a monstrous monolith of stone nearly five hundred feet high. Deeply scarred and furrowed by ages of erosion, it brought to mind an image of an enormous tombstone, marking the grave of dead aeons.

The Sandcat's clattering treads carried it easily over thorny scrub brush and scatterings of stone. The sun was just starting to settle behind the horizon when they left the perimeter of the facility. Already the desert was cooling down and with it came a refreshing breeze. Crowe and Decard rode for several minutes in silence.

Decard leaned his head back and closed his eyes, figuring that it would be the perfect time to catch a few winks. One thing he had learned during his four years of training with the Magistrates was to take sleep where and whenever it could be found. He felt himself drifting off in a light doze.

"Hey, kid," Crowe growled and swatted him on the shoulder. "Wake your ass up. We're almost there."

Decard rubbed his eyes, feeling the sting of lack of sleep. "We are? That was fast. How far out were they?"

"About forty-five miles."

Decard felt his eyebrows rise. He blurted, "But we only left the facility a few minutes ago." Then he noticed it was pitch-black outside the Cat. Crowe was relying on the vehicle's thermal-imaging module to drive.

"You've been asleep for over an hour," Crowe grunted.

Decard was too embarrassed to respond to the statement, so he asked a question instead. "Any idea how many we're going up against?"

Crowe nodded, never taking his eyes off the terrain before them. "Outer sensors indicate about a half dozen approaching."

"A quick sweep then, huh?"

A thin smile creased Crowe's lips. "That's the plan. Drop them fast and then return home with the carcasses."

A chill hand of suspicion stroked the base of Decard's spine. "With the carcasses? What the hell for?"

Crowe shrugged. "Hard-contact Mags make hard contact, ask no questions. It's been a standing order for a couple of months—any and all trespassers are to be killed and their bodies returned to the mesa."

Decard nodded as if Crowe's dismissive response satisfied him. Instead, his suspicions grew.

Suddenly, Crowe braked the Sandcat to a stop. "All right, kid, unleather, lock and load. Let's do this. Try for head shots."

Pushing open the vehicle's gull-wing door, Crowe

unbuckled his harness and climbed out. Decard followed him, overwhelmed by the total silence of the desert night. Back at the facility, there was always noise of some sort, whether it was the constant thrumming of electrical generators, the clangor of repairs or just the snores of his fellow Magistrates. He found the lack of ambient sound disconcerting. Tilting his head back, he glanced up at the constellations glittering cold, white and impersonal in the vast tapestry of the sky.

Crowe took the point, holding his Sin Eater in his right hand, bore pointed skyward. No sound but the careful footfalls of the two men disturbed the brooding quiet. Decard let Crowe get a dozen feet ahead before he flexed his wrist tendons. The weapon slid smoothly into his hand.

Many years of patrolling the Tartarus Pits, as well as the Outlands, taught Crowe to move as silently as a ghost. Decard wasn't quite as proficient as the elder Magistrate. His movements seemed clumsy and untrained in comparison.

They crept through the darkness for nearly ten minutes before Crowe snapped up his fist and sharply brought it down. Decard stopped instantly, watching the older man carefully climb the face of a low dune. At the crest, he held up his left hand, five fingers splayed. A moment later he held up two fingers. The simple signal told Decard that they were facing seven opponents.

In a crouch, he climbed the dune and scanned the

rough terrain ahead and a little below them. Through the light-intensifying visor of his helmet, Decard discerned the seven figures moving slowly across the desert, about twenty yards away. Six appeared to be human adults, while he figured one was a child, due to its small stature. The distance was too great and the light too poor to tell the sexes apart, or even if they were humans, muties or Dregs.

Crowe tapped Decard on the shoulder with the forefinger of his left hand, then ran the same finger across his throat. He then patted the ground. The younger Magistrate knew that he was to stay put and not make a sound. He nodded as Crowe touched his chest and drew a semicircle in midair, indicating that he intended to circle around the seven travelers.

Crowe wanted to catch the outlanders in a classic pincer trap. The slaughter would be over almost before the last outlander knew what hit him or her. The senior Mag moved silently into the desert night, a shadow blending with other shadows. Decard tracked him, not moving a muscle as the seven figures moved toward his position. None of them spoke. The only noise was the steady scuffing of feet against the rough dirt of the desert floor.

As the people drew closer, Decard saw that the group consisted of four males and two females. The smallest one had to have been a child, but he was unable to discern the sex. They were dressed in typical outlander rags, scavenged from ruins or put together from odds and ends of cloth bartered from traders. The males all carried crude knives made of hammered strips of metal that were tucked into the loose strips of fabric around their waists. They glanced around warily.

Decard held his breath as Crowe suddenly appeared in front of the group, as if disgorged by the gloom. He stroked the trigger stud of the pistol, and a triburst ripped into the band of outlanders, dropping two with head shots and knocking another one off his feet, folded around a belly wound.

As the sound of the full-auto fusillade still rang through the night air, Decard stood and leveled his Sin Eater at the outlanders. Killing defenseless people, although it was his duty and what he had been trained to do, rubbed the young Magistrate the wrong way.

The hand cannon belched thunder and flame as round after 9 mm round smashed into the reeling bodies of the outlanders. There was no chance for the people to defend themselves, or escape the cross fire. In mere seconds six of them writhed on the ground, dead or dying.

"Check the bodies," Crowe ordered, keeping his gun trained on the victims.

Decard complied, climbing from the crest of the dune and swiftly crossing the rough ground. All but two of the outlanders were dead, their vital organs having been messily pulped by multiple bullet strikes.

"Two of them are still breathing," he said, noting silently they appeared to be norms, neither muties nor Dregs.

Crowe nodded in satisfaction. "They'll do. Put the survivors down. Head shots."

Decard felt his throat constrict as he glanced down at one of the wounded. She was probably in her late twenties, maybe early thirties, and would have been beautiful if her face hadn't been covered with blood streaming from a scalp wound. A kneeling girl-child clutched at the woman's limp hand, gazing up at Decard with wide but fearless gray eyes. Her long hair was the color of the sand all around them. He guessed her age at no more than ten.

Decard assumed the senseless woman was the little girl's mother. Grateful that she was unconscious, he leveled the Sin Eater and put a single round through her left temple. The child didn't release the woman's hand or even react to the sound of the shot.

Crowe nodded his approval. "Flashblast the other one."

Decard shifted his position slightly, turning toward the other survivor, a man clutching at his bullet-ruptured belly. His dirt-encrusted face was twisted in a mask of agony. Decard squeezed the trigger and put a single round into his head, ending his suffering.

The young girl sat silently watching, no sign of emotion on her face. It was as if she knew her fate and had decided to accept it.

Crowe returned his Sin Eater to its holster and walked up to Decard, clapping him on the back. "You did good, kid. A righteous hardcase, just like your old man."

Decard nodded, not trusting himself to reply.

"Start stacking up the merchandise," Crowe continued. "I'll go get the Cat."

Crowe marched away and Decard worked quietly and methodically, pulling the bullet-riddled corpses into a neat pile away from the blood-soaked site of the slaughter. The girl watched the process in silence, moving only when he dragged her mother's body toward the base of the dune.

Within a few minutes, Crowe brought up the Sandcat. He stepped out of the vehicle and opened the rear door. Working together, the two Magistrates loaded the corpses into the Cat. The child watched the procedure with a blank face, releasing her mother's hand when her body was shoved into the back of the vehicle.

"What about her?" Decard asked, nodding toward the little girl.

"Got uses for her alive." Crowe beckoned to her. "Time to go, sweetheart."

She stood there, not moving, regarding him silently.

Crowe stepped forward and grabbed her by the hair, jerking her head back. "Get in the Cat," he snarled.

Decard felt hot anger building deep in his chest and shame warming the back of his neck. Magistrate or not, he didn't like seeing a child being handled so brutally, even though he had been through simulations during his training. But he stood his ground, keeping his mouth shut.

Finally the young girl made a sound—a cry of pain

as Crowe bodily lifted her off the ground by her hair and hurled her through the open hatch of the Sandcat. She fell onto the corpses, and the elder Magistrate slammed the hatch cover closed. As he turned, he said, "Now only one thing left to do."

"What's that?" Decard asked, stomach churning with nausea as he opened the passenger-side door.

"Fulfilling a termination warrant," Crowe answered quietly. His Sin Eater slapped into his waiting palm. "I'm sorry. You had real potential, but you were too nosy for your own good. Just had to see what a baron looked like, didn't you?"

A soul-chilling fear momentarily froze the young Magistrate's limbs. "Termination?" he husked out.

"It was one thing seeing the barons," Crowe replied, sounding almost regretful. "But listening to a conversation between Baron Sharpe and Samarium—that wasn't meant for grunts like you and me."

Decard's mind raced. He considered lying about it, but knew it wouldn't do any good. But he didn't want to die, either. "How'd you find out?"

Crowe shook his head, either in pity or contempt. "Didn't you know the first thing put back online was the security system? The vid spy eye recorded everything…not just what they said, but the fact you heard it."

"I didn't hear anything I understood," he protested.

Crowe sighed. "It's on the record that Quavell ordered you to stay away from the nursery, too. Remove your helmet, son."

Mind racing, weighing and discarding half a dozen plans inside a second, Decard echoed Crowe's sigh with one of resignation. "All right."

Reaching up, he began to unlock the helmet's underjaw guards. As he raised his right arm, he flexed his tendons and the Sin Eater sprang into his palm. His forefinger was crooked, and the weapon fired instantly.

The burst pounded into Crowe's chest, most of the kinetic energy being redistributed over the armor, but enough was channeled through the polycarbonate to slam him hard against the hull of the Sandcat. He cried out in angry pain. "You stupe son of a—"

Decard didn't give him the chance to finish his invective. Shifting his aim, he depressed the firing stud one more time. A burst of rounds crashed into the frame of Crowe's Sin Eater, amid a flurry of sparks and a deafening cacophony of ricochets. He felt a jarring impact against the left side of his chest. One of the bullets shattered the elder Magistrate's wrist. Clutching at his right forearm, Crowe howled. His knees buckled and he fell to the ground.

Over the man's moans, Decard heard a faint sputter of sparks and peered into the control compartment. Smoke curled from the bullet-holed control panel. At least two rounds had ricocheted into the dashboard. Glancing down, he saw a vertical dent on his badge where another bouncing bullet had nicked it. He smiled grimly. Death had missed him by inches once again.

Stepping to the rear of the Sandcat, he undogged the

hatch and swung it open. The outlander girl sat perfectly still near her mother's body, neither looking at him nor at the corpses. For the moment he ignored her, reaching up to the overhead emergency supply locker and pulling out the rations packs and all the water bottles he could comfortably carry.

For the first time, the outlander child looked up at him with her huge eyes. Gazing at the girl, for an instant the image of Gem's huge, haunting eyes superimposed themselves over her face. Wordlessly, he held out his hand to her. The child hesitated for a moment before taking the offered hand. He helped her out of the Sandcat and past Crowe.

"The Cat isn't going anywhere, Crowe," Decard declared coldly. "A search party will probably come after you by dawn. I can't spare any water, so you'll just have to suffer for a little while."

"You'll never make it, kid," Crowe grated. "If we don't hunt you down and kill you, the desert will do the job for us."

Decard didn't reply. He had nothing to say, since he knew exactly what had just transpired. Magistrate Decard was now an exile, as much of an outlander as the people he had just killed. He would never again be safe in ville territory, and every Magistrate would be out to collect the considerable bounty the barons would surely place on his head.

He realized the child was staring fixedly at the nine-spoked wheel, the badge of his former life, attached to his chest. It hung askew. He touched it and the metal symbol came away in his hands, loosened by the impact of the ricocheting bullet. He held it, noting how it gleamed like freshly spilled blood against the black gauntlet sheathing his hand. With a grimace, he dropped it in the sand.

Then, without a backward glance at Crowe, Decard took the child by the hand and walked into the desert.

Chapter 2

Dawn was just breaking over the horizon in a welter of molten reds when Decard finally stopped to rest. Seven long hours of travel through the desert had left him exhausted. His young companion never made a sound, never complained, as if she were used to such hardships. Removing his helmet, he wiped the film of sweat off his forehead and realized that it was going to get dangerously hot. "Better find us some shelter till nightfall," he told the child.

The girl stared up at him impassively. The young Magistrate shrugged and pulled a canteen off his belt and opened it. Remembering his survival classes, he took only a single swallow and handed the container to the girl. She imitated his action, drinking only a mouthful and handing the canteen back.

"Thank you," she said in a soft voice.

Decard smiled at her crookedly. Those were the first words his companion had spoken during their all-night trudge, and he had begun to believe she was mute. "So you *can* talk," he said. "What's your name?"

In the same quiet tone she answered, "Cassandra. My people called me Cassie."

"What were you and your people doing out here, Cassie?"

"We were on a pilgrimage…to the City of the Sun."

Decard snorted out a derisive laugh and gestured to the horizon. "You'll get plenty of one in a little while but damn little of the other."

Cassie didn't respond. He surveyed the surrounding terrain, seeing little but an endless ocean of beige sand. The monotony of the plains was broken here and there by clumps of sagebrush and a few ocotillo shrubs. A couple of miles to the west, he saw what looked like a long, low outcropping of stone rising from the flatlands. He decided it would be the ideal place to stop and wait out the heat of the day. He started walking. "Let's go."

As the two people walked side by side, Decard asked, "Who told your people there was a city out here?"

"I did. But it's not out here." She waved vaguely toward the horizon. "It's out there."

Her matter-of-fact reply startled him so much, he stumbled over an irregularity in the desert hardpan. Recovering his balance, he bit back a curse, then snapped, "Out there? What gave you the idea there was a ville of any kind 'out there'?"

Cassie eyed him apprehensively, a little taken aback by his anger. "The oracles of Aten told me."

"The who told you how?" he challenged.

The girl touched her forehead with an index finger. "The oracles talked to me inside my head. They called to me, asked if me and my family wanted to join them in their holy city."

Decard gaped at her, disbelief warring with suspicious fear within him. He knew about psi muties, doomseers with extrasensory perception and weird talent who could see into the future and hear the thoughts of others. He had never expected to meet one, certainly not a child.

"The oracles guided me," Cassie went on calmly, "and I guided my family." She lifted a shoulder in a resigned shrug. "That's all there is to it."

"If you're a doomie," Decard demanded, "why didn't you know about me and Crowe waiting to ambush you?"

Cassie blinked up at him in confusion. "What's a doomie?"

He smiled in spite of himself, tapping the side of his head. "Somebody who can see or hear what's up ahead with their minds."

"I can only hear or see if somebody calls," she stated. "And the oracles called to me."

"Are they still calling you?"

Cassie nodded somberly. "Oh, yes."

"Do any of them have names?"

"Only one. Her name is Mavati. She's watching over me even now."

Decard felt his flesh prickling and he cast fearful glances around, but he saw nothing but the rolling plain. He quickened his pace toward the rock tumble, eyeing the position of the sun in the sky. "Let's pick it up, Cassie."

Although he didn't expect to see any signs of pursuit for quite some time, he was fairly certain the tracks made by him and the girl could be spotted by a low-flying Deathbird. By the time a chopper was dispatched from the mesa, he wanted to be deep within the sheltering, stony bosom of the outcropping. With the granite baked by the merciless heat of the day, the Deathbird's instruments would be hard-pressed to achieve a solid fix on their thermal signatures.

Decard forced a jaunty grin to his face, gesturing for the girl to catch up with him. For a reason he couldn't quite identify, confidence in his ability to escape the desert swelled within him. If he utilized his survival training and carefully rationed the food and water, he knew he and Cassie would stroll out of the wasteland and into rich new lives, far from the reach of arrogant hybrid bitches, ruthless barons and treacherous superior officers.

DEHYDRATION RACKED Decard's body as he trudged foot over foot across the cold desert sands. Six days had passed since he and Cassie left their comfortable nook in the outcropping. Six long days of sheer hell, waiting out the blazing sun in whatever shelter they could find, six nights of near freezing temperatures as they traveled inexorably westward.

He had given Cassie the last of the water earlier that evening. She had taken it and drank the tepid water quietly. Not a whimper, not a cry of pain, not a moan of complaint had passed her dried and cracked lips all during their long trek.

Decard admired her strength and tenacity. Although his throat hurt too much to engage in idle conversation, he wished that he could tell her as much. Unless they found water by nightfall, they wouldn't live through the next twenty-four hours.

His survival training had gotten them this far. He had been able to find enough cacti to supplement their rapidly dwindling water supply, but it wasn't enough. An average human had to drink eight glasses of water a day to survive, and in the harsh desert climate, two or more quarts were required to stave off dehydration. He figured that they were running on about half that amount.

The farther they trudged into the burning wasteland, the scarcer the plants became. Now, easily a hundred miles from nowhere, the plants had given way to a sea of broiling dunes. Even the outcroppings that they had been using for shelter had disappeared. He took a feeble satisfaction in the fact they had eluded pursuit, but since he hadn't seen anything resembling a Deathbird or Sandcat, he realized sourly there hadn't been a pursuit. The security staff at the Archuleta Mesa dealt with far more immediate concerns than chasing after a recruit who had gone renegade.

He heard a faint whimpering moan, and he cast a glance behind him. Cassie's strength had finally given out, and she lay loose limbed on the sand. For a second, Decard contemplated drawing his Sin Eater. One shot, and her misery would be ended forever.

Instead, he bent, slid one arm under her legs and the other under her shoulders. Slowly, he lifted her, almost falling as he overbalanced himself, expecting her to weigh more. Her body was nothing more than skin and bones. Her heat-split lips stirred and she murmured faintly, "Mavati…hurry. Help us."

Decard paid no attention. Periodically over the past couple of days Cassie had called the name of Mavati, the imaginary oracle from Aten.

Stoically, he continued to walk westward. Behind him the first rays of dawn broke over the horizon.

An hour later, the full fury of the sun beat down upon them. Decard looked over the dune wastes spread out before them, his eyes burning from the searing light reflecting off the sand. The heat rose in shimmering waves, never relenting. The sun tightened a screw of pain into the back of his head.

He took a step forward—then the thin layer of silicon crust burst upward beneath his right foot. Grit showered him, stung his eyes and he received only a fragmented impression of a creature humping upward through the sand.

It resembled a garden slug, but its leprous gray mass, colored by splotches of tan and gray, was almost six feet long and nearly half that wide. An ugly, featureless head bobbed on the end of a rubbery neck. Two stalks jutted from the head, and Decard saw they bore eyes on the tips. The neck extended out at least three feet and was almost as thick as his arm.

With a moist, sucking sound, a round, pulsing orifice opened on the underside of its head, surrounded by coiling and uncoiling tentacles. The slug emitted a high-pitched, hissing sound, like steam escaping from a faulty valve.

Decard managed to keep from crying out in revulsion, and only a backward stumble prevented the creature's mouth from closing on Cassie's dangling right foot. She still lay unconscious against his chest. He knew the creature from Outlands folklore, the Ouroboros Obscura, the giant worm of the deserts. Anyone born in postskydark America had heard rumors of its existence drifting in from hellzones. Outlanders had sworn to the stories of the predatory beast, mutated and adapted to life underground.

He struck out at the mutant creature's head with his left fist. The Ouroboros hissed angrily and snapped out again, the jaws just missing his wrist.

Decard staggered backward while he attempted to bring his Sin Eater to bear. He adjusted his aim, aligning the unprotected flesh of the creature's head and neck in front of the bore. His finger touched the firing stud and the weapon stuttered.

The burst missed, the bullets gouging furrows in the ground just beside the creature's flat tail. The giant slung almost seemed to sense what he was doing and plunged headfirst beneath the sand.

Cursing, Decard turned and ran, Cassie's legs flopping like those of a disjointed puppet. His only concern was to put as much distance between him and the mutant as he could. For a full minute he ran flat out, scraping the bottom of his last reserves of strength and energy.

He stopped and dropped the girl to the ground. He whipped around, his eyes searching the rippled sand for any sign that the mutant might be in pursuit. Nothing disturbed the desert.

Decard knew that they were not out of danger, but there was no place for them to go. He walked forward, the weapon still gripped in his palm. His heart beat a staccato rhythm against his rib cage. He crept a few yards forward, every one of his senses on full alert, as he had been trained to do.

The hiss of shifting sand reached his ear and he turned his head, his arm following his movements. The Ouroboros Obscura burst up from the dunes, sand sifting down from its mass of rubbery flesh.

Decard fired, the triburst homing in on the mutant's head. The rounds punched holes in its back amid little squirts of dark ichor. Shuddering ripples ran through the slug's gray skin, and it burrowed swiftly beneath the sand, clouds of dirt flying from beneath it. Within seconds, the creature had disappeared from view.

Decard felt grit on his tongue, but he had no moisture with which to spit it out. He scanned the area, turning in almost a complete circle, the Sin Eater trembling slightly in his hand. When he felt a faint rumbling beneath the soles of his boots, he thought for a crazed half second the creature's subterranean progress had triggered an earth tremor. He was suddenly thrown from his feet when the giant slug burst up through the sand directly under him.

He landed hard on his side, the wind forcibly leaving his lungs in a grunt. The Ouroboros Obscura lunged at him, and the round mouth snapped tight around his left ankle. Decard screamed in agony as he felt the bones break under the powerful pressure.

Raising the Sin Eater, he gritted his teeth against the searing agony spreading up his leg, refusing to let it take possession of him. He triggered the weapon, blowing away the slug's left eye stalk and part of its right. The crushing pressure on his ankle subsided instantly, as the wounded creature released him and thrashed wildly like a worm on a fisherman's hook.

Grit-induced tears blurred Decard's vision, as he tried to take aim on the creature's lashing head. He rubbed the back of his left hand against his eye sockets. The Ouroboros Obscura writhed backward, then it opened its round maw wide and emitted a sound like that of a man spitting. A jet of colorless liquid flashed through the air. The fluid splashed into Decard's eyes and he screamed as it blotted out his sight and burned into the flesh of his face like hot coals.

Blinded by the caustic venom, he fired his weapon in panic. Fortunately for him, the wounded creature's head was still in the weapon's arc. The final round punched straight through the mutant's open mouth, burrowing deep into its primitive brain.

Overcome by pain, Decard groped for Cassie, calling out hoarsely to her. She didn't respond and he wiped at his eyes with the heel of one hand. A pattern of shadow and light shifted and he squinted, trying to make out a shape that might be the girl. His temples throbbed and pounded, and his surroundings seemed to spin madly. His belly churned with nausea, and he realized he was suffering a reaction to the slug toxin. Right before he sank into a pool of welcoming blackness, the pattern of light and dark coalesced into multiple blurred images that towered over him.

He was in too much pain to wonder about them. He preferred to escape the agony by crawling into the comfortable arms of unconsciousness.

COVERED FROM HEAD TO TOE in loosely woven tan, hooded robes, four figures stood over the pair of prone bodies in the sand. One kneeled beside the black-armored man and murmured in sympathy as he inspected the wounds covering the youth's face.

"He's alive, but he won't be for long," he said to the other three. "The burrower almost took him. Another hour and his flesh would start to rot away."

A smaller figure knelt before the little girl. Placing

a finger on the child's neck, she announced in a distinctly feminine voice, "Cassie is alive, but she's badly sunburned and dehydrated."

One of the robed men pulled a clay jug from beneath his garments and popped open the top. He poured water over the blisters disfiguring the young stranger's face. With a cloth, he wiped the wounds and repeated the procedure until the damaged flesh looked pinkish, all traces of the slug's venom gone.

The robed woman watched the procedure, then declared, "That'll have to do until we get them back to Aten."

As the man stoppered the jug, he asked doubtfully, "Are you sure this is the child you've been calling, Mavati? The one named Cassandra?"

The girl's lips moved and she whispered, "Mavati…"

"She is the one," the woman announced, thrusting back the hood of her robe. "Yes, Cassandra, it is I."

Despite the unflattering folds of her robe, Mavati's body was slim and graceful. Her long glossy black hair flowed evenly around her shoulders and back. Her lips were full and sensual beneath a small, perfectly formed nose.

Her large brown eyes looked liquid with concern. "We reached her just in time. We must hurry…we have a long journey ahead of us."

"What about this one?" a man asked, gesturing to the armored figure.

Mavati gazed at him dispassionately for a moment before stating, "He comes, too. As the oracles of Aten, it is our duty to offer aid and succor to all who seek entrance to our city."

"But he didn't seek it," the man protested. "Only the child—"

Mavati rose to her full height of five foot five. Her sudden anger made her seem far taller. "Do you dare question the will of the daughter of Aten's queen, granddaughter of mighty Akhenaten himself?"

There were hasty head shakes all around. The four oracles attended to the man and child, gently swabbing their split lips with soft, water-saturated cloths, allowing less than a swallow to trickle into their mouths.

From a pack, they removed bolts of fabric and wrapped the armored man and the young girl in thick folds. They took out several jointed metal rods and swiftly connected them to form a pair of travois.

Once the two people had been secured to the frameworks, the robed and hooded oracles dragged them up the face of a dune and down its opposite side toward a pair of two-wheeled vehicles parked at its base. The boxlike, wooden chassis were overlaid with intricately worked borders of brass, copper and bronze. Both of them bore identical embossed symbols—a half disk surrounded by radiating vertical lines.

Seven feet long, the vehicles were shaped roughly like upside-down, elongated Us. They sat on low-slung platforms atop heavy axles, positioned between two very large spoked wheels. The wheels were of a dark lacquered wood and rimmed with metal. Sunlight flashed dazzlingly from a reflective surface at the rear of the platforms.

The oracles attached the travois to the backs of the chariots, and they climbed aboard. The vehicles were steered by a simple guide bar, the speed controlled by a joystick lever projecting from a very simple gearbox. The dry air vibrated with a low-pitched hum, like a distant swarm of bees, undercut by a steady mechanical clicking, and both chariots rolled forward simultaneously without a lurch.

Mavati said quietly to her companion, "I sense your unease, Sokar. You fear my mother will be displeased with my decision to bring the man in black."

"He was not among those we called," Sokar retorted tersely. "He could be an enemy."

"Aten needs citizens," Mavati countered flatly. "Particularly gifted ones like this child. As for the man in black, Queen Nefron has taught me well the art of turning enemies into friends."

Chapter 3

Thunder Isle, Pacific, one year later

Moving with wolflike stealth, Kane crept along the rock-strewn shoreline, carefully choosing each step on the wet stones. Sin Eater held snugly in his right palm, his eyes scanned the twilight-enshrouded jungle for any sign of the interlopers.

Kneeling, he studied the tree line for movement. His blue-gray eyes absorbed even the most insignificant details of the terrain, even though they stung from sweat. His dark hair hung in damp strands, soaked through with perspiration. The lowering of the sun had done little to relieve the oppressive humidity of Thunder Isle.

Kane wore a black T-shirt, and his jeans were tucked into the tops of laced jump boots. The heat and humidity felt even more debilitating at the juncture of the jungle and the booming sea. Wiping away the sweat trickling down his cheeks and chin, he grimaced at the gritty grate of sand under his fingertips.

In either direction, there was nothing to see except a strip of white beach, black gravel and the long lines of combers rolling against the shoreline. He knew that

Grant and Shizuka were somewhere in the jungle, trying to flank the intruders before they reached Redoubt Yankee. As it was, neither he nor his friends were as concerned about the interlopers reaching the installation as escaping with word of its existence to Wei Quang.

Kane, Grant and Brigid had arrived at the Operation Chronos facility the day before on an arranged visit, like one of many they had made in the past half year in order to make Thunder Isle a viable alternative to the Cerberus redoubt in Montana. Over the past couple of months or so, living in Cerberus had grown increasingly claustrophobic, with the infusion of new arrivals from the Manitius base on the Moon.

But the night before, several of Shizuka's samurai, the Tigers of Heaven, had returned to the main building of the facility, carrying a dead comrade. His skull had been split by a hatchet, and if the method of murder had not been sufficient to identify the culprits as Chinese Tong pirates, one of their boats was found on the beach.

Upon seeing the bright scarlet chops painted on the prow, Kane knew the pirates worked for Wei Quang, the warlord of Autarkic. Quang handpicked his men, and all of them were hardened killers. Their chosen weapon for close-in fighting was a single-bladed throwing ax. The Tong had invaded the Western Islands some decades in the past and had set up an empire there.

The term "Western Isles" was something of a misnomer. Back during the nuclear holocaust, bombs known as earthshakers had been triggered, seeded months before by submarines along the fault and fracture lines of the Pacific Ocean. ICBM missiles had pounded the Cascades and the region from western Canada down to California. The concentrated destructive force had ripped apart the entire coastline.

Tidal waves had swept inward, and pummeled by earthquakes and volcanic activity, California had sunk beneath the waves. When it was over, the Cific coast was barely twenty miles from the foothills of the Sierra Nevada.

After a century, the sea had receded somewhat, leaving islands in its wake where most of the landmass had once been. Many of the islands were the high points of old California, or regions that became more elevated with the shifting of the tectonic plates. Many other islands had been created by the volcanic activity, Autarkic and the New Edo chain—which included Thunder Isle—among them.

Shizuka interrogated the samurai and learned that the group of Tong invaders had been chased into the jungle by some sort of four-legged animal. As the commander of New Edo's military arm, the Tigers of Heaven, she immediately dispatched a contingent of samurai to track down the intruders before they escaped and took word of New Edo's existence back to Autarkic. She didn't have to ask Kane and Grant for their assistance. They offered it without hesitation. Brigid had already returned to Cerberus.

The snapping of a twig brought Kane out of his reverie, and he swung the Sin Eater in the direction of the sound. His heart pounded against his rib cage. He wasn't sure what to expect. The source of the noise could be one of the Tong, a Tiger or one of the many predatory creatures prowling the jungle. Narrowing his eyes, he searched the shadows between the trees for signs of movement.

He didn't search for long. Half-concealed by the leafy ferns that seemed to fill every inch of the jungle, he glimpsed a man dressed in a dark linen jerkin. He crept through the foliage in a crouch, moving with an admirable degree of silence. Kane knew the man was one of the Tong raiders, not a Tiger of Heaven.

The man paused and slowly straightened, turning his head to the left and right, displaying unmistakable Asian features. A strip of white cloth soaked through with perspiration bound his forehead. It bore the red symbol of Wei Quang. Despite the dim light, Kane guessed the Tong pirate to be in his early twenties. He looked half a foot shorter than Kane's six foot one, and weighed at least twenty pounds less than his 180. His black hair sprouted from his scalp in a series of little topknots.

Cradled in the man's bare arms was an ancient hunting rifle. By glancing at the size of the bore Kane could tell that it was probably a .306, but the weapon was so beaten and battered, he wouldn't have been surprised to see it fall apart in the man's hands the moment he pulled the trigger. A wooden-hafted hatchet hung from a red sash at his waist.

The pirate sidled into the murk between trees and seemed to be swallowed by the shadows. Kane briefly considered spraying the area with his Sin Eater, but the impulsive act would also only waste ammunition, it would also instantly alert any other Tong in the vicinity to his whereabouts.

Pushing himself up from the crouch, Kane carefully picked his way over the rocks, staying low so he didn't present an easy profile, in case the man with the rifle happened to linger at the edge of the undergrowth and glance toward the beach.

Kane made it to the edge of the jungle and slid noiselessly into the tree line. Crouching once again, he peered at the thickening shadows. Soon it would be almost impossible to see with the naked eye, and he would have to rely on the light-amplifying capabilities of his night-vision glasses, still tucked in his shirt pocket. He cursed under his breath.

A deeply accented voice suddenly spoke from the murk. "A sec man. What you doing here?"

Kane felt hard, cold metal touch the back of his neck, and he didn't move a muscle. The pirate had the drop on him, screened from sight by the underbrush. "I could ask you why a Tong soldier is so far from Autarkic," Kane replied with studied nonchalance.

The pirate snorted. "Trying to get back to my boat without being eaten by that fucking bone-face or having my head chopped off by them samurai."

Kane understood his fearful reference to decapitation, but not the meaning of the "bone-face" epithet. "What are you talking about?"

The Tong dug the barrel of the rifle hard into Kane's neck. "You just keep that blaster nice and high. If I sees it low, I chills you. Gots that?"

"Gots it," Kane answered as he carefully climbed to his feet, keeping the Sin Eater held high above his head. "Now what?"

"Now drops the blaster, sec man."

Kane seethed in anger at being called a sec man. The term was a slur against the highly trained Magistrates, as it harkened back to the days of preunification, when independent barons called their ragtag security forces sec men. He reached out with his left hand to the buckles and straps of the weapon's holster. He felt the pirate shove the bore of his rifle hard between his shoulder blades. That single move showed Kane the man's inexperience. Only amateurs got so close with a firearm.

"Slow, sec man," he growled. "Slow."

As Kane reached up to unhook the first tab, an eardrum-compressing roar shattered the silence of the jungle. In that instant, he felt the barrel of the rifle jerk away from his back. Kane didn't hesitate for a second. He spun his arms around and the heel of his left hand connected solidly with the barrel of the rifle, knocking it aside. The back of his right impacted solidly against the hinge of the pirate's jaw.

The force of the ram's-head blow slammed the pirate against the trunk of a tree. His finger tightened around the trigger of the weapon, and it discharged with a thunderous boom. Kane felt the shock of displaced air as the round narrowly missed his left ear. Balancing himself on the ball of his right foot, Kane knocked the weapon out of the man's hands with a sweeping kick of his left leg. The battered .306 spun end over end and landed in the brush several yards away.

Recovering quickly, the Tong pirate launched himself away from the trunk of the tree. He slammed a shoulder into Kane's midsection, his momentum carrying both men off their feet. They landed heavily in a tumble of arms and legs, with Kane beneath the man.

Despite being small and slender, the pirate's tensile-steel strength took Kane. The man grabbed Kane's right arm and forced it down against the ground, preventing him from bringing his pistol to bear. He secured a viselike grip around Kane's left wrist, pinning it to the ground, too. Kane whipped up his left leg, pounding his knee into the man's kidney. The pirate grunted, but his grip on Kane's arms didn't loosen.

In retaliation, the pirate smashed his forehead on the crown of Kane's head. The impact drove the back of Kane's skull into the ground, but the cushion of leaves and soft loam prevented him from being stunned by the head butt. Still, it hurt. The pirate tried to follow through by leaning down to bite Kane's right eye. Hot breath that stank of fish oil clogged Kane's nostrils as he turned his head to the side. The pirate's teeth snapped on empty air.

Kane stopped trying to shake off the man and let his body go limp. The pirate, expecting upward resistance from Kane's arms, overbalanced himself and slid forward, losing his grip on his wrists. Kane helped propel the man off him by bridging his back and bucking. The Tong pirate fell into a clump of thorny shrubbery and thrashed his way to his knees. He snatched out his hatchet and cocked his arm for a throw.

Rolling onto his left side, Kane didn't take any further chances. Lifting the Sin Eater, he took quick aim and depressed the trigger stud. The 9 mm round drilled through the pirate's forehead and exited at the back of his skull, pelting the earth and leaves with a mist of blood, brain and bone fragments.

"Kane!"

He turned at the lionlike bellow and saw Grant charging through the underbrush. "I heard the shot."

"Yeah," Kane said grimly. "You and all the other Tong bastards on the island, I imagine."

Standing, Kane gestured with his pistol at the corpse. "You see any more of these?"

Grant shook his head, his long-jawed face locked in a characteristic scowl. Droplets of perspiration gleamed against the coffee-brown skin of his face and bare arms. Standing four inches over six feet tall, Grant was an exceptionally broad-chested and -shouldered man with a heavy musculature.

Gray sprinkled his short-cropped, tight-curled hair at the temples, but it didn't show in the sweeping black mustache curving fiercely out from either side of his grim, tight-lipped mouth. He wore camou pants and an olive-drab T-shirt. His own Sin Eater was strapped securely in its power holster around his right forearm, and a Copperhead subgun hung from a strap around his left shoulder.

A chopped-down autoblaster, the Copperhead was less than two feet in length. The magazine held fifteen rounds of 4.85 mm steel-jacketed rounds, which could be fired at a rate of 700 per minute. Even with its optical image intensifier and laser autotargeter scope, the Copperhead weighed under eight pounds.

"I wish we knew how many we were up against," Kane said. "But they're not going anywhere. I knocked a hole in the bottom of their boat myself, and two Tigers are guarding it."

As Grant opened his mouth to reply, another tremendous roar seemed to rattle the leaves around them. "What," he asked quietly, "the fuck was that?"

"Probably whatever was chasing the Tong," Kane answered. "In this damn place, it could be anything from a baby Monstrodamii to a saber-toothed tiger."

Grant understood his oblique reference to the offspring of the vicious Daspeltosaurus nicknamed Monstrodamus. "Or a saber-toothed baby Monstrodamii," he said darkly. "Want to split up, or should we stick together?"

"Where's Shizuka?"

Grant jerked his head to the right. "She's on the trail of at least two of the bastards. She'll catch up with them any time now."

Kane nodded, relieved that Brigid Baptiste had agreed to return to Cerberus a few hours earlier. With her no longer out in the field, there was one less potential casualty to worry about.

"Let's stick together from here on in," Kane said as he moved into the woods, unconsciously taking the point.

Both men moved swiftly and stealthily as they wended their way through the darkening jungle, pausing long enough to put on dark-lensed glasses. The electrochemical polymer of the lenses gathered all available light and made the most of it to give them a limited form of night vision. They also carried Nighthawk microlights but they were loath to use them, fearing the glows they produced would pinpoint their positions to night hunters far more dangerous than the Tong.

They heard no sound except for their own respiration. It was a clear sign that there was serious danger about, when even the crickets and other night creatures of the jungle ceased their noise. That didn't sit well with either man. But then, very little about any of the Western Isles did, New Edo included.

New Edo had been settled by the House of Mashashige, fleeing political unrest in Japan. The daimyo, Lord Takaun, went into exile with as many family members, retainers, advisers and samurai as a small fleet of ships could hold. They set sail into the Cific, their destination the island chain once known as the Hawaiians.

But a storm drove the little fleet far off course, and they had no choice but to make landfall on the first halfway habitable piece of dry ground they came across. This turned out to be a richly forested isle, the tip of a larger landmass that had been submerged during the nukecaust. Evidently it had slowly risen from the waters over the past two centuries, and supported a wide variety of animal and vegetable life. Lord Takaun decreed it would support theirs, as well. The exiles from Nippon claimed it as their own and named it New Edo, after the imperial city of feudal Japan.

The mission by which they had been introduced to the inhabitants of New Edo also brought them to Thunder Isle—and the primary Operation Chronos installation, a major subdivision of the Totality Concept.

The Totality Concept was the umbrella designation for predark American military supersecret researches into many different but interconnected subdivisions. The many spin-off experiments were applied to an eclectic combination of disciplines, most of them theoretical—artificial intelligence, hyperdimensional physics, genetics and new energy sources.

The primary subdivision of the Totality Concept was Overproject Whisper, which in turn spawned Project Cerberus and Operation Chronos.

Whereas Cerberus dealt with the transfer of organic and inorganic matter from one location to another, Chronos focused on transtemporal interphasing—time travel, or in the vernacular of the Totality Concept scientists, time "trawling."

The seat of Operation Chronos, code-named Redoubt Yankee, was built on one of the Santa Barbara or Channel Islands, disguised as a satellite campus of the University of California. As one of the finest and most secret research establishments in the world, its engineering and computer centers were second to none.

It was a place Kane, Grant and Brigid assumed had been uninhabited and forgotten since the nuclear holocaust of two centuries before. Only much later did they find out the installation was inhabited by an old enemy—Sindri, the brilliant but deranged dwarf.

Sindri's tampering with the technology caused it to become dangerously unstable. With a contribution from Brigid, the dilator overloaded and reached critical mass, resulting in a violent meltdown of its energy core.

When the radiation in the installation ebbed to a nonlethal level, Kane, Grant and Brigid returned. No trace of Sindri was ever found, but none of them believed he had perished, since he had escaped what appeared to be certain death twice before. In the weeks following the incident, Brigid and Lakesh made several visits to Redoubt Yankee, salvaging what could be salvaged. There turned out to be a surprising amount of equipment, most of which had yet to be cataloged. They didn't need the task to be made even more difficult by the depredations of Tong pirates. If a single one of them escaped with even a whisper of the redoubt's existence, then Thunder Isle and its neighbor, New Edo, would be overrun by Wei Quang's raiders within weeks, if not days.

"If the Tong don't have a boat, then we could just let Thunder Isle kill them," Grant muttered. "It's bound to happen if they stay here long enough—hell, it's bound to happen if *we* stay here long enough."

"And here I thought you planned to set up housekeeping with Shizuka next door to this place," Kane replied distractedly.

"If I did," Grant growled, "the first thing I'd do is—"

Whatever else he had to say was drowned out by an eardrum-compressing, bawling cry that pierced the murk. It was followed by a deep-throated croaking roar that stopped them both in their tracks.

Chapter 4

Shizuka glided wraithlike through the shadow-shrouded jungle, eyes darting from the almost imperceptible depressions in the grass to the broken stems of bushes. She had trailed the pair of Tong pirates for more than an hour and she was hot, tired, hungry and wanted to rejoin Grant as soon as possible.

The last thing she had expected to do when she boated over from New Edo to meet with Kane, Grant and Brigid was to be led on a chase through the darkness, in pursuit of a band of cold-blooded killers.

A small, delicate woman, Shizuka stood little over five feet tall. She wore her luxuriant black hair tied back in a long braid, framing a smoothly sculpted face of extraordinary Oriental beauty. Her complexion was a very pale gold with peach and milk for an accent. Beneath a snub nose, her petaled lips were full. Her dark, almond-shaped eyes glinted with the fierce, proud gleam of a young eagle.

She wore a partial suit of armor, not the full battle dress of the Tigers of Heaven. Her body armor was a lightweight lacquered *hara-ate*, which consisted of segments of flattened metal linked together by tiny chains. Because of the heat, she wore a rough pair of shorts that covered her legs to midthigh. *Sune-ate*, shin protectors made of heavy cloth, rose from her ankles to the base of her knees. Two scabbarded swords, a long bladed *katana* and a shorter *tanto,* were strapped crosswise across her back. Simple sandals covered her bare feet.

Shizuka flitted from tree to tree, not even cracking a twig in a demonstration of stealth that perhaps only real tigers could have equaled.

Several minutes before, Shizuka had heard a gunshot, clearly identifiable as a report from a Sin Eater. The sound brought a cold smile to her lips. She hoped that either Kane or Grant had found and killed one of the Tong they were pursuing. The sudden roar, on the other hand, made her exceptionally nervous. She knew the kind of creatures that lived and hunted on Thunder Isle, and few of them belonged there.

She remembered Sindri's explanation of how, when he investigated the Operation Chronos installation, he found that the temporal dilator's chronon wave guide conformals ran wild on random cycles. They either reconstituted trawled subjects from the holding matrix or snatched new ones from all epochs in history. Thus, everything from people, animals and plants were randomly trawled from past epochs.

The murmur of voices reached her ears, causing her to stop dead in her tracks. Shizuka tilted her head in the direction of the sound and listened intently. She wasn't able to make out what they were saying, but knew the pirates were only a scant dozen yards ahead of her on the other side of a wall of shrubbery.

Inch by inch, she crept up on the Tong and peered through the screen of brush. The two pirates, both fairly young men, sat on an old log, breathing heavily and sweating profusely. She could smell the fear on them, an odor as pungent as their perspiration. Judging by their youth, Shizuka guessed the mission to Thunder Isle hadn't been ordered by a superior, but was one they undertook independently as a way to gain face among their brotherhood.

Shizuka's hand closed around the hilt of her *katana* and slowly she drew the weapon, not wanting to rush it. The slightest sound would alert the two pirates to her presence before she was ready, and she didn't want that.

Just as the blade cleared the wooden scabbard, a series of heavy thudding impacts shook the thick brush just behind the Tong. With cries of surprise mingled with fright, the two men jumped to their feet. One drew his hatchet from the sash around his waist while the other pulled out an old, rust-pitted revolver.

The ferns trembled and swayed violently. Then, with a hoarse bellow, a huge form burst through the undergrowth at the fringe of the little clearing. During the years Shizuka had spent on New Edo and her few visits to Thunder Isle, she had witnessed a number of monstrous animals, snatched from all epochs of history by the temporal dilator. But nothing she had seen up to that point had prepared her for the creature that crashed through the brush.

The animal dimly resembled a bear, but its bloated body was propelled forward by four bowed legs the diameter of medium-sized tree trunks. Thick, bony protuberances jutted from a massive, shovel-jawed head, the heavily muscled neck drooping with the weight of it. The long, extended jaws gaped open, much like those of an alligator's. Jagged teeth glistened wetly, many having been broken off in the past. The two eyes, sunk deep beneath knobs of bone, held a red gleam.

The four limbs were heavily muscled and ended in three-toed paws, tipped by curving talons nearly five inches in length. Shizuka had time to register the fact that the creature's hide resembled wart-pebbled leather, covered by a sparse pelt of coarse black hair. She estimated it was twelve feet in length, measuring from its blunt-horned snout to the tip of its tail. She had no idea if the monster was one of the prehistoric samples trawled to the island by the temporal dilator or a mutant, but its pedigree was unimportant.

A Tong pirate brought up his pathetically small ax and scrambled backward, trying to get away from the fanged jaws champing open and shut inches from his face. His fellow pirate aimed the revolver at the head of the bear-beast and pulled the trigger three times. The barrel of the weapon lipped flame, smoke and thunder.

Each round struck one of the flanges of bone sprouting from its skull and ricocheted, chipping away fragments. Other than enraging the monster, the bullets had little effect.

Roaring in fury, the beast swung its huge head, and the bludgeons of bone slammed into the pirate with the revolver. The protuberances crushed the man's chest, and blood erupted from his mouth as the impact flung him ten feet away. He struck a tree with the back of his head and he fell, limp and unmoving.

The Tong with the hatchet turned and ran, heading straight for Shizuka. She stepped aside as the pirate raced past, screaming in mortal terror. The bear-beast lumbered after him in pursuit. She, too, felt a surge of unreasoning terror at the sight of the monster, but she forced it down. Shizuka scrambled around the trunk of a tree, hoping that the bear-beast would not catch sight of her or a whiff of her scent. She brought up her sword and held it over her head, both fists wrapped around the handle. Her heart pounded within her chest as the monster tore through the underbrush after the interloper. She listened to the creature crashing its way through the brush, then the sound of its violent progress stopped. She heard a small cry, as shrill as it was brief.

Taking a deep breath, Shizuka slid her small body around the trunk of the tree. She scanned the brush, hunting for the creature. Its passage wasn't difficult to find, as the trail was covered in broken branches, trampled ferns and clods of earth torn up from the jungle floor in the bear-beast's wake.

Just over thirty feet from her position, the bizarre quadruped had stopped. Shizuka heard snuffling sounds, then the grisly crunching of bones being crushed between powerful jaws. The bear-beast had overtaken the pirate and now feasted on the man's flesh.

Not wasting any time, Shizuka crept away from the tree, hoping that it was too intent on its meal to notice her. She kept her eyes on it as she backed away, increasing the distance between her and the creature.

KANE STOPPED AND HELD UP his fist at the sound of the commotion in the distance. He turned and looked at Grant when he heard the rage-filled roar. "I don't like the sound of that."

"Me, either," Grant bit out. "How far do you figure?"

"About two hundred yards," Kane said, staring into the darkness, "give or take. That's where Shizuka's supposed to be, isn't she?"

"Yeah."

Grant's eyes suddenly narrowed, and he jerked up the Copperhead. From the look in his eyes, Kane knew that something was right behind him and he lunged forward, around Grant.

As Kane moved, Grant's finger curled around the trigger of the Copperhead and squeezed. A jackhammering burst tore from the barrel of the rifle and slammed into the monstrously malformed head of the beast that had appeared out of the murk behind Kane.

Diving forward, Kane hit the ground and rolled onto his side as he brought up his Sin Eater. He hesitated for a split second when he caught sight of the creature Grant fired upon. It was without a doubt one of the most hideous things he had ever had the misfortune of laying eyes on, but he recognized it from pix he had seen.

Fear caused his finger to depress the trigger stud of the weapon, and his blaster joined Grant's in a duet of steel-jacketed death, pumping round after round into the monster's upper chest and neck.

The bear-beast lowered its bone-shielded skull in an instinctive attempt to protect its vital organs from the barrage of fire, but to little avail. The twin streams of lead tore through tough flesh, dense muscle and heavy bone, drilling deep into the creature's body.

A lucky round penetrated one of its eyes before finally stopping in the thick cranial bone at the back of its head, having destroyed the creature's brain on the way. It voiced a single anguished bellow before toppling over, the impact of its massive body shaking the jungle floor around them.

Seconds ticked by as Kane and Grant stood before the beast, watching its tail twitch in postmortem spasms. Kane finally broke the silence. *"That's* what was chasing the Tong? No wonder they were so scared."

Grant ejected the spent magazine from his Copperhead and toggled a fresh one home. "What the hell is it? Some kind of mutie?"

Kane shook his head. "Not on this island. It's called a dinocelphalian—that means 'terrible head.' It's from the Permian age. Fossils were found in Russia, South and North America."

Grant gazed at him doubtfully and speculatively. "How do you know that?"

Kane shrugged, popping out the clip of his Sin Eater, checking the load and slipping it back into the butt of the gun. "When Brigid and Lakesh found a computer record of all the time periods the temporal dilator had been focused on before Sindri took control of it, I did some research on the kinds of animals that might have been trawled here."

Grant nodded. "Let's find Shizuka and join up with the other Tigers. If there are any more of these 'terrible heads' around here, we better hook up for safety. I just hope that the Tong are having as much fun as we are."

Kane chuckled humorlessly. "I can't imagine why they wouldn't be."

SHIZUKA HEARD the stuttering reports from a Copperhead, followed almost instantly by the thunder of a Sin Eater. She was off and running in the direction of the fusillade immediately, knowing Grant and Kane had met the murderous bear-beast. She heard its bellows of pain and anger and then nothing.

Movement in the corner of her eye caused the samurai captain to skid to a halt. Swiftly she brought up her *katana*. Her blood froze in her veins as another of the bone-headed beasts seemed to appear out of nowhere, only a scant handful of yards from her. Its head was turned toward the sound of the gunfire and the death cries of the other creature—either its mate, sibling or parent.

The creature snarled and lumbered off in the direction of the cacophony, totally ignoring the Japanese woman. Shizuka watched as it went blundering noisily through the underbrush. She ran her sleeve across her forehead, wiping away the film of sweat. Kane and Grant would need her assistance, so she fell into step after the creature, making sure that she was far enough behind that it wouldn't notice her presence.

After only a score of yards, she saw that the creature had stopped and stood on its hind legs, the misshapen head sniffing the air around it, as its tiny, bone-encrusted eyes stared off into the darkness. Turning to the right, it growled as it dropped to all fours. Shizuka remained motionless, watching as the monster lumbered off.

Soft footfalls reached her ears, and she molded her body against one of the numerous trees that surrounded her. Lowering her arm, she dropped the point of her sword to the ground, in the off chance that whoever was approaching might be Grant or Kane or one of her own samurai.

Two more Tong pirates sidled through the overgrowth, looking around alertly and fearfully. Like the others, they were young men, dressed in linen jerkins. The expressions on their dirty, sweaty faces were those of stark fear.

The two pirates passed by her position and she raised her sword, resting the hilt and half the blade along her left forearm. Shizuka counted ten beats of her heart before she glided away from the tree and crept up behind the Tong. Staying low, she moved with the speed and stealth of a stalking tiger, her prey totally unaware of her presence.

Shizuka leaped into the air, kicking out with her right foot, connecting solidly between the shoulder blades of the pirate slightly in the lead. At the same time, she slashed down with the *katana,* the razor-keen edge of the blade dragging across the back of the other man's neck. She felt it grate against his vertebrae.

The pirate she kicked staggered forward, all the air driven from his lungs. The man whose throat she had just sliced wide open reached up with both hands to try to stanch the flow of blood. Neither pirate could make an outcry.

The man with the cut throat writhed on the ground, mouth working, eyes rolling. His companion managed to grab a sapling and keep from falling. He spun and his eyes flickered with fear at the sight of the blood-stained blade. Then he realized he faced a woman, and the fear on his face was replaced by a deep anger.

Shizuka knew that as far as the pirate was concerned, a woman with a sword was still only a woman.

The pirate stepped toward her, holding his hatchet out before him, waving it to and fro. The Japanese woman feinted with her *katana,* deliberately letting the tip of the weapon fan empty air a good foot from the man's stomach. The Tong reflexively brought his own weapon down swiftly in an attempt to block.

Shizuka smiled mockingly and backed away. "Not much of a challenge."

The Tong growled in fury, his hand tightening around the haft of his hatchet. He took the bait and moved to attack, raising his arm to slash down with the ax with all his might, seeking to split her skull.

Anticipating the move, Shizuka gracefully dodged out of the way and slashed upward with her own weapon, cutting the man's fingers to the bone on the hand that held the ax handle. He cried out in pain as the weapon dropped from his slashed fingers, two of the digits falling free amid squirtings of blood.

Smiling coldly, Shizuka ducked under his flailing arms and slashed out with the blade, cutting a long, deep gash across the man's chest. When he tried to bring up his good arm to block, she slashed it from elbow to wrist, slicing the flesh to the bone.

The Tong pirate wailed in pain and fear as he backpedaled from the whirling, mirror-bright blade. Shizuka pressed on, letting months of frustration and anger out in one vicious attack. She hated all the Tong, since they preyed on the weak and helpless. She had every intention of making an example out of this particular man. Her sword blade moved blindingly fast, cutting and slicing the hapless pirate until his body was a bleeding patchwork of shallow gashes and slashes.

The pain from the wounds forced the man to his knees. He held his hands up before him, tears cutting runnels through the blood on his cheeks. In broken English, he pleaded, "Please, stop. Just kill me, don' keep cuttin' on me, just kill me."

Shizuka poised herself to deliver a decapitating stroke. Before she could move, a huge paw reached out from between a pair of trees and latched onto the man's head. The force the paw exerted was so tremendous that it caused the man's skull to implode as his body was dragged back into the brush.

Unable to repress a yelp of fright, Shizuka jumped backward and almost screamed out loud as she felt her body connect against something hard and unyielding. She tried to whirl around, bringing the *katana* up to slash at the attacker, when a heavy hand wrapped around her wrist, stopping the attack dead.

Chapter 5

"Easy, sweetheart," Grant said calmly.

"Kaibutsu!" she cried, momentarily lapsing into Japanese. She pointed to the spot between the trees where the pirate had been dragged. "Monster!"

"We know—we saw it," Grant said, letting her go.

Kane appeared a moment later, breathing heavily in the night air. "You okay?" he asked Shizuka, genuine concern in his voice.

She nodded and pulled away from Grant. "Yes. What is that thing?"

"Kane calls it a dinocelphalian," Grant answered.

She eyed him suspiciously. "A what?"

"It means 'terrible head,'" Kane said helpfully.

"Here." Grant handed her his Copperhead assault rifle. "You'll be better off with this than your swords, believe me. It's got a full clip, so just point and shoot."

Shizuka didn't argue with him, despite the samurai code, which scorned firearms. Resheathing her *katana,* she gripped the weapon tightly, bracing the butt against her hip. "I hear something."

Immediately following her announcement, six Tong

raiders burst through the brush, armed with an eclectic variety of weapons, including a couple of rusty pistols. One even had a crude crossbow cradled in his arms. Upon spying Grant, Kane and Shizuka, they rocked to clumsy, thrashing halts. Four of the Tigers of Heaven appeared next, brandishing their own bladed weapons, clearly excited at catching the interlopers who had eluded them for so long.

It was at that exact moment the dinocelphalian decided to join the melee, bursting out from the screen of underbrush, with the arm of the pirate dangling from its jaws.

The prehistoric beast slurped the torn limb into its gullet and bounded toward the group of Tong pirates. Screaming in fear, they turned and ran—right into the waiting swords of the samurai. Shizuka held the Copperhead low and fired from the hip, the rounds smashing into the hind legs of the dinocelphalian, but to little effect. It bellowed in pain as it scrabbled around to face her.

Acting in tandem, Kane and Grant lifted their Sin Eaters and aimed at the head of the creature. Kane's finger caressed the trigger stud, and the weapon stuttered with a short burst that chopped splinters out of the sproutings of bone on the creature's head.

The rounds fired by Grant smashed into the dinocelphalian's upper left shoulder and torso. The wounds were unsightly, but didn't hamper the creature's movements. If anything, the pain just made it angrier.

The samurai were engaged in a vicious hatchet-to-sword battle with the pirates. One particularly large Tiger, almost as wide as he was tall, faced off against the Tong raider wielding the cobbled-together crossbow.

The samurai raised his *katana* over his head to strike. At the same time, the pirate shouldered his crossbow and thumbed the trigger switch. The metal-tipped bolt ripped a bloody furrow across the back of the samurai's hand. He grunted in pain, his fingers opened and the sword fell to the ground.

In the same smooth movement, the Tong pirate dropped the crossbow and drew a hatchet from his sash. As he whipped the double-bladed weapon out, the large samurai backed off and drew his shorter *tanto* sword with his left hand. He whirled the blade in a glittering arc around his head as he shifted position, standing so his right side faced the pirate.

Bending his knees slightly, he spun the sword in a downward, half-clockwise circle so the flat blade rested under his armpit. The samurai held his injured right hand out toward the raider palm up, then he gave the man the finger.

The Tong pirate blinked in surprise, then his lips peeled back over his teeth in a silent snarl. He brought the hatchet down in a long arching curve toward the crown of the samurai's head. The Tiger of Heaven seemed to lean backward less than an inch, but the ax missed its target.

Almost negligently, the samurai slid his *tanto* from between his arm and body and used the tip to swat the hatchet out of the Tong's hand, taking a good chunk of the man's thumb with it. The pirate instinctively clasped his hand against his chest, and the Tiger followed through, driving the sword through the stomach of his opponent, impaling the man and pinning him against the tree just behind him.

The samurai's victory was short-lived. Smelling the blood, the enraged dinocelphalian swiveled about and caught sight of the Tiger withdrawing his *tanto* from the body of the raider. Kane yelled a warning, but it was too late. The long, daggerlike claws slashed across the samurai's back, tearing away the armor, rending the flesh beneath and severing his spine as if it were made of rotted twine. The Tiger of Heaven had time to gasp once, then he tumbled face forward into the brush and lay motionless.

Shizuka cried out shrilly in anger and grief. Grant fired his Sin Eater again, holding down the trigger stud. The prolonged burst drilled straight through the creature's huge paw, smashing away clots of tissue and talons. The dinocelphalian bellowed in agony. Grant maintained his finger's pressure on the trigger, then the firing pin clicked loudly on an empty chamber.

Shizuka's Copperhead hammered as she fired a long burst at the rampaging prehistoric creature. Blood erupted from the wounds perforating the animal's right side. It turned its head to snap at the pain as she kept her finger crooked tight around the trigger. But with only a 15-round magazine, the subgun could be fired dry in a couple of seconds and Shizuka did so. Eyes flashing with fear, she thumbed the magazine release and looked over at Grant for another.

"Grant!" Shizuka cried as the dinocelphalian took a stumbling step toward her.

Seeing the woman in mortal danger, Grant threw himself between Shizuka and the creature. The beast swiped at him with his good paw. The claws tore four horizontal rents in Grant's shirt, inflicting shallow cuts on his chest.

Biting back a cry of pain, Grant took the first action that occurred to him—he grabbed two of the protuberances of bone extending from the creature's jaw and used them to vault onto its back. The dinocelphalian reared, bucked, kicked out with its massive hind legs. One paw struck a Tong pirate like a battering ram directly in the face, turning his features into a red jelly smear and catapulting him a score of feet into the foliage.

Grant managed to wrap his arm around the beast's squat neck as it bellowed in frustration. It violently shook itself, trying to dislodge the human astride its back. The sight of the mad struggle caused the combat between the Tigers of Heaven and the surviving pirates to cease as they stared with openmouthed amazement.

It required all of Grant's considerable strength to hold on as the dinocelphalian tried to shake him loose.

He tightened his arms around the neck of the creature and dug his knees into its back, pushing out with them to add even more leverage to his attack. With a gasping grunt of exertion, the animal rose onto its hind legs and tottered madly about the clearing.

Shizuka dropped the empty Copperhead and drew her *katana*. She swiftly slid into position and lashed out with the blade at the most vulnerable area within reach—the dinocelphalian's oversized testicles. One swift, corkscrewing stroke removed them from the juncture of the prehistoric animal's legs. Trailing a little stream of blood, they flopped wetly into a bed of crushed ferns.

The creature stopped in its tracks. It stood motionless for several long seconds. Then it began to shake all over, so violently that it actually managed to dislodge Grant from its back as it started to scream, throwing its massive head back. It wasn't a simple animal cry of pain, but an agony-laced cry of outrage and fear.

Stepping up beside Shizuka, Kane fired a single 9 mm round into the beast's wide-open mouth. The shot blew a fist-sized chunk of flesh and bone from the dinocelphalian's upper jaw. Instantly blood began to course down its throat, drowning out the scream as he fired again. The second shot drilled straight through the roof of the creature's mouth.

The scream became a liquid gurgle as the beast toppled backward, narrowly missing Grant as it crashed to the ground. It shuddered once, then breathed out a long, rattling exhalation. The death of the creature broke the stunned spell that had overcome all of the combatants, and they once again engaged one another with murderous fury. The fight was over before Kane, Grant and Shizuka could rejoin it. Within seconds, the last two Tong raiders writhed on the ground, their lifeblood seeping from numerous wounds, soaking into the earth beneath them.

"And that, as they say," Kane muttered, "is that."

The Tigers of Heaven stood there silently, staring at Grant for several long silent seconds, before he demanded impatiently, "What?"

Laughter echoed through the trees as the samurai resheathed their swords, shaking their heads. Shizuka shook her own head as she said, "Grant, that was either the bravest, or the stupidest thing I ever hope to see you try."

The big man shrugged as he rammed a fresh clip home into the Sin Eater and chambered a round. "Something had to be done."

Shizuka returned her *katana* to its scabbard, then stood on her tiptoes and kissed Grant's chin. *"Arigato, kawaii hito,"* she whispered.

Repressing a smile, Kane turned away. Because of his presence and those of the samurai, Shizuka's display of gratitude was very restrained, almost formal. But he could tell by the glint in her dark eyes she intended to thank Grant very thoroughly and far more informally as soon as they were alone back on New Edo.

The Tigers busied themselves searching the Tongs. Kane wasn't eager to join them as they plundered the dead. He said, to no one in particular, "Somebody ought to call the samurai I left guarding the Tongs' boat and let them know to come in."

Shizuka nodded and produced a black square of pressed plastic from beneath her breastplate. It was a smaller version of the trans-comms used by the Cerberus personnel. As she made the call to the absent samurai, Grant gestured to the Tong corpses. "What are we going to do about the bodies?"

Disdainfully, one the Tigers retorted, "Let Ikazuchi Kojima—Thunder Isle—deal with them."

Neither Grant nor Kane felt like arguing with him. The island sometimes seemed like one hungry mouth and empty belly. Within an hour, all of the corpses, the dinocelphalian's included, would be divided up among a variety of digestive tracts.

"I'm going back to New Edo for the night," Grant told Kane. "You figure you can make your way back to Cube without ending up as a meal?"

The Cerberus personnel called the main building of the Operation Chronos installation the Cube, because it resembled a square mountain of black stone. It held within it a mat-trans gateway.

Kane smiled sourly. "Nothing's gotten me yet."

Shizuka swiveled her head toward him. "It only takes once, or so I'm told." She didn't smile when she said it. "Be careful, Kane-san."

Kane nodded in acknowledgment and set off through the jungle. Wryly, he realized the visit to Thunder Isle hadn't gone according to plan, but that wasn't particularly unusual.

A humming mosquito lit on his face, and he impatiently brushed it off. He experienced a slight sensation of surprise that Grant and Shizuka were still determined to spend a couple of days together a month, despite their respective duties that kept them apart most of the time. Until recently, it had been Grant's intent to leave Cerberus altogether and live in the little island monarchy of New Edo with Shizuka, particularly after the arrival of the Manitius Base personnel and the hybrid woman Quavell. But after being captured and tortured by the sadistic Baroness Beausoleil, Grant realized the struggle remained essentially the same—there were just new players on the field. The war itself would go on and would never end, unless he took an active hand in it, regardless of his love for Shizuka.

Well, Kane reflected, let them enjoy each other while and when they could. God knew both of them had earned a little happiness, the hardest way possible.

Kane's own recollections of romance were few and far between. He remembered the few hours spent with the Celtic priestess Fand, or the kiss stolen from Brigid during the time-travel trip to New Year's Eve 2000. But more often than not, the image of Quavell would insinuate itself into his mind—her fall of silken, white-blond hair the perfect frame for the inhuman loveliness of her face.

The details of the days in her company during his captivity at Area 51 were locked away in some secret part of his mind, pushed far back into the rear of a mental vault.

Suddenly the vegetation and foliage dropped away as if the jungle dared not cross an invisible boundary. Before Kane stretched a flat, sandy plain at least half a mile across. Rising from the center of the dead zone was the dark mass of the Cube. It resembled a fortress, but one with streamlined architecture. It loomed above a complex of smaller structures like a squared-off mountain peak.

As always, the dark, windowless edifice awakened a quiver of dread within Kane. As he approached the defoliated zone, he stepped onto a marshy patch and sank ankle deep into foul-smelling sludge.

Grimacing, he pulled his foot free and muttered to himself, "You're not out of the woods yet."

Chapter 6

Reba DeFore, the de facto physician of Cerberus, strode down the lengthy main corridor of the redoubt, her footsteps echoing hollowly on the vanadium alloy flooring. Built more than two hundred years earlier, the Cerberus complex had been constructed to last close to forever as part of the Totality Concept's Overproject Whisper. It had been designed to be the home of at least a hundred people, and for the first time in nearly two centuries, the actual population was nearing that number. What occupied DeFore's thoughts now was a potential new resident, a newborn one.

DeFore's stride held purpose and she knew exactly to whom she needed to talk to about the situation that had developed since the arrival of the pregnant Quavell, nearly four months before. When she reached her destination, she stopped before the closed door and lightly rapped on its surface.

"Come in," said a melodic voice, muffled by the doorway.

DeFore twisted the door handle and entered the workroom. Rows of drafting tables with T-squares hanging from them lined one wall. Only a few lights were on, but she saw Brigid Baptiste sitting at a long, low trestle table at the far end of the room. A goose-neck lamp struck flame-colored highlights from her mane of red-gold hair. Soft music filtered from a CD player, something with haunting horns and tinkling piano keys, a form of predark music she had heard Lakesh refer to as "cool jazz."

Walking across the room, DeFore saw Brigid crouched over a laptop, her gaze fixed on the information scrolling swiftly across the screen. Resting atop the table next to the computer was an object that resembled a very squat, broad-based pyramid, made of smooth, dully gleaming metal. Two of the sides were missing and revealed a confusing mass of circuitry and microprocessors within. Barely one foot in width, the device didn't exceed twelve inches in height.

Brewster Philboyd, an émigré from the Moon colony, probed and prodded the interior with a tool not much thicker than a blade of grass. An astrophysicist in his midforties, he was a little over six feet, long-limbed and lanky of build. Pale blond hair was swept back from a receding hairline. He wore black-rimmed eyeglasses, and his cheeks appeared to be pitted with the sort of scars associated with chronic teenage acne.

He glanced up when DeFore came to Brigid's side, his expression flickering with annoyance. "What is it now?"

"Now?" DeFore repeated exasperatedly. "You two are in the exact same positions as the last time I looked."

"That was when you asked if we wanted to go to lunch," Brigid replied distractedly.

"Exactly," DeFore stated. "And it's now way past dinner. If you leave now, you might just get in under the wire for a midnight snack."

Brigid lifted her gaze, emerald eyes blinking perplexedly behind the rectangular lenses of her wire-rimmed glasses. Her fair complexion was lightly dusted with freckles across her nose and cheeks. A high forehead gave the impression of a probing intellect, whereas her wide mouth with the full underlip hinted at a sensual nature.

A mane of red-gold hair fell in loose waves almost to her waist. Her tight-fitting white bodysuit, identical to DeFore's and Philboyd's, showed off her willowy figure to full advantage.

The corners of her lips quirked in a slightly abashed smile. "Putting back together what Danaan technology tore asunder is proving more time-consuming than I thought."

DeFore narrowed her brown eyes as she gazed at the pyramidion. "Putting back together? Isn't this a completely new interphaser?"

Brigid took off her glasses and neatly folded them next to the keyboard. "Pretty much, except for cannibalizing some parts left over from the prototype that

Lakesh cobbled together and never used in either the first or second versions."

The interphaser had evolved from the Totality Concept's Project Cerberus. More than two years before, Lakesh had constructed a small device on the same scientific principle as the mat-trans gateways, a portable quantum interphase inducer designed to interact with naturally occurring hyperdimensional vortices. The interphaser opened dimensional rifts much like the gateways, but instead of the rifts being pathways through linear space, Lakesh had envisioned them as a method to travel through the gaps in normal space-time.

During the investigation of the Operation Chronos installation on Thunder Isle, a special encoded program named Parallax Points was discovered. Lakesh learned that the Parallax Points program was actually a map, a geodetic index, of all the vortex points on the planet. When these coordinates were fed into the interphaser's targeting computer, the interphaser became more than a miniaturized version of a gateway unit, even though it employed much of the same hardware and operating principles. The mat-trans gateways functioned by tapping into the quantum stream, the invisible pathways that crisscrossed outside of perceived physical space and terminating in wormholes.

The interphaser interacted with the energy within a naturally occurring vortex and caused a temporary overlapping of two dimensions. The vortex then became an intersection point, a discontinuous quantum jump, beyond relativistic space-time.

Evidence indicated there were many vortex nodes, centers of intense energy, located in the same proximity on each of the planets of the solar system, and those points correlated to vortex centers on Earth. The power points of the planet, places that naturally generated specific types of energy, possessed both positive and projective frequencies, and others were negative and receptive.

Lakesh knew some ancient civilizations were aware of these symmetrical geo-energies and constructed monuments over the vortex points in order to manipulate them. Once the interphaser was put into use, the Cerberus redoubt reverted to its original purpose—not a sanctuary for exiles, or the headquarters of a resistance against the tyranny of the barons, but a facility dedicated to unfathoming the eternal mysteries of space and time.

"Is building another interphaser that important?" DeFore asked.

Brigid stood up from the stool and stretched her willowy body, working out the kinks that had settled in her lower back during her long hours at the worktable. "Not at the moment," she answered wryly. "We could use a break. Brewster, would you mind checking in the galley and seeing what you can scrounge up for a late dinner?"

Philboyd hesitated, looked to be on the verge of

voicing an objection, then he smiled ruefully, patting his stomach. "I didn't know I was so hungry until food was mentioned."

Once the man had left the workroom, DeFore commented, "I didn't think Brewster believed the interphaser even worked. What did he say it reminded him of?"

Smiling, Brigid turned to DeFore. "An incense burner from a sixties head shop, whatever that was supposed to be. What's up?"

DeFore brushed a wisp of ash-blond hair back from her forehead. "I've been studying what we know about the hybrids ever since Quavell arrived. Since she's now part of our little—" DeFore paused for a second, groping for the proper term "—family, I figured it would be best if I knew what to do if she ever became sick or injured."

"I see," Brigid replied, her brow furrowing as she leaned a hip against the table. "And what's the conclusion you've reached?"

DeFore held up her right hand and extended two fingers, saying, "Conclusions, plural. We know that the barons need annual treatments to replace their tainted blood to strengthen their autoimmune systems, and that they require an infusion of fresh genetic material, or they sicken and die. I've asked Quavell if she'll require the same kind of treatments, and she's been evasive."

Brigid could already see where DeFore was going.

"And you have come to the conclusion that we don't have the medical equipment necessary to perform the procedures of replacement and infusion if she needs it?"

"Exactly. The equipment brought down from the Moon base helps to synthesize the nutrients she needs, but since the DNA specimen I took from her fetus defies every identifiable pattern, the other conclusion I've reached is that she's carrying a totally new form of homo sapiens. If her gestation period is anything like that of a human female's, then she should be reaching the end of her third trimester."

"Which means that when the delivery time comes," Brigid replied, anticipating the doctor's line of thought, "you'll want all the help you can find, even if that means combing every redoubt connected to the Cerberus network to procure any and all medical equipment."

DeFore smiled wanly. "I wouldn't go that far. I can think of only two places where we could find what we may need."

The tall red-haired woman repressed an involuntary shudder. "Since the Dulce facility is destroyed, that leaves only Area 51."

DeFore sighed heavily. "Unless there's another place we don't know about."

Brigid pondered the matter for a moment, searching the dark corners of her memory for anything that could possibly offer a solution. Contemplatively she said, "Lord Strongbow had the equipment to concoct the mutagenic virus that created his Imperial Dragoons."

"That would mean a trip to England," replied De-Fore. "But since Kane and Grant helped overthrow the imperium, I'm sure the Celts wouldn't be adverse to letting us take any equipment that might still be intact."

Brigid started to respond, hesitated, then said, "You know, I believe there might be a place closer to home. Remember when we checked out the various redoubts we thought could have the facilities necessary for the barons to receive their treatments?"

"Yeah," DeFore said dryly. "The end result is that we have Quavell here."

Brigid didn't reply to the comment. "I recall reading about a small facility located in the Guadalupe desert that was attached to Overproject Excalibur."

Overproject Excalibur was one of the many branches of the Totality Concept, the final phase of a millennia-long conspiracy that led to the skydark and the eventual enslavement of humanity to the barons. Overproject Excalibur dealt with genetic engineering and one of its subdivisions, Mission Invictus, was devoted to altering human beings so they could survive and thrive in the postholocaust environment.

"No one was sent to inspect the installation, right?" DeFore asked.

Brigid shook her head. "Lakesh claimed that it was too small for the needs of the barons and the hybrids."

DeFore's smile widened. "Too small for the baronial oligarchy, but not too small for a single hybrid?"

"Maybe not. I'll talk to Kane and Grant about a scouting mission."

"Shouldn't we discuss it with Lakesh?" DeFore asked.

Brigid shrugged. "Not right at the moment. I want to talk to Kane before we go any further."

DeFore looked at her quizzically, then nodded. "Okay, just let me know. Since it also involves Quavell, I believe that she should be in on the mission, as well."

"Good thinking. After all, she was a technician at the Dulce facility and would recognize the equipment needed. Although I don't know how safe making a mat-trans jump would be for the baby."

Nibbling at her lower lip, DeFore considered the possibility. At length she blew out a frustrated sigh. "Since she's the first hybrid ever to be impregnated by a human, there are too many variables to take into account. I'd hate to endanger her baby in the process of trying to help it."

Brigid nodded. "Very true." Even though her expression and tone didn't reflect it, she felt a little jealous. Over two years before, on a mission beneath the Black Gobi desert in Mongolia, she had been exposed to a strange radiation and suffered chromosomal damage. She had been rendered barren.

"I can say this," DeFore stated. "Quavell appears to be perfectly healthy, and all signs point to this being a normal pregnancy. But I'm not sure I would want her going on this trip, unless we can figure out an easy way for her to make it."

"I'll talk to Kane tonight," Brigid said. "He gated back from Thunder Isle about an hour ago. He popped in to let me know everybody was all right. He's in the armory now."

"Okay, let me know what he has to say on the matter," DeFore said as she went out into the corridor.

For a few minutes, Brigid stood there, staring at but not really seeing the interphaser. She couldn't deny she had been hurt when Kane finally opened up about what he had been forced to endure during the two weeks that Baron Cobalt held him captive in Area 51. It was a mutual pain, as she could sense his anger and humiliation as he related the details of his imprisonment. But now, the pain was closer to home, since the baby Quavell was carrying might indeed be Kane's.

She swallowed a curse and strode across the workroom and into the adjacent Cerberus armory. She knew that Kane was inside the big room, stripping and cleaning his Sin Eater, as was his habit after returning from an op.

Her long-legged gait swiftly took her to the entrance and into the huge storeroom. Everywhere she looked she saw wood and metal boxes, filled to the brim with firearms, ammunition and various other instruments of death. There were enough weapons stored in the room to supply a medium-sized army.

Kane sat on a long metal crate stamped with the logo Property Of The U.S. Army. His arm was outstretched and he was flexing the tendons in his wrist. The Sin Eater sprang from its holster and slapped snugly into his waiting hand, then withdrew as he relaxed. Behind him, like a pair of silent sentries, stood two suits of black, formfitting polycarbonate armor on steel frameworks. The armor belonged to Kane and Grant, reminders of the time when they were the epitome of what it meant to be Magistrates.

Looking up, Kane nodded curtly to Brigid. "Baptiste. You and Brewster done rebuilding the interphaser?"

She smiled wryly. "Not quite. I'm still a little surprised Lakesh is allowing us to upgrade his original design."

Kane matched her wry smile. "He's a changed man…in more ways than one."

"So are you," Brigid replied.

"Prove it."

"That's one reason I'm here."

"What's on your mind?" Kane unhooked the straps that secured the Sin Eater's power holster around his forearm.

Taking a deep breath, she began to talk. "There may be a problem with Quavell."

If she hadn't been watching for it, Brigid would have missed the flicker of unease in Kane's eyes at the mention of the hybrid woman's name. He placed the holstered Sin Eater on the metal box next to him and rubbed his hands on the thighs of his pants, wiping off the residue of gun oil. "Isn't there always some kind of problem with Quavell? What is it now?"

"She very well may need autoimmune-boosting treatments prior to her delivery date, to insure the baby is born alive and healthy."

Kane angled challenging eyebrows. "And?"

Brigid sighed. "And we don't have the equipment needed here in the redoubt."

Pursing his lips, Kane stared at his hands before he stood up and slung the holstered Sin Eater over his shoulder. "What about all the stuff brought down from the Moon base?"

Crossing her arms under her breasts, Brigid answered, "That helped synthesize the kind of food she needs, but Reba is worried there could be complications during the birth if she's not at optimum health—or whatever passes for it with a hybrid."

"Where do you propose we find this equipment?" Kane asked without a trace of emotion in his voice. His face looked as if it had been carved from granite. "Dreamland?"

"Not necessarily. There's a medical redoubt located in the Guadalupe desert. It's Totality Concept related, so it has a gateway. I think it might have the equipment needed for gene therapy, but we'll have to make a recon first."

Kane narrowed his eyes slightly. "Where's the Guadalupe desert? Mexico?"

"California, actually, about 150 miles north of what used to be Los Angeles."

"The Barrens?"

Brigid raised one eyebrow questioningly. "I suppose the area is still called that. It falls within the outlying territory of Baron Snakefish's jurisdiction."

"Any idea of what we could expect to find out there besides a redoubt?"

"Sources mention a city named Aten fairly close to it."

"Aten?" Kane echoed. "What kind of name is that?"

"Egyptian." Brigid saw the text in her mind as she called upon her eidetic memory. "Aten was the ancient Egyptian sun god. His worship was advanced by a pharaoh named Akhenaten, who had modeled the modern city of Aten on Heliopolis, forced the citizens to dye their hair black and bathe in dye to darken their skin."

Kane snorted in incredulity and disgust. "Typically fused-out for a preunification Outland settlement. If nothing else, the Program of Unification put most of those deranged despots out of work."

"I suppose that's one thing it was good for," Brigid agreed. "Historical records say that Akhenaten was killed and his daughter, Nefron, took over as ruler of the city."

"So, they traded one baron for another, then."

"In this case, I believe the term pharaoh would be more appropriate," Brigid corrected him dryly.

Kane shrugged. "Whatever. If this city was fairly

close to the redoubt, who's to say that they didn't strip it of anything useful a century ago?"

"I can't answer that. We have to do the recon. I'm sure that you'd rather go there than back into Area 51."

"Sounds like a long shot, at best."

Brigid nodded. "True, and we'd need Quavell's technical expertise, so taking her with us might present another problem. The interphaser isn't finished, so we have no choice but to use the mat-trans to get there."

"After a hundred years, I wouldn't get my hopes up about finding much," Kane said, crossing the room to a glass-fronted gun case. He opened the door and placed the Sin Eater on a hook.

"To be honest, I don't. There's always a chance something valuable was overlooked. But let's discuss the pros and cons with Lakesh, and anybody else who wants to go on the expedition."

Kane nodded curtly. "Might as well get this little expedition organized, then. But I don't expect Grant back until some time tomorrow morning."

A slight smile tugged at the corners of Brigid's lips. "Page me when he gates in. I just hope he's not too tired to make another jump."

Kane turned toward the entrance of the armory. "Even if he is, he wouldn't mention it. His image, you know."

Chapter 7

The next day, shortly before noon, Kane and Grant entered the redoubt's large cafeteria, where most of the briefings were convened. Brigid sat at a corner table talking quietly to Lakesh. Reba DeFore was seated opposite the two, her attention fixed on several sheets of paper. Quavell sat beside her.

Kane's eyes locked briefly with the inhumanly large, crystal-blue eyes of Quavell. She tilted her head slightly in greeting as she shifted in her chair, trying to find a comfortable position. Her tiny form was encased in a silvery-gray, skintight bodysuit. It only accentuated the distended condition of her belly and the slenderness of her limbs. The material of the one-piece garment was a synthetic polymer with a high degree of elasticity, and it provided adequate support.

The two men took seats on either side of Lakesh and Brigid. As he sat, Kane reached out and grabbed a cup from a nearby table and filled it with coffee from a pot at his elbow. "So we've come up with the plan?"

"Yes, friend Kane," Lakesh said, a lilting East Indian accent underscoring his cultured voice. "The good doctor has been providing us with a laundry list of everything to look for at your destination."

Mohandas Lakesh Singh was a well-built man of medium height, with thick, glossy black hair, a dark olive complexion and a long, aquiline nose. He looked no older than forty-five, despite a few strands of gray at his temples.

Kane still felt more than a little disconcerted every time he looked at him, seeing a man who physically didn't look more than fifteen years his senior, but who was in reality just a year or so shy of celebrating his 250th birthday. The change in Lakesh's appearance had taken place several months earlier, his youth and vigor miraculously restored by Sam, the imperator.

Glancing around the table, he inquired, "*My* destination? I'm not going alone, am I?"

Grant leaned back in his chair and crossed his arms over his chest. He scowled as he said, "Until we know more about the destination in question, it's a little premature to say anybody is going. What is this place?"

"The installation was attached to Overproject Excalibur, specifically Mission Invictus." Lakesh spoke tersely. "The head researcher for the mission was Dr. Connaught O'Brien. You may recall me speaking of her."

Kane and Grant nodded. Everyone at the table knew Overproject Excalibur and its many subdivisions attempted to create life-forms that would survive in a world laid waste by nuclear war. They had been responsible for the first generation of scalies, stickies, swampies and other muties that had ranged over the country in the late twenty-first century.

Lakesh continued. "The mandate of Mission Invictus was to create the missing link, the biological bridge between predark and postdark man, a superhuman designed to thrive in the world created by the atomic Armageddon. Our database has several extensive files pertaining to the genetic engineering work she conducted in the Guadalupe redoubt—at least up until the time of skydark."

"Dr. O'Brien didn't achieve the objective of her mission until after the nukecaust," Brigid declared. "A staff of twelve was settled in the installation out in the Guadalupe desert. Dr. O'Brien developed a synthetic mutagen for phase three of the mission, and the man known as Akhenaten was the end result of her work. He grew to be a powerful telepath and possessed several different psionic abilities. He had been obsessed with ancient Egypt from the time he was a child. He took his name from a rather radical pharaoh who reigned during the eighteenth dynasty."

Grant eyed her skeptically. "So this mutie from a test tube built an Egyptian city out in the middle of the Barrens?"

Brigid glanced at him. "I was getting to that. Apparently the city was already in place. It was built during the 1920s as a movie set for the silent version of *The Ten Commandments,* directed by Cecil B. DeMille."

"A ready-made ville, just waiting for someone to come in and take it over?" Kane inquired doubtfully.

"Why not?" Lakesh interjected, sipping at a cup of the green Bengali tea he favored. "With a little creative thinking and some technical expertise, it wouldn't take much effort to tap into the water tables beneath the desert and set up hydroponics. With the information stored in the redoubt's database, they had half the work done for them before they even started."

Kane shook his head. "I don't recall seeing any mention of a city or even a tar paper Outland settlement in any of the Mag patrol reports coming out of Snake-fish."

"There isn't any way in hell that a city like that would go undetected even in the Barrens," Grant observed dourly. "Me and Kane have been on enough extended Outland patrols to know that every settlement is investigated, a census taken, and depending on which ville's jurisdiction the settlement falls under, what baron ends up controlling the resources, if there are any."

Kane nodded in agreement. "And since there is no record of any settlement in the Barrens, I'd say the place is long gone."

Quavell's large eyes focused on Kane, pinning him to his seat with her stare. "It is possible that the city does still exist. If the ruler did indeed possess powerful psionic abilities, it's not unreasonable to assume that they could have been passed down to his offspring.

The descendants could have encountered Magistrates before and mind-wiped the encounter, leaving no memory of what had transpired."

"We're engaging in a lot of pointless speculation here," DeFore declared impatiently. "It's the redoubt we should be concerned about, not if a city is still there or not. This is all hypothesizing based on anecdotal data that's a hundred years old."

Lakesh laughed shortly, conceding the point. "Very true. However, we receive a live transit line signature, so the gateway in the installation is still functioning. The question now is who wants to be on the jump team."

"I should," DeFore said to the surprise of Kane and Grant. "I can determine if any of the medical equipment is still intact. That way we can make a preliminary list for Quavell to go over when we get back."

Before Kane could raise his objections, Brigid spoke up. "I have to agree with you, Reba. You, Grant and Kane should make the first jump, and when you get back, we'll go over the report and then decide what to do next."

Kane cast her a swift, suspicious glance. "You usually insist on joining these field trips, Baptiste."

She shrugged. "It's just a simple scout-out, right? Besides, I'm busy rebuilding the interphaser, remember?"

"Yeah," Kane said dourly. "Just a simple scout-out." He briefly wondered how Brigid would react if he suggested Philboyd accompany them on the jump, but decided not to press the issue. It annoyed him that she seemed to prefer the company of the lanky, myopic astrophysicist to his, at least lately. He didn't understand what she found so appealing in him, even if she was drawn to his intellect.

Curtly, he said, "Sounds like a plan to me, Baptiste. When do we want to leave?"

"The sooner, the better," Grant grumbled. "Let's gear up and meet in the mat-trans chamber in thirty."

PRECISELY TWENTY-NINE MINUTES later, Kane and Grant stood outside the brown-tinted armaglass walls of the jump chamber. Both men wore midnight-colored shadow suits that absorbed light the way a sponge absorbed water. Although the black, skintight garments didn't appear as if they would offer protection from fleabites, they were impervious to most wavelengths of radiation.

Ever since they had absconded with the suits from Redoubt Yankee on Thunder Isle, the suits had proved their worth and their superiority to the polycarbonate Magistrate armor, if for no other reason than their internal subsystems.

Manufactured with a technique known in predark days as electrospin lacing, the electrically charged polymer particles formed a dense web of formfitting fibers. Composed of a compiled weave of spider silk, Monocrys and Spectra fabrics, the garments were essentially a single-crystal, metallic microfiber, with a very dense molecular structure.

The outer Monocrys sheathing went opaque when exposed to radiation, and the Kevlar and Spectra layers provided protection against blunt trauma. The spider silk allowed flexibility, but it traded protection from firearms for freedom of movement. The suits were climate-controlled for environments up to 150 degrees and as cold as minus ten degrees Fahrenheit. Flat, square pouches were attached to the small of their backs by Velcro tabs.

DeFore joined them, dressed in a pair of khaki shorts, high-topped jump boots and a long-sleeved blouse. Normally the woman shied away from firearms, but strapped to her waist was an old-fashioned 9 mm 1914 Browning handgun. Her rucksack contained a medical kit, several packets of MREs, a laptop and a small vid camera.

Grant's and Kane's Sin Eaters were strapped securely to their right forearms. Kane secured a small motion tracker to his left wrist and turned it on, watching the tiny LCD screen beep as people moved about the control chamber. Satisfied that it was working properly, he switched it off and gave the strap one last tug. "Ready to go?"

DeFore nodded nervously. "As ready as I'll ever be."

Kane glanced out the door leading to the operations center and gave Bry the thumbs-up gesture. Bry, seated at the master control board, nodded in acknowledgment and his fingers flew over the keyboard, inputting the coordinates of the destination gateway. "Transmission codes locked in, so whenever you're ready," he announced.

Kane lifted the wedge-shaped handle of the jump chamber and the heavy door opened easily on counterbalanced pivots. Entering the chamber, he took up a position leaning against the wall opposite the doorway and tried to relax. Grant entered, his face a stony mask, but Kane knew that his partner was filled with trepidation. Kane could sympathize with him, as he also disliked using the chambers, but without access to an interphaser, the gateway was their fastest form of travel. DeFore sat between the two men on the metal hexagonal floor plates, nervously dry-washing her hands.

"You sure you're good to go?" Grant asked her.

DeFore managed to force a grin. "As good as you are."

Grant grunted and pulled the door shut, the solenoids clicking soundly in place and initiating the automatic jump sequence. As tendrils of mist began to curl up from the chamber floor, Kane closed his eyes and waited for the transition to begin.

Chapter 8

Kane squeezed his eyes shut against the harsh light. He placed his hands against his temples, fearing for a moment the sudden surge of pain within his skull would blow his head apart. Within seconds, the agony receded. He had to admit that he had been through far worse when making other mat-trans jumps.

He was lying flat on his back, which wasn't unusual. One of the enduring mysteries of the gateway process was how a jumper could begin a transition standing erect, but almost always ended it lying down. Forcing his eyes open, he looked around.

The armaglass walls of the gateway were a pale rust color, which was fairly easy on the eyes compared to some of the more garish color codes he had seen. Flexing his wrist tendons, he let his Sin Eater slap into his waiting palm, and slowly climbed to his feet.

Both DeFore and Grant were starting to stir. The big man opened his dark eyes and gazed at Kane accusingly, then closed them. "I'm getting too old for this shit," he whispered hoarsely.

"How do you feel?" Kane asked, extending a hand.

Grant took it, and allowed Kane to heave him to his feet. "Like always after a jump. Like shit. I hurt all over."

"Maybe you shouldn't have wrestled with that dinocelphalian then," Kane commented unsympathetically, turning toward DeFore. "How're you doing, De-Fore?"

The bronze-skinned, buxom woman didn't attempt to stand. Instead, she lay motionless on the floor of the gateway. Weakly, she said, "Give me a minute."

Unleathering his own Sin Eater, Grant took a position to the right side of the door. He and Kane waited patiently for DeFore to regain her equilibrium. Both men were used to the side effects of the hyperdimensional jumps, and recovered quickly. DeFore had only traveled by the mat-trans a handful of times, and hadn't grown accustomed to having her molecules transformed into digital data and sent hurtling through the quantum stream.

After a moment, DeFore carefully stood. She nodded curtly to both men. "Ready."

"I'll take point," Kane said, more for DeFore's benefit than Grant's.

He reached for the handle on the door and lifted it up. The heavy door swung open smoothly and silently, revealing a small anteroom. As with all the redoubts they had been in, the chamber led into a room containing a number of computers and monitor screens. Past the electronic equipment, Kane saw a narrow corridor. Fluorescent light strips glowed feebly from narrow channels recessed into the ceiling. Stepping down from the platform, he moved out of the anteroom, computer room and glanced into the hallway.

Strange markings were painted on both walls of the corridor. It took Kane a moment to realize that they were hieroglyphs. He had no idea of their meaning, but from what Brigid had told them during the briefing, he was positive that they were in the right place.

Grant and DeFore joined him at the entrance to the corridor. Holding up his wrist, Kane looked at the tiny LCD of the motion tracker. The small device registered nothing moving ahead of them. He knew from unpleasant experience that a lack of motion didn't mean the redoubt was uninhabited, so Kane proceeded down the passageway with extreme caution.

The corridor ended at a partly ajar door, which Kane gently pushed open with a foot. Nothing jumped out at him as the door opened fully. He saw a very small unfurnished room. The opposite wall was perforated by a metal-sheathed disk surrounded by three concentric collars of steel. Affixed to the wall beside it was a keypad. A square plastic sign beneath the keypad warned in bright red letters: Biohazard Beyond This Point! Entry Forbidden To Personnel Not Wearing Anticontaminant Clothing!

Kane cursed under his breath, suddenly fearing a possible biological hazard beyond the metal door. Both he and Grant had seen similar warnings in other places. The surge of momentary fear subsided. He looked behind him and nodded for DeFore and Grant to join him.

Grant entered first, followed by DeFore. She looked at the warning on the wall and said, "This facility must have dealt with some serious pathogens during its researches."

Kane threw a questioning glance at his partner, raising his eyebrows slightly. Grant shrugged and stepped back, pulling Reba DeFore with him. Kane punched the enter button on the keypad and a green light flashed. With a rumble and a squeak of hydraulics, the metal disk rolled to the left.

The room beyond was dimly lit by weak and wavering overhead lights, but Kane could make out the outlines of trestle tables. The motion tracker on his wrist remained silent as he stepped into the chamber, his eyes adjusting to the dimness around him.

Lights blinked on overhead, pushing back the dimness and revealing the room's contents. Heavy tables lined the walls. A heavy pane of transparent armaglass comprised the right-hand wall, which ran the entire length of the chamber. Directly across from Kane was a twin of the door that they had just passed through. He could also see the outlines of where equipment had once taken up floor space, but nothing remained of it, not even a shard of broken glass.

"Looks like this place was cleaned out," he told his companions. "Probably a long, long time ago."

DeFore entered the chamber and looked around. "We still have the rest of the redoubt to explore."

Kane crossed the room and punched the enter key on the pad next to the round hatch, and as with the other, it blinked green. The heavy slab of metal rolled aside. Beyond it stretched another corridor, with doorways on either side. The main sec door at the end was a massive portal of vanadium steel.

Kane moved quickly and silently down the corridor, pausing only briefly to peer into each doorway as he passed. Several of the rooms clearly were sleeping chambers, while another was a combination of galley and kitchen. Another contained bathing facilities, and two more were apparently storage closets. When he reached the end of the corridor, he swept the motion detector around one last time. It registered no movement.

"All clear," he called to DeFore and Grant.

The big man ignored the rooms as he walked past them to join Kane; DeFore, on the other hand, stopped at the first of the storerooms and paused at the threshold, looking apprehensively into it.

"This place is bare!" she exclaimed in dismay.

"Yeah, that's what 'cleaned out' generally means," Kane retorted dourly.

"As long as we're here, let's make sure," Grant grunted.

They split up and began to inspect the small redoubt. Unlike many Totality Concept–related installations, this one wasn't a multileveled labyrinth of corridors and control rooms. It was stripped down and Spartan.

There were a total of eighteen beds divided up between three dormitories, which indicated the maximum personnel of the place. The bathroom was small, but held five toilet stalls and three urinals. Three showerheads projected from a tiled wall in an enclosure, and there was a six-and-a-half-foot-tall, bullet-shaped cylinder located in one corner. Kane recognized it as a Medisterile chamber, a decontamination unit used in the Mag Divisions to clean up Magistrates who might have strayed too near a hellzone or hotspot during a field op.

Kane searched an office suite that held six desks enclosed by partitions, each one equipped with a computer terminal. None of the machines were powered up, and he wasn't sure if they could be. Two gray metal filing cabinets stood against one wall.

Curiosity got the better of Kane, and he opened the top drawer of a cabinet and lifted out a file folder. Thumbing through the files contained in the folder, he saw most of them were written in scientific terminology that he found all but impossible to understand. His mind flashed to Brigid, thinking that if she were with them, it would take the woman only a glance to decipher the meaning of the file in his hands. He tamped down a surge of irrational anger that she had chosen to remain in Cerberus and tinker with one of Lakesh's toys, instead of joining the team. At least he hoped she was tinkering with only a toy.

DeFore entered and broke his paranoid train of thought. "What are you reading?" she asked.

"Not really reading," Kane replied, passing the folder to her. "I can't make head or tails of it."

DeFore flipped through the sheaves of paper and then dropped the folder back into the filing cabinet. "Nothing of real importance in that."

As she walked around the room, peering into the cubicles, she said, "I'm afraid I've got bad news."

Kane knew she was going to say that. He rolled his eyes toward the ceiling and leaned against a filing cabinet. "Let me guess—this place is as bare as Baron Cobalt's conscience."

She nodded, her expression troubled. "It's like you said…the redoubt was cleaned out quite some time ago. All the medicine, medical equipment and laboratory equipment is missing. There are signs that the place has been visited in the past few years, though."

Crossing his arms over his chest, Kane regarded DeFore critically. "Probably a Mag force when they checked out all the redoubts a couple of years ago, searching for us."

"That's what I figured, too." Reaching into the back pocket of her shorts, DeFore produced a small square box of transparent plastic containing a number of CD jewel cases.

DeFore placed the box on a desk and opened it,

pulling out one of the disks and turning it over in her fingers. As she flipped it, Kane noticed a red triangle with three vertical lines bisecting it. He recognized the symbol of Overproject Excalibur, which had later been adopted as the insignia of the Archon Directorate. Imprinted below the image, he saw a series of numbers. They read 1/18/08.

Kane asked, "Is that some kind of journal or log?"

DeFore studied the numbers and slowly nodded. "I'd have to guess that's the case." She picked up the box and flipped through the disks, one by one. "They're all dated."

"Maybe we can learn something from the information," Kane suggested. "They might contain the locations of other medical redoubts that could have the same kind of equipment that we need."

"At the very least, they'll make for interesting additions to the Cerberus database," DeFore commented as she placed the disk back into the box and snapped it shut.

Grant strode into the room, scowling as always. "Nothing of use here. Might as well jump back home."

Kane pushed himself away from the cabinet. "I want to have a look around outside first," he said.

"Why?" Grant asked, his eyebrows knitting at the bridge of his nose.

"Curiosity, mainly," Kane responded. "If a Mag force was responsible for cleaning the place out, we'll probably find some evidence outside."

"What Mag Division would've done it?" Grant asked.

"My guess is Cobaltville."

Grant nodded in agreement. "That's right. Baron Cobalt was already making incursions into Snakefish territory."

"Then he might have sent out teams to retrieve any equipment that would have been even remotely of use to him in Area 51," DeFore interjected. "And since this place was used for genetic engineering, it makes a certain amount of sense."

Kane and Grant left the office and walked to the huge vanadium steel door. Grant stood by the green lever on the steel frame and pushed it up. Kane trained his Sin Eater on the rectangle of alloy as a complicated system of gears and pulleys began raising it. DeFore stood a few feet behind him.

A wave of brilliant sunlight poured into the redoubt, almost blinding the three people. Shading their eyes, they squinted out at the desert wasteland that stretched out before them as far as their eyes could see. The drifting dunes of saffron and ochre seemed endless.

Kane waited for several seconds, letting his eyes adjust to the harsh glare reflecting off the dunes. The heat against his face felt like it radiated from an open oven, and sweat formed on his brow. He stepped out of the interior of the redoubt and stood beneath an overhang, examining the terrain. Grant joined him, but DeFore stayed just inside the door. Neither man said a word as they took dark-lensed glasses from the pouches at the small of their backs. They walked a dozen or so paces forward, then turned around to study the exterior of the redoubt. It was a gray half dome, nearly buried on all sides by high drifts of sand.

Grant crouched, running his fingers over the sifting sands. He glanced up at Kane and announced matter-of-factly, "Tracks."

Kane squinted down to where Grant pointed. Two narrow, parallel grooves showed faintly against the desert hardpan beneath a layer of sand. "A wagon or a cart of some kind?"

Pursing his lips, Grant stood. "Of some kind. I suppose we could try and follow the tracks, see where they lead. They may take us to the medical equipment."

Kane put his hand over his eyes to shield them from the sun, as he stared out over the desolate landscape. "That seems like a hell of a long shot to me."

"Me, too." They turned as DeFore braved the heat to join them. "Roamers probably made the tracks. We might as well return to Cerberus and make secondary plans."

As they turned to reenter the redoubt, Kane thought he saw sunlight glinting off metal to the north of their position. He roughly pushed DeFore toward the redoubt's open door. "Inside," he commanded.

The medic obeyed instantly, even though the narrow-eyed glance she cast over her shoulder showed she was a little irked at the rough treatment. Sin Eater in hand, Grant moved to the right of Kane. Stealthily,

Kane crept toward the glitter. Light flashed from the crest of a dune, no more than twenty-five yards away.

Keeping to a crouch, Kane scaled the face of the dune and found a half-buried glass bottle, sunlight reflecting from its surface. He released his breath in a profanity-seasoned sigh, and pulled the wind-scoured bottle from the sand.

Turning toward Grant, he called, "Just some litter!"

"What kind?" his partner asked.

Kane held the bottle over his head. A thunderous crack suddenly split the still desert air. Kane jumped and swore as the bottle shattered in his hand, spraying his shadow suit with shards of glass. Instinctively, he threw himself off the dune. Grant rushed over, eyes and gun barrel questing for a target.

"That was a fucking Sin Eater!" Grant snarled.

Spitting out grit and knuckling sand from his eyes, Kane rose swiftly to his feet. His rejoinder of "You think?" fairly dripped with sarcasm.

Together, the two men backed away from the dune toward the open entrance to the redoubt. A swift glance showed him DeFore just inside the doorway, her autoblaster in hand. "I don't see anybody!" she half shouted in agitation.

"Let the rest of the Barrens know they've got the drop on us, why don't you?" Grant bit out. "Get to the gate room and stand by!"

The medic hesitated a moment, then turned on her heel and ran into the darkness of the passageway.

"What the hell could Mags be doing out here?" Kane snapped, eyes sweeping their desolate surroundings.

"Probably not Mags," Grant retorted. "Some Roamers who stole a Sin Eater, more than likely."

At that instant, a lone figure appeared on the crest of the dune. He wore ebony Magistrate armor and brandished a Sin Eater.

Chapter 9

Both Kane and Grant tracked the armored figure with their pistols as it stopped and stared down at the pair.

"He doesn't look much like a Roamer to me," Kane murmured.

"You think?" Grant replied sardonically, his finger brushing the trigger stud of his pistol. "Whoever he is, it's best if we get the first shots in, then get back to the mat-trans and gate the fuck out of here."

About a dozen men appeared atop the dune and spread out in a line on either side of the Magistrate. "I don't think we'll make it," Kane commented wryly.

All of the men were similar in physique and clothing. Naked except for loosely woven white linen kilts threaded through with gold wire, they were very dark skinned, the breadth of their chest and shoulders enormous. Glittering collars of hammered gold enclosed the bases of their muscular necks. Only their heads differentiated them from one another.

Each man wore jeweled, helmetlike headpieces that completely covered their faces and rested on their broad shoulders. They all followed a different design, fashioned after the appearance of an animal; Grant and Kane saw ones that depicted falcons, cats, jackals, bulls, snakes and even a bug.

Neither man saw anything that resembled a traditional blaster among the group assembled atop the dune, but all of them held long, slender silver rods, tipped by V-shaped prongs.

Grant side-mouthed to Kane, "One Mag, one Sin Eater and a bunch of fused-out sec men with fishing poles—I think we could make it."

Kane didn't immediately agree with Grant's assessment. The silver rods reminded him too much of the infrasound wands used by the hybrids. For several tense seconds, the two groups stared at each other, neither side moving or speaking.

Then the Magistrate stepped forward. "Don't let the armor fool you," he said in a surprisingly youthful voice. "I'm like you."

As the Mag descended the face of the dune, his booted feet starting miniature avalanches of sand, Kane noted he had a slight limp, favoring his left leg. Although the black polycarbonate exoskeleton was standard Magistrate issue, the red badge was missing from the left pectoral. Kane walked forward to meet him. Grant maintained his position, his eyes and gun never straying from the dozen figures arrayed on the crest of the dune.

"What did you mean," Kane asked quietly, "that you're like us?"

The Magistrate lowered his weapon and responded to Kane's question with one of his own. "What are you doing here?"

"That's really none of your business," Kane answered.

"That's where you're mistaken," the armored man replied tersely. "This redoubt and everything inside it are in my jurisdiction. You're trespassing, and unless you have a damn good reason for being here, I might have to consider this a hostile incursion."

"I might consider somebody shooting a bottle out of my hand the same thing," Kane told him coldly. "Or was that just the way you say hello in these parts?"

"I'm waiting," the Magistrate said autocratically.

"Officious little son of a bitch, aren't you?" Grant rumbled.

Kane smiled as he stared into the tinted visor of the Magistrate's helmet. He couldn't make out the man's eyes, but he could tell by the rounded softness of his chin and relatively unlined face the Mag was very young, probably not even twenty.

Kane tired of the eye-wrestling contest and lowered his weapon. "All right. We wanted to check out the equipment that might have been stored inside the redoubt."

"Why?"

"To help a friend."

"A friend?" The Magistrate made something of a show of holstering his Sin Eater. Reaching up, he removed his helmet. The man was even younger than Kane had imagined, probably eighteen at the most. "From what I hear, you and Grant don't have a whole lot of friends."

"Where did you hear that?" Grant asked genially.

"Ragnarville," the youth said. "Then I was stationed at the Archuleta Mesa, right after I graduated the academy. That was where I stayed until you two destroyed the place."

Kane didn't bother to argue the point. Although he and Grant were directly responsible for the destruction of the facility, the act had been inadvertent. He still felt guilty about it, remembering how his and Grant's actions had caused the deaths of almost two thousand newborn and toddler-aged hybrids.

"So, you know who we are. That's not much of a surprise." Kane maintained a calm, almost disinterested tone. "But why are you here? This is a hell of a long way from either the mesa or Area 51."

The Magistrate cocked his head quizzically. "Area 51? What's that? I've never heard of the place."

Kane waved the question away. "Never mind. You know who we are, but who are you?"

The young man smiled. "Name's Decard." He gestured over his shoulder at the men standing silently on the crest of the dune. "And those men are Incarnates, the guardians of Aten."

Neither Kane nor Grant replied for a long moment. Then Grant inquired, "The city still exists?"

Decard nodded. "I've been there for about a year now, ever since I was forced to turn my back on the Magistrates and run for my life." He smiled, but there wasn't much humor in it. "That's why I said we were the same."

"What—or who—forced you to do that?" Kane asked.

Decard's lips twisted as if he tasted something sour. "Two barons were on an inspection tour of the facility and I overheard something they said. I was found out. A senior Mag named Crowe tried to issue my termination warrant."

Kane nodded, fully understanding what the young man was telling him. "So you fought back."

"Yeah," Decard replied grimly. "Yeah, I did. I grabbed what supplies I could and made a run for it. If it weren't for the oracles of Aten, I would have died in the desert. But they found me and nursed me back to health."

"Lucky you," Grant grumbled somewhat sarcastically, his tone and bearing skeptical.

Decard eyed Grant superciliously. "That brings us to the big question. What made you think there was anything in the redoubt?"

Kane looked at Grant, who raised his shoulders a fraction of an inch. Turning back to Decard, Kane said, "We have our sources, as I'm sure you've heard."

Decard wiped at the sweat accumulating on his brow. "How'd you even know there was a redoubt out here?"

"Once again," Grant retorted curtly, "we have our sources. But there's nothing in there now."

"What do you need it for?" Decard demanded.

Kane felt his hackles starting to rise. "Like we said, to help a friend."

"Who?"

Kane's lips compressed in a tight angry line. "Does it make any difference?"

"It might. If you tell me what kind of equipment you need, I might be able to work out some sort of arrangement."

"So the stuff we need has been removed to Aten?" Grant asked.

Decard shook his head. "I never said that. I said that if you told me what you need it for, and who you need it for, then I could possibly help you."

"Who would you be working out this arrangement with?" Kane wanted to know.

The young man's lips curved in a smirk. "Hand me a name and I'll hand you one back."

Kane snorted contemptuously, turned his back on Decard and stalked toward the redoubt. "Forget it, boy. It's too damn hot to stand around playing guessing games with you."

"Give my regards to Quavell," Decard called after him.

Astonishment leapfrogged over shock in the pit of Kane's belly. He stopped in midstep but he did not turn. "What did you say?"

"You heard me, Kane."

For once, the scowl on Grant's face lifted, replaced by a mask of surprise. Eyes narrowing to angry, suspicious slits, Kane spun on his heel and glared at the younger man. "Where did you hear that name, boy? The mesa?"

Decard met Kane's aggression with a calm demeanor. "She's who you needed the medical equipment for, isn't it?"

Kane raised his Sin Eater and aligned Decard's forehead with the bore, even though he saw the Incarnates pointing their strange staffs at him and Grant. "How do you know about her?"

Decard's composure faltered slightly and he swallowed hard. "I knew her in the mesa complex, like you figured."

"And how do you know she was the reason we came here?" Kane half snarled. "Is that the reason you and your menagerie are out here?"

Carefully, Decard dabbed at the sweat pebbling his forehead. "You'll have to come with me to learn that, Kane."

"Come with you where, boy?"

Decard bristled slightly at being addressed as "boy" again. "Aten, where else? You can talk to Queen Nefron and learn everything you need to know."

Grant snorted. "Forget that. We're not stupes."

Decard shrugged as if the matter were of little importance to him. "It's your choice. I give you my word as a former Magistrate that you won't be harmed if you come with us. You could negotiate with Queen Nefron for the equipment that Quavell needs, if we have it. And more besides."

The blazing sun beat down on the heads of everyone as Kane stood there, staring at the young Magistrate. Although he had acted in the role of an ambassador before, striking agreements with other groups of people, even in foreign countries, the eerie aura exuded by the animal-headed Incarnates made him distinctly disinclined to put his trust in Decard.

The reference to a Queen Nefron didn't soothe his apprehension, either. He remembered Brigid noting that a Nefron had taken power in Aten—over a hundred years ago. The likelihood that the two Nefrons were one and the same didn't seem high, but he and Grant had encountered astoundingly long-lived entities before.

"I don't think so," Kane said at length. "At least not under these circumstances. Maybe later, I can return with—"

Decard cut him off with a sharp gesture. "A one-time-only invitation, Kane. I'm breaking the law as it is. But since you and Grant are something special…" The young man trailed off and shrugged again.

"Thanks," Kane replied dryly. He gave the group of Incarnates one last look before he turned back toward the redoubt. "Well, it's been pointless knowing you."

He wondered if Decard was experienced enough to

recognize a bluff, or the deliberate show of disdain, by keeping his back to him and his Incarnates. Kane and Grant had crossed less than half the distance to the entrance when DeFore came running out of the doorway, her face registering excitement and fear. "The gateway's been activated. We've got inbound jumpers!"

Grant and Kane rocked to a halt. "Could it be someone from Cerberus?" Grant demanded.

DeFore shook her head. "Not unless a hell of an emergency blew up in the last couple of hours since we've been gone. I didn't stick around to see who was coming through."

"Who the hell is that?" Decard barked. Kane turned at the sound of the young man's approach.

"Reba DeFore, our medical expert," Grant stated.

"And what's the problem?" Decard demanded.

"Your redoubt has an unauthorized jumper," DeFore answered.

Decard gestured to the animal-headed men on the dune. Immediately, the Incarnates fanned out and moved with enviable speed and agility across the dunes toward the entrance of the redoubt, to take up positions on either side of the open door.

"I don't think it's any of our people," Kane declared. "It could be a group of Magistrates, coming from one of the villes."

"I doubt that," Decard replied worriedly. "There hasn't been any activity around here since—" He broke off, then said, "We're not expecting anybody."

"Anybody else, you mean," Kane corrected him flatly. "It's pretty obvious you were expecting us."

Decard didn't deny the assertion and Kane dropped the subject. He stared into the darkness beyond the threshold of the entrance. "We shouldn't take any chances."

Grant tapped DeFore on the shoulder and gestured to the dune where Decard and the Incarnates had first appeared. "Reba, get behind that. If the shit hits the fan, you should be safe from any stray fire."

Her mouth a grim line, the medic nodded and half ran, half stumbled across the sifting sands and disappeared behind a dune. Grant watched her go.

"What about you?" Decard asked, looking between the two men.

"Your territory, your show," Kane said tonelessly.

For a few seconds, Decard looked uncomfortable, then he spun on his heel and ran to join the Incarnates, who had positioned themselves strategically around the entrance to the redoubt. Both Kane and Grant joined DeFore behind the base of the dune.

An eternity seemed to pass before there was a hint of activity inside the doorway. Then, a single figure enshrouded by a beige-hooded cloak stepped with a strange grace over the threshold and stood in the sand. It carried a long spear, almost half again the size of the person carrying it. The figure stooped over slightly as it inspected the ground, then walked forward another few yards, stepping in such a way as to suggest an unusual foot structure.

"Like they're walking on tiptoes," Grant whispered.

"Or the sand is burning their feet," Kane retorted.

As the words left his mouth, a second figure joined the first, dressed identically, but with a rifle of an unusual design strapped across its back. It looked heavy and clumsy, larger even than the Barrett sniper rifle Grant favored.

"Ever see a rifle like that before?" Kane asked Grant in a whisper.

"No, not ever," Grant replied in the same low tone of voice. "Not even pix."

The two figures bent their hooded heads toward each other and seemed to be exchanging words.

"At least," Kane commented, "they're not Mags—"

The words caught in his throat as the first of the figures stood tall and threw off the robe. There was no mistaking the feminine curves, with the tawny mane of dark golden hair rippling down her back and full, firm breasts. But the resemblance to a human woman ended there.

Her legs were disproportionately long and slender, but her feet were very large and had only four clawed toes. Her head was round with a flat face tapering to a narrow chin. The big slanted eyes gleamed scarlet in the iris. The wide mouth showed sharp teeth, with filament-like whiskers quivering slightly in the breeze.

Her big ears rose to sharp points on either side of her skull. Sleek, black-striped tan fur covered her body.

It lightened into a rich shade of creamy white at her throat.

"What," Grant husked out, "the fuck is that? And where did it—*she*—come from?"

"At the moment," Kane murmured, "I'm more interested in what *she's* doing here."

Chapter 10

Brigid Baptiste inspected the Mercator map and asked, "How long have they been gone?"

She stood in the central control complex of Cerberus. A long room with high, vaulted ceilings, it was lined by consoles of dials, switches and computer stations. A huge Mercator relief map of the world spanned one wall. Pinpoints of light glowed in almost every country, and thin phosphorescent lines networked across the continents, like a web spun by a rad-mad spider. The map delineated all the locations of all functioning indexed gateway units all over the world.

"Less than two hours," Lakesh replied from the main ops console. "Well within reasonable time parameters. I thought you were preoccupied with retooling the interphaser."

Brigid turned to face him, a slightly abashed smile on her face. "I turned it over to Brewster for a little while."

"Having second thoughts about sitting out this mission?" Lakesh inquired genially.

Only Domi, Lakesh and Quavell were present in the

redoubt's nerve center. Brigid guessed Lakesh had volunteered to sit in for Bry while he took a meal break. In the wake of the recent assault on the redoubt, the man had actually earned a long vacation, working as he had almost nonstop to restore the operational functions of the installation. The major repairs had only recently been completed, although a few of the subsystems were yet to be tested and debugged.

"It's only a recon," Brigid replied a little defensively. "Or supposed to be."

"They're fine," Domi said reassuringly from the medical monitor station.

Brigid turned toward the girl. An albino, Domi was dressed far less formally than anyone else in the command center, or the entire redoubt for that matter. She wore very high-cut khaki shorts, a white tank top and nothing else. She almost never wore shoes while in the redoubt and not very often while outside of it either, since her feet were thickly callused on the soles.

Born a feral child of the Outlands, Domi was barely five feet tall and weighed every ounce of a hundred pounds. Her unruly bone-white hair was cropped close to her head, and her bright red eyes shone like polished rubies on either side of her thin-bridged nose. Her forehead still showed a purple discoloration, a memento of Maccan's infrasound gauntlet.

On the screen she saw an aerial topographical map of the state of California. Superimposed over it flashed three icons. The telemetry transmitted from Kane,

Grant and DeFore's subdermal biolink transponders scrolled in a drop-down window across the top of the screen. The computer systems recorded every byte of data sent to the Comsat and directed it down to the redoubt's hidden antenna array. Sophisticated scanning filters combed through the telemetric signals using special human biological encoding.

The digital data stream was then routed to another console through the locational program, to precisely isolate the team's present position in time and space. The program considered and discarded thousands of possibilities within milliseconds.

All of the icons, including Kane's, glowed green, much to Brigid's relief. Images spun in the depths of the monitor, memories from even further back than her first meeting with Kane. For a shaved splinter of a second, she saw him as a young man of nineteen or twenty, sword in his hand as he charged to rescue her from the Norman soldiers who held her captive.

Kane had worn another name then, another form, but the name that had been chosen for him by Morrigan, the blind nun from Ireland's Priory of Awen, fit him best: *anam-chara.* In the Gaelic tongue, it meant "soul-friend." The dreams both of them had experienced during different mat-trans jumps and crisis points suggested that they'd lived past lives, each continually intertwined with the other in some manner, never knowing true love.

She ran her fingers through her hair and tried hard

not to think about the message conveyed from the future Kane of twenty-seven years hence, regarding their relationship. She was glad she and Kane hadn't discussed the issue at length. For all his fighting prowess—or maybe because of it, Brigid wasn't sure—Kane thought first with his emotions. That was alien to everything Brigid Baptiste held dear.

To survive, one needed a clear head. She worked hard to keep hers that way.

"I hope they find something of use there," she announced to no one in particular.

"Even if they don't, just knowing there's nothing there is of use, right?" Domi asked ingenuously.

Lakesh laughed and arose from the ops console, coming to stand beside Domi. "That's a very Zen observation, darlingest one."

The albino girl slid an arm around Lakesh's waist and pressed her head against his hip. Lakesh smiled down at her fondly and gently stroked her bone-white hair.

Brigid studiously avoided paying too much attention to the open display of affection. She wasn't sure if she didn't prefer it when the two people kept their intimacy a secret.

From a computer station, Quavell spoke up in her soft, almost childish voice. "This is interesting."

Almost gratefully, Brigid turned toward her. "What is?"

"The information I found in the database relating to the Mission Invictus redoubt and Dr. O'Brien."

The Cerberus control complex contained five dedicated and eight shared subprocessors, all linked in a mainframe system. The advanced model used experimental error-correcting microchips of miniature size, which even reacted to quantum fluctuations. The biochip technology that was employed contained protein molecules sandwiched between microscopic glass-and-metal circuits. Almost the entirety of human knowledge could be accessed by a few keystrokes or mouse clicks.

"I thought we went over that at the briefing," Lakesh said a little stiffly.

"Superficially I suppose we did," Quavell responded smoothly. "But I did a little more research into her and the various branches of Overproject Excalibur."

"What did you uncover?" Brigid asked.

"As I'm sure you're aware," Quavell answered, "a great deal of the Overproject Excalibur research was directed toward the creation of the hybrid race, although for some reason much of the engineering regarding advanced psionic ability was omitted during the final phase of our creation. I find that to be somewhat disconcerting."

"How so?" Lakesh prompted

Quavell made a diffident gesture with one hand, her kind's equivalent of a resigned shrug. "Apparently, such abilities were actually desirable during the initial Mission Invictus experiments but were not actively pursued afterward. But it's obvious much of the research conducted there before the nuclear war, served as the template for my kind...not to mention all the other genetically engineered life-forms that grew from Overproject Excalibur subdivisions."

"Wouldn't that make you related to some of the stickies, scalies and other muties, then?" Domi's voice held an apologetic note.

Quavell inclined her head ever so slightly. "That is true. But unlike those creatures who were designed to be soldiers, my kind were bred to lead, not fight or follow."

Brigid ran her hand through her fall of hair. "Where are you going with this, Quavell?"

An insistent electronic beep interrupted the discussion, and Lakesh disengaged himself from Domi and returned to the master ops station. Touching a key on the board, he narrowed his eyes at the data appearing on the monitor screen. "I've got a signal on a gateway activation."

All eyes in the chamber turned to look at the Mercator map spanning the wall. All the lights glowed a steady yellow.

"It's not registering on the index," Brigid stated. "That means it's not part of the official Cerberus network, but one of the modular units."

"I'll trace the jump line. One moment." Lakesh bent over the keyboard, his fingers a blur of motion. He returned his attention to the map, announcing triumphantly, "Got it."

On the Mercator map, a light appeared in the

African subcontinent. Glancing at the machine language scrolling across the monitor screen, Lakesh said, "From the coordinates, the jump line originates from Egypt…from the vicinity of the Sphinx in Giza."

"Egypt?" Brigid echoed incredulously. She stared at the brightly glowing pinpoint of light on the map. Then the tiny bulb went dark.

"That was exciting," Domi said sarcastically.

Brigid turned questioning eyes toward Lakesh. "Did the bulb burn out or what?"

Lakesh rubbed his chin thoughtfully, looked at the data on the screen again and then shrugged. "It's possible that it was merely a computer glitch, one of the subroutines not operating properly yet. Mr. Bry hasn't run a diagnostic on everything yet."

Stifling a snort, Brigid said, "I don't think it's a coincidence—Giza in Egypt, Aten in the Barrens."

"No, that doesn't seem to be likely, does it?" Lakesh looked back up at the map.

"Is it possible there's a mat-trans in the vicinity of the Sphinx?" Quavell asked.

Lakesh tugged absently at his nose. "Not only possible, but very probable, now that I think about it. Before the nukecaust a much-debated chamber beneath the Sphinx was finally located and entered. The discoveries were immediately given the highest secret classification. A research station had been set up nearby, under the guise of an archaeological dig. A modular gateway was installed in the chamber."

Brigid glanced quizzically at Lakesh. "Did you ever learn anything about the findings there?"

"Not much, I'm afraid."

Even Quavell looked interested in what he had to say. "Enlighten us, if you would, please."

Lakesh sighed. "As you may know, there are many pyramids and monuments built up and down the Nile River in Egypt. They were considered to be places of ascent, the point of departure for the deceased on his journey to the heavens to join the gods."

"What does that have to do with what was found beneath the Sphinx?" Domi asked in a bored voice.

"I'll get to that," Lakesh said with a smile. "The pyramid monuments were preceded by brick tombs called mastabas. They contained burial and special chambers set up so that the loved ones of the deceased could offer food and other goods that could be used by the individual in the afterlife. This style was changed during the Third Dynasty, when Imhotep placed a series of stone mastabas on top of one another in a graduated design, which formed the step pyramid at Saqqara. This pyramid was built to house Djoser, who ruled the country from 2630 to 2611 B.C.

"This first pyramid was 204 feet in height and comprised of six separate layers, or steps if you will, each one smaller in size. The base of the pyramid was 358 feet by 411 feet. The layers were covered with limestone and were surrounded by a complex of buildings, replicas of those erected to celebrate sed festivals. The entire structure and its surroundings measured 1800 feet by 900 feet in total, and the roads were paved in limestone."

"The ancient Egyptians didn't do things in half measures, did they?" Brigid inquired, taking in every word for possible future reference.

"You might say that," Lakesh replied. "It was quite amazing, actually. The entire site was itself a miniature city, with its own priests. The items found in the tomb were equally amazing."

"Such as?" Quavell asked.

"I'm getting to that." Lakesh paused to take a breath. "Other step pyramids were started soon after Djoser's rule, but the true pyramids didn't appear until the Fourth Dynasty, during the reign of Snofru from 2575 to 2551 B.C. Snofru ordered the construction of two pyramids at Dashure and finished his father's pyramid at Meidum. It was from these monuments that the traditional pyramidal complex evolved. The great pyramids at Giza are the best known of them all."

"How many were built?" Domi asked, now appearing to be more interested.

"There were seventy other such monuments erected, stretching the length of the Nile, as far south as the Sudan, but few of them were as large or as grand as the ones located at Giza. The so-called Great Pyramid of Khufu covered thirteen acres."

"What was the point of building these things? Just as mausoleums?" Domi's tone was skeptical.

"Not exactly," Brigid said. "There were astronomical and religious traditions involved, too."

"Those aspects were only the proverbial icebergs," Lakesh stated. "Because of the sheer size of the pyramids and their strategic positioning of the building, many scholars thought they served as beacons."

"For who?" Domi demanded.

Quavell gave the albino girl a rare smile. "The Annunaki, I would imagine."

Brigid nodded knowingly. "We already have a little evidence that Enlil was believed to be the god Set by the ancient Egyptians. So it's possible the Annunaki hid something beneath the Sphinx."

"I'd say so," Lakesh agreed, "Khephren, who ruled from 2520 to 2494 B.C., constructed the great monument at Giza. It remained untouched for over a thousand years until Tuthmosis IV of the Eighteenth Dynasty had it repaired. Tuthmosis, who had been a prince at the time he first laid eyes on the great monument, had a dream in which the Sphinx appeared to him and complained rather vehemently about its deteriorating condition, and told him that he would become the pharaoh when he had restored the statue to its former glory."

The albino girl laughed out loud. "The statue came to him while he was sleeping and said that?"

Lakesh merely smiled at the young woman, but didn't answer.

She suddenly stopped laughing and turned solemn. "What was found?"

Just as Lakesh began to reply, the beep sounded again. All of them turned toward the map, just as the light began to glow. "What's going on now?" Brigid asked anxiously.

Lakesh sat down at the console and began inputting commands into the keyboard. "This is no glitch, I'm afraid. We've got a jump in progress. Definitely from Egypt."

No one moved in the big room as Lakesh's fingers flew over the keyboard. "I've got a trace on the transit line."

"Well, don't keep us in suspense," Brigid demanded impatiently.

Lakesh lifted his eyes and met hers unblinkingly. "The Guadalupe redoubt—that's the destination lock."

Chapter 11

The cat-woman drove the butt of her spear into the soft sand and dropped to all fours, sniffing at the ground before her.

"She looks like a panther!" Grant breathed in amazement. "Never even heard of a mutie like that—or a hybrid."

Although Kane didn't reply, he agreed with his friend's comment. The woman definitely was a hybrid blending of human and feline. He found himself entranced by her beauty. There was a beast's blaze in her eyes, but something startlingly innocent there, too.

The woman stopped sniffing and stood, facing the dune behind which Grant and Kane were hidden. Her lips curled in an unmistakable snarl, revealing her mouthful of needle-tipped teeth. Her cloaked companion unlimbered the strange-looking rifle, swiftly raising it to a shoulder.

Simultaneously, the Incarnates rose from the top of the dune. They held the V-pronged rods before them, aiming the weapons at the two newcomers. Snarling, the feline female bounded backward, into the doorway of the redoubt, tearing her spear from the ground in the process. Her robed companion backpedaled rapidly. A shrill, fierce scream of defiance came from within the shadows cast by the cowl, and for a second, Kane glimpsed a face more falcon than human, beaked and feathered with eyes like beads of onyx swimming in little pools of molten silver.

Leaping to his feet, Decard rushed down the face of the dune, his Sin Eater firing a full-auto fusillade. The 9 mm steel-jacketed bullets pounded a sand-spurting line toward the falcon face.

Screeching a high-pitched howl that had a faint echo of lost humanity in it, the cat-woman hefted her spear and cast it in a swift, looping overarm throw. The bronze point crashed into Decard's chest. Although the molded polycarbonate was designed to withstand even heavy-caliber rounds, the impact of the spear was still sufficient to knock him off his feet.

The Incarnates split up into three groups of four. The first group maintained its position atop the dune, kneeling in the burning sand, weapons pointed at the redoubt. The second group sprinted across the ridgeline, intending to approach from the rear of the installation. The other group charged from the opposite direction. All of the helmeted men moved with uncanny grace and speed over the heavy sand, and Kane had to grudgingly admire the skill they displayed. The desert was their territory, and they knew it well.

The falcon-faced figure triggered the rifle. A thunderous boom shattered the still desert air, and a bull-helmeted Incarnate atop the dune flailed backward, his head exploding in a slurry of blood, bone and brain matter. The helmet provided no protection whatsoever.

Apparently unmoved by the sudden death of their companion, the surviving Incarnates extended their weapons. A strange buzzing noise caressed Kane's eardrums, like the vibration of an insect's wings. Flares of energy, almost invisible in the sunlight, burst all around the redoubt's entrance.

The cat-woman was struck several times from different angles. Little halos of energy danced up and down her body, causing the fur to stand on end. She screamed in agony, a shockingly human howl, and fell face first to the ground just outside the doorway. She writhed briefly, then moved no more.

Energy flashed along the barrel of the falcon face's rifle, and he recoiled dropping the weapon. Outnumbered and outgunned, the hooded and cloaked figure shrieked in rage and spun on a heel, disappearing into the redoubt. All of the Incarnates broke from their positions and raced down the dunes and across the sand toward the entrance.

The unmistakable sound of heavy gears grinding reached Kane's and Grant's ears as the huge, multiton door of the redoubt began to fall. Several of the Incarnates reached the entrance and dropped to their bellies. They raised their silvery rods and fired beneath the rapidly descending door. It sealed with a booming thud.

The helmeted men got to their feet and clustered around the keypad controls of the sec door. Kane and Grant rose and walked down toward the redoubt. While Grant helped a groaning and cursing Decard to his feet, Kane continued toward the body of the fallen cat-woman. Kneeling, he placed a finger on the side of her neck, absently noting the softness of her fur as he felt for a pulse. He stood, shaking his head as DeFore approached him.

"Dead?" the medic inquired, eyeing the body.

"As a fried flounder," Kane replied. He stepped over to the threshold and picked up the rifle the falcon face had carried. He gauged its weight as more than thirty pounds.

Opening the breech, he ejected a shell, catching it deftly in his hand. As Grant walked up, he tossed it to him. "Looks like a .50 caliber."

Grant examined it closely and then nodded. "For sure. Depleted-uranium core round. It'll punch through the skin of a Sandcat like it was made of paper."

Grant held out his hand toward the rifle and Kane passed the weapon to him. He hefted it, grimacing a little at the weight. "Not exactly made for foot soldiers."

Decard, wincing at the pain in his chest, joined them. "One for one, not exactly the kind of trade-off I like. Nefron won't like it, either. Apis was one of her favorites. I've been pushing her to allow me to get the Incarnates to start wearing helmets made of metal instead of wood. If she would have listened to me, things might have turned out differently."

"Not against uranium rounds," Grant said. "Not even your own armor would have saved you."

DeFore knelt beside the felinoid, turning her head back and forth on her neck. The expression of animalistic ferocity on her face was almost demonic due to the crimson glint in her glazed eyes. "I don't see any wounds. What kind of weapons did your Incarnates use on her?"

Decard hesitated before saying, "They're called *metauh* rods. I'm not sure exactly how they work, but they operate on an ancient principle about channeling *sekhem*, the life force. Takes years of training to use them."

"And what about Miss Kitty here?" Grant demanded. "I get the distinct feeling this isn't the first time you've come up against her…or creatures like her."

An Incarnate wearing a headpiece resembling the likeness of a crocodile stomped angrily up to Decard. "I don't know how he did it, but that damn Horusian somehow managed to lock out the codes. We can't get in."

Kane and Grant exchanged quizzical glances. "Horusian?" Kane echoed.

Decard affected not to have heard. "Maybe we can rewire the controls."

"I don't know how to do that," the crocodile

snapped, his voice eerily distorted from within the helmet. The scaled and fanged snout turned toward Grant and Kane. "Do either of you?"

Kane stalked to the door. "I'll crack it, but I want some answers afterward."

Reaching into the pouch, Kane removed a small flat device shaped like an elongated circle with a slit down the middle. He attached the device to the keypad, touched a tiny stud projecting from the center of it and watched.

"I wish I hadn't left my Syne back in Dulce," Decard said wistfully. "Would have come in handy several times since I left."

Grant nodded, but didn't reply. The Mnemosyne, or Syne, as it was more commonly known, was essentially an electronic lock pick. Given time it would eventually crack any locking code, encryption or security protected device. It allowed access, be it to a lock, or even in some cases, computer programs. The device rarely failed to work except when deliberate countermeasures were installed.

There was a sudden loud pop, and a flurry of sparks erupted from the lock. Kane ripped the device off almost instantly, but the damage had been done. He examined it briefly, then tossed the now useless device into the sand.

"A power surge," he snapped. "Fried the Syne."

"I thought they were built to withstand something like that," Decard commented. "What could have caused it?"

Tilting his head to the right, Grant looked at the young man. "Could have been anything. The lock might have been boobied, or Hawk-face could have shorted out the circuits on the other side."

Kane scratched idly at his chin with his hand, staring at the damaged keypad, and then he glanced over at Grant. "Be a fairly long hike back home," he said, trying to sound nonchalant.

"Yeah, that's a safe bet," DeFore said grimly. "From California to Montana. I doubt we'd make it by supper."

Turning to Decard, Grant asked, "Do you think you might be able to get the spare parts we need to fix this in Aten? Or possibly transport?"

The young man ran his tongue over his teeth as he pondered the question. Very slowly, he nodded. "Yeah, I think we can work something out, one way or the other."

"We need to get word back to Brigid and the others before too much time passes," Kane said quietly to Grant. "I don't want them jumping in blind, especially if there might be hostiles waiting inside."

"Yeah, but how?" Grant asked. "Without the satellite uplink we have in the Sandcats, we're pretty much cut off."

"We have a sophisticated comm system in the city," Decard said. "So, again, maybe we can work something out."

"We're working lots of things out today," Kane said,

the suspicion carrying clearly in his tone. "How very convenient for you."

A frown spread over Decard's face. "I gave you my word you can trust me, and that's something I don't break."

Grant cleared his throat. "I guess we'll have to find that out for ourselves. Let's get going. The sooner we arrive in Aten, the sooner we can figure out a way out of this mess."

Decard's eyes moved back and forth between Kane and Grant and he shrugged. "Follow me, then." He turned on his heel and walked past the corpse of the cat-woman. Addressing the crocodile-helmeted Incarnate, he pointed to the body and said, "Let's take her with us. Queen Nefron will want to see her."

The Incarnate heaved the corpse up over his broad shoulder. All of the Incarnates followed Decard past the dunes. Kane, DeFore and Grant fell into step behind them. Two of the animal-helmeted men carried the body of Apis. Blood dripped from his bullet-blasted skull, spattering the desert with an artless pattern.

Eyeing the position of the sun, DeFore said, "I hope this place isn't far, because we've still got several hours of pretty hot daylight left."

"It's about thirty miles away," Decard said over his shoulder.

Grant made a spitting sound of disbelief. "Even by a forced all-night march, we won't get there until some-time tomorrow—if we're lucky."

Decard laughed. "You don't seriously think all of us hoofed it through the damn desert dressed like this, do you? We would've dropped dead inside of three miles."

Kane shrugged. "I guess we hadn't really thought about it."

As they rounded the dune, Decard gestured theatrically to ten big-wheeled carts that reminded Kane of nothing so much as chariots—minus horses or any other means of locomotion.

Eyeing the two-wheeled vehicles skeptically, Grant asked, "That's how you get around in the Barrens?"

Decard nodded. "They're not very fast, but they get you there in the end."

Kane and Grant walked around the chariots, both men silently admiring the design, which was functional and elegant in its simplicity. Pointing to a stacked array of concave mirrored squares within an open box at the rear of the chassis, Decard stated, "Semiconductor chips, converting solar energy to electricity. They make enough power to run the chariots for miles, as long as you don't drive them too long at night."

"Or on a cloudy day," Grant commented, noting how the angle of the mirrors could be changed by a small crank handle projecting from the side of the box.

"Let's get moving," a ram-headed Incarnate announced. "We might make it back before the evening meal."

"Hold on a second," Grant said, facing Decard. "If we don't gate back to our home base soon, or if our people don't hear from us within a couple of hours, somebody will come looking for us."

"Yeah," Kane interjected. "Assuming they can get the redoubt door open, it would be a nice gesture if you could leave one of your men here to tell them what's going on and escort them to Aten, if necessary."

The young man considered Kane's suggestion for a handful of seconds, then nodded. He gestured toward an Incarnate who wore a helmet resembling a narrow-snouted dog's head. "Anubis, you don't mind staying here for the night, do you?"

The canine head turned toward him, then shook from side to side. "I guess not. I've got field rations and water."

"That's mighty accommodating," DeFore observed quietly.

Decard threw her a slightly abashed smile. "He's my brother-in-law."

"Brother—?" Kane said, startled. "You're married?"

Decard's smile widened into a prideful grin. "Into the royal family no less. But don't feel you have to show me any special courtesy."

"Don't worry," Grant muttered. "We won't."

Kane climbed into a chariot with Decard, sitting at the edge of the platform beside the solar-cell battery. The young man engaged the drive with a purring hum, and the vehicle moved smoothly forward.

Grant, sharing a chariot with the crocodile-helmeted man and the corpse of the cat-woman, caught Kane's eye and said sourly, "Just a scout-out. When will I learn not to listen to you?"

LAKESH KEPT GLANCING from the monitor screen to the Mercator map. His fingers flew across the keyboard, and he hissed in angry impatience as he studied the copy glowing on the screen.

"It's not a glitch in the sensor web," Brigid Baptiste said, peering over his shoulder. "It definitely registered a mat and demat cycle. Someone—or thing—gated into the redoubt from Egypt and a few minutes later gated back out to the same place."

From the biolink terminal, Domi said, "Whatever stimulus caused their vital signs to spike must be over. They've pretty much gone back to normal."

Lakesh rubbed his eyes. "They would have jumped back here by now if they were able. We still receive an active read on the Guadalupe gateway unit. Something damn strange is going on there."

Brigid nodded thoughtfully. "What are you thinking of doing, then?"

With a sigh, Lakesh shifted his eyes from the terminal to her face. "I'm thinking that we should make a reconnaissance to the redoubt. They might need our help." Reluctantly, Brigid found herself agreeing with Lakesh. "When do you want to go?"

Lakesh stood up quickly. A flicker of pain crossed his features as he felt a stabbing sensation in his right knee joint. "As soon as possible, while there is still daylight."

He turned toward Domi. "Darlingest one, do you wish to accompany us?"

The petite albino girl grinned. "You have to ask?"

Lakesh returned her grin. "I'll go to the armory and pick out a weapon that would be suited to my skills."

Brigid's eyes narrowed in surprise. Even though Lakesh had gone on away missions before, he never carried a gun, usually passing the responsibility for "packing the musketry," as he called it, to Kane and Grant.

"Don't look so astounded," he said to her, a harsh note undercutting his tone. "I promise I won't get in the way."

"I never thought you would," Brigid said defensively. "Let's meet back here in ten."

EVEN THOUGH LAKESH was primarily responsible for moving most of the equipment into the redoubt over a period of many years, he was still staggered at the sheer magnitude of weapons of destruction that were housed in the Cerberus armory.

He walked past the stands, between the rows of rifles, handguns, crates of explosives and mountains of ammunition. He stopped and looked at a rack containing several dozen CAR-15 carbines, which looked like smaller versions of the standard M-16 A-2 assault rifles used by the American military right up to the skydark.

Pulling one of the weapons off the rack, he examined it swiftly. The firearm felt strange in his hands, even though he had spent many an hour on the outdoor firing range, honing his skills until he was a passable marksman. He pulled back the cocking mechanism, feeling it move smoothly and easily in his grip. Lakesh picked up a magazine from the rack and placed it in the weapon, letting the weapon's cocking mechanism click back in place, pushing a single round into the chamber.

Lakesh slung the weapon and took a bandolier from the rack, then spent several minutes fitting six fully loaded magazines into it. Once finished, he headed deeper into the armory and went to a display case holding a number of handguns. One of the weapons he had practiced with was the old standby Colt .45. The ammunition for the pistol was plentiful, and the weapon was reliable. He selected one from the case, as well as four fully loaded magazines and a hip holster for it.

Satisfied with his weapons of choice, he made his way to the back of the armory and took a Kevlar-weave jacket from a rack. How things have changed, he reflected sourly.

A little less than a year before, he had been an old man who could barely walk a hundred feet without pausing to catch his breath. Ever since that fateful day when Sam had restored his youth and vitality by the introduction of cell-repair nanites into his body, he had felt he was living in a dream world.

Now the dream was inexorably entering the realm

of nightmare. The results of a recent medical examination had shown that the nanites in his body were now inert. They no longer worked to maintain his metabolism at its restored levels. If Sam had exerted control over them, he had either relinquished it on his own accord as a way to punish him, or the influence was broken for another reason. Regardless of the reasons, DeFore's prognosis was that he would begin to age, but at an accelerated rate.

He had no choice but to agree with her gloomy diagnosis. The worst-case scenario she offered had him back to his prerestoration physical condition inside of a year. The absolutely best-case situation would be one where he simply began to age normally, from the point the nanites stopped working, but he knew that was an unrealistic hope at best.

Without the help of Sam's nanomachines, his body simply couldn't maintain its present state. In fact, the possibility existed that his cardiovascular system wouldn't be able to withstand the strain of rapid aging and would shut down. He had kept the prognosis to himself so far, although he knew eventually he would have to apprise Domi of it. But he was fairly certain that the girl's razor-keen perceptions had already noted his gray hairs and how he grimaced at the return of old aches and pains.

Lakesh didn't want to return to his former decrepit condition, but the only way to retain his youth was to cut a deal with Sam, and that meant betraying Kane,

Brigid and the other Cerberus exiles. He had suffered through many a sleepless night, debating all the ramifications of joining forces with Sam once and for all.

He always came up with a good reason to remain loyal to his friends, people he now felt to be his family, despite the problems among them that had occurred over the years. Despite the frequent disagreements and arguments, they always looked out for one another, and genuinely cared for each other's well-being. In some ways, the exiles of the Cerberus redoubt's ties were stronger than that of blood kin.

As far as Lakesh was concerned, the three people in the Guadalupe redoubt were his best friends, his colleagues, even his children, and he was going to bring them back home, no matter what the risk might be.

Chapter 12

It was the kind of sunset seen only in the Outlands. The sky looked like a lowering curtain of blues and purples, smeared with lurid flame-red streaks and molten brass. All around was basically flatland, without even the first sproutings of desert scrub to relieve the monotony of the terrain.

Decard braked the chariot to a halt and gestured to the rolling dunes, waving from left to right. "There we are. The kingdom-city of Aten."

Kane stared out over the desolation, wondering if the young man had gone mad from exposure to the heat. "I don't know if you're aware of this," he ventured mildly, "but there's nothing there."

"That's because it's hidden."

Kane continued to scan the windswept wastes, searching for anything that might indicate the location of a city or even an outhouse. "You're sure?" he asked skeptically.

Decard grunted in exasperation. "Yeah, I'm sure. I live there, remember? C'mon, let's get out of this heat and have something to eat. This armor is really starting to chafe my ass."

With that, the young Magistrate engaged the drive of the chariot and guided it toward the crest of a small dune. The Incarnates followed him in their own chariots, and Kane and Grant exchanged questioning looks, but didn't say anything.

For the third time over the past twenty minutes, Kane squashed the desire to boot Decard out of the chariot. During the two-hour ride from the redoubt, the youth had steadfastly refused to answer any of Kane's questions, deflecting them with either smiles or head shakes.

Kane's instincts, what he called his point man's sense, told him that a number of events were swirling around the Barrens, and the redoubt and Aten were focal points. He knew he and his friends had been expected in the redoubt, and he was almost as certain that the arrival of the cat-woman and her hawk-faced companion hadn't come as a complete surprise to Decard, either. Regardless, he didn't feel as if he and his friends were being led into a trap. At least, he could only hope not.

When the chariots crested the dune, the terrain changed slightly. Kane couldn't quite put his finger on it, and then a moment later, he realized that it appeared as if the desert itself were actually moving. The sand seemed to be shifting, rippling from a faint breeze.

"A mirage," Grant ventured, looking out at the wavelike rising-and-falling phenomenon.

"Thermal inversion maybe," DeFore suggested.

Decard chuckled, turning the chariot slightly to the right. Then Kane realized the desert wasn't actually flowing before the wind, but huge sand-colored nets moved with the breeze. They stretched out over the land and were staked down in place by a network of large, sturdy poles.

"I'll be damned," Grant said, impressed by the camouflage. "No wonder they've kept themselves hidden for so long. Unless a Deathbird crew knew exactly where to look, they couldn't spot this from the air."

The netting covered large plots of land in which all manner of crops grew. As the chariots rolled past, they identified wheat, barley, tomatoes, corn and many other vegetables growing out of rich, dark soil. Irrigation canals twisted through the fields, carrying water to the crops. Dozens of men and women, all naked except for a simple white kilt wrapped around their waists, toiled in the hidden fields.

"Haven't you seen a farm before?" Decard asked.

"Not like this, I haven't," Kane said in all honesty.

Decard grinned. "If this impresses you, wait till you see the city it feeds."

As the chariots rolled past the men and women, the workers stopped and stared at the newcomers with mild curiosity. Kane studied each face they passed, searching for any sign of hostility or fear. Several of the men nodded courteously to him, and even one of the women smiled saucily, flaunting her toned and proud-bosomed body.

After almost five minutes of rolling through the tarp-covered fields, the ground slowly declined into a shallow coulee that Kane guessed to be a dry streambed. It pitched sharply downward the farther they traveled along it. The channel stretched between two bastions of rock. On either side of the outcroppings stood four burly men. They wore gold-trimmed kilts and odd headpieces made of striped cloth, and all were armed with military-issue Stoner M-207 autorifles.

Grinning, Decard braked the chariot to a halt and disembarked. He clasped one of the men by the forearm and spoke briefly to him. The man smiled and nodded to the other three guards, who stepped aside and left the streambed clear for them to navigate.

Decard gestured and everyone climbed from the chariots. "We walk from here on out," he told the three outlanders.

"Who is that?" Grant asked. "Another brother-in-law?"

"Nothing of the kind," Decard replied. "An uncle-in-law."

"These people here don't seem to be afraid of us," DeFore said quietly.

"Why should they be?" Decard countered as he entered the cavern.

The scorching heat of the desert faded as a cool breeze played over their faces. On it Kane detected the odors of cooking fires, food, spices and other pleasant odors, mixed liberally with the unmistakable odor of human sweat. But his nose didn't catch a whiff of decay or excrement that was always prominent in the Tartarus Pits or in the outlander villes.

The long streambed wound through a tunnel beneath the desert hardpan, the channel cut by a long-ago subterranean waterway. Bronze lamps hanging from hooks driven into the stone provided a steady, flickering illumination. By the time they had traveled half a mile, they had taken no less than a dozen sharp turns. At each turn stood a pair of guards, some armed with assault rifles. None of them made any move to stop them or appeared hostile in any way.

When the group rounded another corner, they reached a T intersection and the Incarnates marched down the left-hand passageway. Decard led Kane, DeFore and Grant along the right tunnel. It widened significantly. The young man stopped on a long, wide ledge and gestured for the three outlanders to look out over the city of Aten.

Below them spread out over a broad canyon was a bustling settlement. But it was more than either a settlement, or even a city. It came very near to meeting Kane's definition of a metropolis. Scattered almost as far as he could see, up and down the valley floor, were mud, brick and clay huts, all of them expertly crafted, many covered in hieroglyphs. Everywhere they looked, they saw men and women engaged in day-to-day chores, cleaning clothing, preparing meals. They saw small shops of every sort, stalls selling meats and vegetables, artisans plying their skills. The impression of the city was essentially one of compactness.

Situated in the center of the city, a huge sculpted structure made of a dark, dully gleaming material rose from the valley floor. In height and breadth, it was not even close to the monstrous proportions reached by the D&M Pyramid of Mars, or even the ziggurat they had seen in Amazonia, but for a hidden valley in California, it was an impressive sight.

All three outlanders had seen pix of the Sphinx on the Giza plains of Egypt, and the giant statue bore a superficially similar outline, that of a human-headed lion in repose, with both forelegs outstretched. But it was completely black, apparently wrought from a single gargantuan stone by an art that surpassed mere craft.

The outer edges of the black Sphinx were cut cleanly and sharply, and the head rising from the beast's body was meant to depict the epitome of male beauty. A square-cut headdress framed a sculpted face that evinced strength, nobility, pride and a touch of arrogance. The eyes were the most unsettling feature of the face—they were represented by red gems or blood-colored glass, making the giant effigy appear even more fearsome.

Kane surveyed the statue with a critical eye and estimated the Sphinx was close to two hundred feet long, measuring from the extended forepaws to the hindquarters, which flowed into a valley wall. The top of the human head towered a minimum of seventy-five feet above the canyon floor.

In a voice hushed by awe, DeFore said hoarsely, "Holy shit."

Decard actually laughed. "I know, I know. I had the same reaction a year ago, when I first stood on this ledge and looked down at the city."

Grant glanced up at the sheer walls of the valley rising at least two hundred feet on either side of the city and made a soft sound of surprise. Kane followed his gaze and noticed the skies above were not clear, but the air still had a clarity about it. Then he realized a huge swatch of beige mesh was stretched over the entire declivity. It filtered the light of the sunset, but without impairing illumination. Evidently the mesh had been anchored to the valley walls to obscure what lay below from aerial observation.

"Even with these precautions," Grant said, "I can't understand how this place stayed hidden for as long as it has. This many people, the crops that you have to grow—there are just too many things to give your presence away to the barons years ago."

"We've managed to stay out of the barons' eyes—you can't argue that," Decard retorted. "At least until recently."

Kane cast him a challenging look. "What do you mean?"

Decard waved the question away. "Later. If the queen wants you to know what I mean, she'll tell you."

"Take us to her, then," Grant declared brusquely.

Decard shrugged his armored shoulders. "We can find out if she'll see you. She might still be in audience with an emissary that arrived yesterday. I can't promise anything."

Kane suspicions suddenly flared. "Emissary from where? I thought your kingdom was secret."

Decard started walking along the ledge without responding. He strode down a ramp that slanted steeply into the valley of Aten. Despite Kane's anxiety, his eyes scarcely left the magnificent view spread out before him and his friends.

The skill displayed in the architecture was even more impressive up close. Each building was constructed of dried bricks, painstakingly fit to perfection, and many were covered in a thin dirt coating so smooth that not even the slightest irregularity could be seen.

Colorful hieroglyphs decorated the facades of many of the structures, most showing idyllic scenes of day-to-day life, while others denoted what trade was plied, or wares sold, in a particular building. As with the farmers aboveground, the people they passed showed no signs of fear or hostility. A few of the citizens regarded them with curious glances, and others bowed their heads as they passed by.

"This is starting to creep me out," Kane said under his breath.

Grant tipped his head in agreement. "Yeah, it

doesn't seem right. The people are way too friendly if they've lived in isolation for a hundred years or more."

Walking between the two men, DeFore demanded icily, "What is it with you two? Are you only happy when someone is trying to kill you?"

"I wouldn't say happy," Kane replied.

"It's just what we're used to," Grant remarked.

The comment was met with an appreciative chuckle from Decard. "I know what you mean."

Kane noticed they had picked up a group of followers, a group of seminaked children. They followed at a discreet distance, whispering and giggling among themselves. Kane found himself missing Brigid. He knew that she would enjoy the city, and her incredible memory and historical insights could prove invaluable.

Pausing, he turned around to face the gaggle of children. It would have been difficult to ascertain the sex of the youngest children if it weren't for the fact they were essentially naked. They all had their heads shorn, except for a single braid of hair tied in a small ponytail.

Decard turned and waved his hands at the children, shooing them away. "Go home. It's almost time for your dinners and your parents will be worried."

Almost reluctantly, the group of children dispersed into the streets. He said apologetically, "Sorry about that. Strangers are still a novelty here."

"Even with emissaries arriving?" Kane asked sharply.

Decard shifted his eyes uncomfortably. He began to speak, then broke off.

"What?" Kane prodded.

Shaking his head, Decard said, "Forget it. It's not my place."

Kane's point man's sense began to sound a faint alarm. "You said we could trust you."

Decard took a deep breath. "Things have been changing here, like I said. Queen Nefron doesn't necessarily think keeping ourselves hidden for another century is the best tactic. But before we raise our profiles any higher, we need to know if we have allies out in the world."

"What kind of allies are you talking about?" Grant asked, brow furrowed.

"I can't say any more, sorry."

Decard continued to lead them through the winding streets. Over the years, the Aten citizens had tunneled into the valley walls, and openings gaped like dark mouths on either side of the canyon. Kane detected the smell of water on the air, and heard the low rumble of a swiftly moving river. They reached a dike built along a narrow concourse of rushing water. There they saw people filling buckets. Others were fishing, and several more were bathing.

As Decard led them deeper into the city, Kane noticed that there were schools, as well as small guard posts, shrines, and it seemed that every single home, from the smallest mud brick hut to the largest noble estate, had a garden. The gardens not only provided natural beauty, but food for the families, as well.

There were pens for livestock, mainly goats and a few cows. They didn't see any idlers. Everyone seemed to be working. The outlanders received the impression that all of the adult citizens had a purpose, a function to fill. The number of artists was surprising. They saw men and women painting, creating sculptures and carving wood into shapes resembling animals.

The craftsmanship of all the items was beautiful, and it was clear that the artisans took great pride in their work. As they passed an open jeweler's stall, Kane saw a fine gold chain with a teardrop-shaped emerald nestled in a ring of gleaming silver. The emerald put him in mind of Brigid's eyes, and he thought of how nice it would look hanging from her neck.

The vendor, a small dark man in his sixties, noticed Kane's interest and held out the pendant toward him. "I see you are thinking of a special woman who would look good wearing this."

Keeping his expression and tone neutral, Kane asked, "Am I that obvious?"

The vendor just smiled fatuously.

When Kane noticed Decard grinning at him, he snapped harshly, "What?"

"She must be pretty special," the young man said.

Kane refused to be baited. He gestured to the street ahead of them. "Continue the tour."

Decard headed toward the center of the valley and

the massive Sphinx. The closer the people drew to the structure, the larger it seemed to grow. Fifteen-foot-tall walls surrounded the entire effigy. Men who were clearly sentries walked back and forth along the parapets, almost lazily, but they had their eyes on everyone and everything around them.

A huge gate stood open at the front of the wall, and people passed in and out as they pleased. Sentries were posted at the entrance, and they stood in such extreme postures of attention, Kane would have mistaken them for statues if not for the rising and falling of their bare chests.

Rising from the ground directly behind the guards loomed a statue carved out of a reddish stone. It depicted the likeness of a powerfully built man with incredibly broad shoulders and a massive chest. The figure wore the traditional kiltlike garb of the Aten citizenry, but atop his head was an elaborate headpiece sporting a rearing cobra. The figure's arms were crossed, one holding a scepter, the other what appeared to be a beaker. Even though the figure had been carved out of stone, there was no mistaking the godlike perfection of the features. They were identical to those of the Sphinx.

"Akhenaten," Decard commented. "The royal father. Shortly after Nefron took control of the kingdom and relocated it into this valley, she had statues of her father erected in his memory. If she lets you tour the palace interior, you'll find hundreds of statues like this scattered around it."

Kane managed to tear his eyes off the massive stone figure and fixed them on Decard's face. "Are you telling us that your current Queen Nefron is the daughter of the original pharaoh of Aten?"

Decard nodded. "She is."

"Then she'd be over a century old!" DeFore exclaimed incredulously.

Decard only nodded again and repeated, "She is."

"Her palace is inside the Sphinx?" Grant demanded. "It is."

Decard continued on toward the Sphinx without another word. The three outlanders exchanged resigned glances and fell into step behind him. He followed a narrow gravel-covered path leading between the outstretched forelegs. The exterior of the colossal statue was almost perfectly smooth, showing once again an expert craftsmanship characteristic of Aten.

A wide, square-cut doorway gaped open in the chest of the Sphinx. Decard marched purposefully through it and into a wide, brightly lit passageway. The walls were covered in murals and hieroglyphs, depicting many different scenes. One sequence in particular drew the attention of Kane, Grant and DeFore.

The scenes showed a group of seven people, five males and two females, one with long red hair of such a flaming hue it seemed unnatural. They stood outside of what was unmistakably a representation of the redoubt in the desert.

The next sequence of images showed the people

being treated as prisoners, and the flame-haired woman being brought before Akhenaten, his lust for her clearly, if exaggeratedly indicated. Another collection of scenes showed the woman standing over the mutilated body of the pharaoh. She had apparently killed him with her own hands.

The following scenes displayed a slender young woman with crimson eyes being crowned queen and then reading proclamations from a scroll. Another sequence depicted many men and women walking through the desert, carrying their meager belongings on their backs and shoulders being led by the young queen. The images continued on, showing the construction of Aten.

"If you follow the entire wall," Decard said, "you'll see where it loops around to the history of ancient Egypt, then back to the time of skydark. It took me weeks to go through it all, since it sort of starts from the end."

"Speaking of starting out from the end," DeFore said acidly, "can you tell us where we're going?"

Decard turned right and strode beneath a stone-linteled archway. "Here."

Grant, DeFore and Kane came to an unsteady halt. The bathing chamber was brightly lit by large braziers filled with glowing coals and oil lamps attached to the walls. A huge square pool dominated the center of the room.

Several statues of cherubic children holding jugs

were stationed at each corner of the pool. A steady stream of fresh water flowed from the jugs into the pool, which drained slowly from a small grate in the center of the pool. Even though the water constantly drained away, the fresh water flowing from the statues always ensured that the pool's level was maintained.

A number of thickly padded benches lined the walls around the pool, and a single table was set up near the only exit from the room. Like the passageway, the walls were covered in murals, depicting ancient waterways filled with bathers, as well as fishermen and people hunting crocodiles and hippopotami.

Soothing music filtered into the room from hidden grates and the air was smoky and fragrant, as the braziers burned incense almost nonstop. A pair of lithe girls, naked except for a single string of beads around their slim waists, stood knee deep in the water, holding large towels over their arms as they watched a young woman relaxing on her back in the center of the pool.

She looked to be less than twenty years old, slim and graceful of build. When she stood, her glossy black hair fell to her hips, flowing evenly around her shoulders and back like a cloak. Beneath a small nose, her full lips were creased in a welcoming smile.

Decard strode to the edge of the pool and extended a hand to her. She waded over to him, completely at ease with her nudity. Her eyes flicked from Decard to the three newcomers.

"I'm back, Mavati," he said. "The emissaries were waiting for us, just as you and the other oracles foresaw."

The girl smiled. "You have done well, husband. I'll let Mother know negotiations can soon begin."

Kane managed to focus past the young woman's nakedness and demand, "What do you mean negotiations?"

"Mavati, I'm very impressed by the power of your oracles," declared a melodic female voice from behind the three outlanders. "Now all the offers can be put on the table."

Despite the acoustics of the bathing chamber and the subtle note of mockery in the voice, Kane instinctively recognized it. Stomach contracting in fear, he whirled and dropped into a crouch. His Sin Eater slapped firmly into his hand. He froze when he glimpsed the tall woman with finely chiseled features, surrounded by a thick mane of hair so black it shone with blue highlights.

Ebony-hued pants hugging her long, lithe legs fell over stilt-heeled boots that gave her the aspect of being taller than she actually was. Her waist was tightly cinctured by a red sash, and the narrow shoulders of her indigo tunic were lifted by tapered pads.

The satiny fabric was tailored to conform to the thrust of her full breasts, which were accentuated by scarlet facings. Her violet eyes calmly swept over the three people, surveying DeFore first, then Kane and finally settling on Grant.

Grant voiced a growl of surprise as his own pistol sprang into his hand. "Erica van Sloan."

Decard had led them into a trap after all.

Chapter 13

It took every last atom of Kane's willpower to restrain himself from firing his weapon at the violet-eyed woman. "Just stay where you are, Erica."

Erica van Sloan smiled coldly at him, her eyes boring into his skull. She looked considerably different from the last time Kane had seen her, rigged out in the revealing, gauzy ceremonial robes of a Shakti priestess. Four imperial troopers were with her, all wearing midnight-blue boots, helmets and coveralls with facings of bright scarlet. The faces under the overhangs of the helmets were of an Asian cast. They carried compact SIG-AMT subguns.

"I don't plan on going anywhere," Erica retorted, her lips quirking in a half smirk. "I was here first."

"Put the blasters down," Decard said sharply. "She's not here to fight with you."

The barrels of Grant's and Kane's Sin Eaters didn't waver. "That would be a first," Kane snapped. "Just why *is* she here?"

"Put the blasters down," Decard repeated. "She's a guest just like you are."

"Have her soldiers lower their weapons," Grant growled, "and we'll do the same."

Erica nodded very slightly, and the four men lowered the subguns, letting the bores point to the floor. Only then did Kane and Grant holster their own side arms.

"What are you doing here, Erica?" Kane demanded.

Erica van Sloan's smile widened. "I could ask you the same question, Kane. Where is your usual complement of troublemakers? Mohandas, Brigid and that little albino bitch?"

"They'll be along directly," Grant replied gruffly. "Answer Kane's question."

From the pool, Mavati said, "She is here to open negotiations with the city and Queen Nefron."

"Negotiations for what?" DeFore asked.

Mavati walked toward the edge of the pool, her arms held out to the sides, water dripping from her supple limbs. The two girls began to dry her off with towels.

"To join the imperator's new order," the girl said matter-of-factly.

"Why the hell would you want to do that?" Kane demanded, his voice rising slightly. He glanced toward Decard. "Don't you know who this is?"

Decard nodded. "I've been told…and of the history you and your group have with her."

Erica regarded Kane haughtily. "An alliance with Sam would allow the people of this kingdom to come out of hiding for the first time in over a century. Far too long have they lived in fear of coming to the attention of the barons."

Completely dry, Mavati left the pool and walked over to Decard, who held out a robe for her to slip on. Taking him by the arm, she led him to the bench. Decard stared at her in adoration. One of the handmaidens handed her a solid-gold, gem-encrusted cup.

"So far," Mavati said dismissively, "the imperator's emissary hasn't convinced either myself or the queen of the benefits of such an alliance."

"She's more than the imperator's emissary," Kane snapped. "She's his mom."

Mavati smiled over the rim of the cup. "We know. She didn't tell us that, but we know."

Folding her arms over her ample breasts, Erica snorted. "And my son knows about the powers that you, your mother and many of the citizens inside this city possess. Sam shares similar abilities."

"And so you believe," Mavati inquired casually, "that because we might share a few psychic talents, that is enough for us to want to join forces with him?"

Erica shrugged. "Would that be such a bad thing? Look at what you've accomplished here. You have peace, prosperity, no one goes without, no one fears starvation or crime. You have created the blueprint for a new order in the Outlands. No longer would your people live in fear of the barons, or the Roamers. With Sam's help, in a matter of a few years we could reshape the nation, and then bring the Aten model of society to the rest of the world."

Grant uttered a derisive laugh and shook his head. "You tried the same thing only a couple of months back with your Scorpia Prime scam, using the natives of Assam as patsies. You're pulling the same con on the people here."

Erica glared at him, lips peeling back over her teeth. "We offer the people of Aten the chance to live free, without having to stay hidden any longer."

"Free?" Kane snapped. "They're free now, not answering to the demands of any of the barons. They don't need you, or your mutant son." Kane made the last word sound more like a curse.

All the while Decard sat beside Mavati, listening quietly to the exchange between the two people. Erica clenched her fists, then relaxed, forcing a smile to her face. "There's no point in discussing things any further, unless the queen is here."

"For once, we actually agree on something," Kane shot back.

Suddenly, Mavati and Decard rose to their feet, squaring their shoulders and stiffening their spines. They stared at the entrance to the chamber. "The queen *is* here," Decard said in a voice hushed by awe. "All of you must pay her homage."

Kane's head swiveled to follow Decard's and Mavati's gaze. A second later, he heard the measured tread of tramping feet, then a retinue of animal-helmeted Incarnates marched into the hall, all of them holding *metauh* rods across their bare chests. They took up position on either side of the doorway in a crescent formation.

A woman strode through the entrance and paused, striking a pose with her right hand on her hip, her slim body gleaming like polished bronze. There was no doubt in Kane's mind she was Queen Nefron.

Decard instantly dropped to one knee, bowing his head. Erica van Sloan and her guards followed suit. For a moment, Kane's rebellious nature kept him on his feet, but the diplomat he had lately matriculated within himself told him to kneel, although he didn't take his eyes off the woman as the others around him had. DeFore and Grant followed his example.

Kane gazed up at her with a frank appraisal. Dressed in a white silken gown with a neckline that plunged between her firm breasts and cut high on the right side, Nefron's warm bronze skin seemed to glow in the lamplight. She was not tall, shorter even than Mavati in her black-laced sandals, but she held herself with a regal dignity that easily dominated the entire room.

Kane admired the beautiful structure of bones beneath the sun-bronzed flesh of her face. It looked very young, no doubt due to costly and time-consuming cosmetic care, but certainly not even close to half a century old, much less a full one hundred years. The resemblance to Mavati was so strong, the two women might have been twin sisters of the same age, rather than mother and daughter. Painted on her forehead in what appeared to be gold leaf was a winged-disk sun symbol.

Nefron's sweeping eyelashes were kohled and shining, framed by a mass of black hair coiffed, upswept and glittering with diamonds and silver threaded among the locks. Jewels and gold glittered at her throat, her wrists and ankles.

Nefron's gaze met Kane's and he barely managed to keep the shock from registering on his face. There were no whites to her eyes, only irises of bloodred with hugely expanded pupils that seemed to reflect only shadows.

Nefron's eyes slid away from Kane and she gestured imperiously to Decard. "Stand, young prince." Her voice was musical, but it held a sharp edge, as of metal striking metal at the back of her throat.

The young man stood, but kept his eyes lowered. "Yes, my queen."

Kane felt his eyebrow rise as Nefron referred to the young man as a prince, but he said nothing.

"I see you brought the outlanders into the city. You have done well."

"Thank you, my queen. But there was an incident." Decard spoke very softly, almost reluctantly. "One the oracles did not foresee."

"Tell me."

"A Bastian and Horusian arrived at your father's birthplace. There was a struggle. The Bastian was slain, but so was Apis."

Nefron's expression of detached calm didn't alter. "I understand. And the bodies?"

"I returned with them to Aten," Decard answered.

Nefron nodded as if the matter were now closed, and her crimson orbs settled on Kane. He felt an involuntary shudder slip up and down his spine, but he had encountered telepathy and mind-touch before, and he wasn't afraid of them. "You and your friends may rise, Kane."

Kane, Grant and DeFore did as she said.

"You have many questions," the woman said. She wasn't asking a question.

Kane took a half step forward and cleared his throat. "First of all, we want to know if you might have some of the medical equipment from the redoubt."

"What else?" Nefron prompted.

"We also need some tools, and maybe some electronic parts to repair the door to the redoubt, so we can use the gateway to return home. If you don't have that, would you be willing to allow us access to your communication gear, so we can let our home base know that we're okay?"

Kane felt very uncomfortable making the requests. Nefron studied him silently with those solid, bloodred eyes, and Kane resisted the urge to avert his gaze. He stood perfectly still, not looking away. At length, a small smile appeared on the queen's full lips. "At this time, I am willing to grant one of your three requests."

Kane stood, waiting for her to say more. He didn't wait long.

"I have just come from my oracles. They tell me

there is no need for you to use our communication equipment to inform your friends of your status. Nor is there any need to repair the door of the installation. Your companions arrived there a short time ago and are being escorted to the city even as we speak."

Kane kept his face as neutral as possible even though his heartbeat sped up. The dismay he felt wasn't evident in his voice. "What companions?"

Nefron's lips pursed. "I do not know their names. Two women and a man, that is all I know."

Kane nodded as if he expected the reply. "Do you have the medical equipment?"

"We do. But there is much to discuss regarding its disposition. I am not willing to let it go without an agreement that will benefit both parties."

"Like what?" Kane asked, a sensation of dread washing over him. He felt DeFore's eyes boring into the back of his skull, and he resisted the urge to turn and glower back.

"A possible alliance, between your people and my city." She looked away from Kane, glancing down at Erica. "Which would possibly involve the imperator."

"Be damned to that," Kane snarled. "We'll get what we need elsewhere, then. If you knew the kind of creature the imperator is—"

Nefron held up a peremptory hand. "I am aware of the bad blood between you and the imperator's faction. But I am also aware you cannot make unilateral decisions for the faction you represent. You should wait until your companions arrive before reaching a possibly rash decision."

Kane saw the superior smirk crossing Erica van Sloan's face, and he fought down the urge to unleather his weapon and kill the conniving bitch on the spot. He said nothing, but his jaw muscles knotted as he clenched his teeth in frustrated fury.

"Is that really too much to ask?" Nefron asked smoothly. "You could gain much from an agreement…the least of which is a method to save what could very well be your child."

Kane's rage mounted as his sense of disorientation grew. The queen, Erica van Sloan, Decard—everyone in the city of Aten seemed to have the advantage over him and his friends. He felt shame, as well, that he had been duped, lured into the city, but he wasn't quite sure how it all happened and who was the real culprit.

In a low, soothing voice Nefron said, "I can see in your heart you would not want any harm to come to the babe, or to the mother, Quavell. You can't hide the truth from me."

Flatly, Kane said, "If that's the case, you know I won't make any deals with van Sloan. I'm willing to cut a deal with you, but no way in hell will Cerberus bargain with her."

Erica climbed slowly to her feet. "Don't be so fast to make those decisions, Kane. Once you've heard our proposal, you might very well change your mind."

The Gold Eagle Reader Service™ — Here's how it works:

Accepting your 2 free books and mystery gift places you under no obligation to buy anything. You may keep the books and gift and return the shipping statement marked "cancel." If you do not cancel, about a month later we'll send you 6 additional books and bill you just $29.94* — that's a saving of over 10% off the cover price of all 6 books! And there's no extra charge for shipping! You may cancel at any time, but if you choose to continue, every other month we'll send you 6 more books, which you may either purchase at the discount price or return to us and cancel your subscription.
*Terms and prices subject to change without notice. Sales tax applicable in N.Y. Canadian residents will be charged applicable provincial taxes and GST. Credit or debit balances in a customer's account(s) may be offset by any other outstanding balance owed by or to the customer.

If offer card is missing write to: Gold Eagle Reader Service, 3010 Walden Ave., P.O. Box 1867, Buffalo, NY 14240-1867

NO POSTAGE
NECESSARY
IF MAILED
IN THE
UNITED STATES

BUSINESS REPLY MAIL

FIRST-CLASS MAIL   PERMIT NO. 717-003   BUFFALO, NY

POSTAGE WILL BE PAID BY ADDRESSEE

GOLD EAGLE READER SERVICE
3010 WALDEN AVE
PO BOX 1867
BUFFALO NY 14240-9952

GET FREE BOOKS and a FREE GIFT WHEN YOU PLAY THE...

Lucky 7

SLOT MACHINE GAME!

Just scratch off the silver box with a coin. Then check below to see the gifts you get!

YES!

I have scratched off the silver box. Please send me the 2 free Gold Eagle® books and gift for which I qualify. I understand I am under no obligation to purchase any books, as explained on the back of this card.

366 ADL D34F   **166 ADL D34E**

FIRST NAME	LAST NAME

ADDRESS

APT.#	CITY

STATE/PROV.	ZIP/POSTAL CODE

7 7 7	Worth TWO FREE BOOKS plus a BONUS Mystery Gift!
🍒 🍒 🍒	Worth TWO FREE BOOKS!
♣ ♣ ♣	Worth ONE FREE BOOK!
🔔 🔔 🍒	TRY AGAIN!

(MB-04-R)

DETACH AND MAIL CARD TODAY!

Kane actually laughed. "Yeah, and on that day, Baron Cobalt will embrace me like a brother."

Nefron made a gesture of impatience. "Once your companions arrive, we will begin the negotiations in earnest. I am willing to give you access to the material you need, but first you must hear out the imperial mother. If, when she is finished, you still won't agree to the bargaining terms, you and your friends will be expected to leave."

With that, Nefron turned and marched with a lithe grace out of the bathing chamber, followed by the Incarnates. As soon as they were gone, Kane whirled on Decard, barely able to restrain himself from grabbing the youth by the throat.

"What the hell is going on here?" he demanded in a voice made guttural by fury. "What have you gotten us into, you little son of a bitch?"

"Do not speak to my husband so disrespectfully," Mavati said angrily, gliding forward to stand beside Decard.

Feeling awkward and more confused than ever, Kane exchanged questioning glances with DeFore and Grant, who could only shrug or shake their heads in commiseration.

"You knew we were coming here?" he asked.

"Yes," Mavati said. "And my husband told me all about you."

Grant raised one eyebrow, and the woman shrugged. "Whatever you've heard, it's probably blown totally out of proportion."

"Not always," Kane interjected.

Mavati placed her arm around Decard's shoulders and leaned her head against his. "I know that if you hadn't destroyed the mesa facility, I might not have met him."

Kane and Grant both shrugged.

"The Outlands people have heard of you and your friends," Erica declared. "They know the barons are not as all-powerful as they were conditioned to believe. There is a new rallying cry echoing across the Outlands, and your names are at the forefront of that cry."

Grant, Kane and DeFore all eyed the tall woman suspiciously. "It's a little late to try to swing us to your side, Erica," Grant told her. "Your bitch of a baroness, Beausoleil, tortured me with an infrasound wand not too long ago. You might have forgotten that, but I haven't."

"I'm not trying to recruit you," Erica responded crisply. "I'm simply stating a fact. But without the support of Sam, your insurrectionist work against the barons is doomed to failure."

"I think you're forgetting," Kane intoned in a low voice, "that Sam tops our list of targets."

The tall, violet-eyed woman shook her head. "You are such fools. Sam will rule with compassion. He has no desire to see the people of the world suffer any longer. There is no need for the humans and hybrids to live apart, and Sam will insure that with your help, and others who are drawn to our cause, that a new age will be ushered in."

Grant rolled his eyes and groaned, "Oh, for the love of—"

Erica pressed on, speaking with such confidence and reverence, the outlanders knew it was a rehearsed speech for the benefit of the rulers of Aten. "Sam was born to unite the nine baronies under his leadership, and eventually unite the world. In the end, we will answer to the imperator, and the imperator alone."

Mavati chuckled. "Countless despots and dictators have said those exact same words throughout history. My own grandfather for one."

Erica sighed and rubbed her hands together. "Perhaps. But unlike them, Sam is not ruled by his own thirst for power. He follows the great plan."

Mavati's eyes burned hotly as she gazed intently at Erica van Sloan. "So you said when you arrived. But no matter what you say, power breeds only a thirst for more power."

"Exactly," Kane said, relieved that he appeared to have a sympathizer in Mavati. "He'd want to add your city to his list of holdings."

Erica didn't appear to have heard him, but she said, "Would it help our position to strike a treaty that would keep your kingdom safe for all time? We have no interest in annexing Aten, unlike the baronies, who would only absorb it into their territories and enslave your people."

She gestured to Kane, DeFore and Grant. "They can offer you nothing except to involve you in bloodshed and struggles with barons that would put Aten at risk of being discovered."

"And you wouldn't?" Grant demanded, sweeping a hand toward the imperial soldiers. "You already brought Sam's forces here."

Mavati scowled. "Enough of this. All proposals will be given serious and due consideration…but in the council chambers, not here."

Erica tilted her head slightly. "As you wish. I'll be in my chambers until I am summoned."

Her tone of voice was so calculatedly contrite, so unctuous, Kane could barely control his gag reflex. Gesturing imperiously to her soldiers, she left the chamber. When she was gone, Decard asked, "Mavati, why does your mother listen to her? Even I can tell she's not to be trusted, and I don't have psi abilities."

Mavati shrugged. "You can't deny she has a sharp mind and her proposals are quite intriguing."

"Neither you nor your mother seem too worried about the imperator," DeFore pointed out.

Mavati smiled. "Why should we be? Until the oracles say otherwise, we have no reason to fear her or her son."

"Don't trust her," Kane said vehemently. "Don't believe her."

Mavati laughed. "My mother doesn't trust anyone from the outside, until they prove themselves. I don't trust anyone whose mind the oracles can't sense. Never fear, once we have discovered her true intentions, then the queen will make a final decision."

"Who the hell are the oracles?" Grant demanded.

Instead of answering the question, Decard stepped forward, hooking a thumb toward the doorway. "C'mon, I'll take you to your quarters so you can get something to eat and wait for your friends to get here."

Reluctantly, Kane, Grant and DeFore followed the young man out of the bathing chamber and into the passageway. Once they were in the corridor, Decard said quietly, "Sorry. I didn't know you had such a history with van Sloan. I should've warned you."

"There are a lot of things you should've done, son," Kane said in a steely tone. "Not rigging the redoubt door controls is the least of them."

Clamping his mouth shut, Decard didn't reply, which told Kane his guess was dead on target. He continued walking along the corridor, not bothering to see if three outlanders followed him or not.

"Why does this shit always have to happen to us?" Grant muttered darkly to no one in particular.

Chapter 14

Decard led the three people through an open gate and into the courtyard of a small, walled estate. The lawn was richly grassed and full of decorative, aromatic flowering plants. The house was significantly larger than most of those they had seen on their way through the city.

As soon as Decard walked through the door of the house, he began to open the seals of his armor. With a groaning sigh of relief, he pulled off the breastplate, stating, "It's been a long time since I've worn this thing. I'd forgotten how heavy all this shit can be."

Grant, DeFore and Kane followed the young man into a large open room, circular in shape, almost like a pavilion. A single low wooden table rested in the center of the floor surrounded by six very large, overstuffed pillows. The windows were covered by curtains made of strung-together beads, intertwined with strips of dyed gauze. Oil lamps burned on small pedestals, shedding a flickering, yet strangely comforting illumination.

A young woman hustled from an adjacent room, her

slender body draped in the flimsiest of coverings. Her heavy black hair rested on her shoulders, and impudent breasts swayed beneath the thin material. In one hand she carried a tray laden with sliced fruit and chunks of well-cooked meat. With her other hand she carefully balanced a tray containing four large clay mugs. She placed both trays on the table and stood by as Decard handed her pieces of his armor.

"Help yourself," he said, nodding toward the table.

None of the three people made a move toward it. "If I wanted to kill you," the young man said testily, "I wouldn't poison you."

"What about drugging us?" DeFore asked, narrowing her eyes.

Decard grimaced in exasperation, then took a piece of meat from the tray and bit into it. He chewed and swallowed noisily, defiantly. "You're in my house," he said flatly. "You're my guests, so I won't be poisoning you or drugging you."

Eyeing the maid, Grant inquired, "How many people live here with you?"

"Mavati, my wife, her maid Qerhet here and Cassie."

DeFore picked up a mug and sniffed its pale amber contents tentatively. "Smells like beer." She sipped at it and murmured, "Not bad. Who's Cassie? Your child?"

Decard kicked out of his boots. "Adopted child, I guess you could say. Without her I wouldn't have met Mavati or still be alive, for that matter."

"Where is she now?" Grant asked.

"Divination school, in training to be an oracle. She's naturally gifted."

"Divination school," Kane murmured, reaching down and picking up a pair of mugs. He handed one to Grant. They clinked mugs.

"In training to be an oracle," Grant drawled. "Just an ordinary family."

Decard's eyes darted first to Kane, then to Grant. "I know this has been a lot to lay on you, but—"

"That's where you're wrong," Kane broke in harshly. "You haven't laid nearly enough on us. That's the problem."

Decard unzipped the one-piece Kevlar weave undergarment and peeled it off, apparently completely comfortable being nude in front of his guests. Qerhet took the coverall and handed him a loosely woven cotton robe. Shrugging into it, he said defensively, "I'm trying to earn your trust. You've been allowed to keep your weapons."

"So has Erica van Sloan and her imperial goons," Grant snapped. "We're still outgunned."

"No one will harm you here," the young man declared confidently. "As guests of Aten, your safety and well-being are guaranteed by the queen herself."

"That makes me feel *so* much better," Kane said with undisguised sarcasm. "You still haven't told us how and why we were expected here."

Decard gestured to the cushions around the table.

"Sit, eat and in a little while I'll do my best to explain."

The three people exchanged uneasy, questioning glances, then sank down on the pillows. Qerhet carried away Decard's armor. Kane took a healthy swig of the liquid in the mug and then gasped for breath as it scorched a path down his throat and into his stomach. "What in the hell is this?"

The young man laughed, "It's called *heneket,* the local brew. It's pretty strong, but you get used to it after a while."

Kane favored DeFore with a frown. "You might have told me it was so strong."

She shrugged. "You might have taken a little sip to test it first."

Grant took an experimental swallow and repressed a shudder. "It packs quite a punch for beer."

Decard selected a piece of fruit from the tray and bit into it. "Like I said, you get used to it."

Kane stared at him levelly. "You seem to have gotten used to a lot of things in a short time."

"What do you mean?"

"I mean you're ville born and raised, and trained to be a Mag. Yet you fit right into this place and something about that just doesn't feel right to me."

Decard's eyes flashed with anger. "And why is that, Kane? Because people are happy and well fed? Because there are no Tartarus Pits, no high towers, no shortages of goods, no slavery?"

"There's that," Kane said with a genial smile with only a trace of mockery in it, "and the fact that a settlement this size has remained hidden for so long."

Qerhet reappeared, placing a pitcher of *heneket* on the table. As she did so, she whispered a few words into Decard's ear and he nodded in satisfaction.

After she left the room, DeFore asked sardonically, "No slavery?"

Decard's boyish features colored slightly from embarrassment. "She came with the house, actually."

"So, things aren't quite so different here than the villes," DeFore countered.

Decard shook his head. "No, you're wrong there. See, even though Aten has its ruling class, and working class, servants and nobles, people are treated with respect and equality, no matter what their position is."

Leaning an elbow on the table, Kane commented, "Why do I doubt you?"

Decard shrugged. "Probably because you're a cynic. The reason that everyone is treated with equal respect in Aten is because it's drilled into them from the moment they're born that they have a responsibility to the community. All the citizens have roles to play. The nobles make the laws, settle disputes and provide jobs.

"The working class builds the homes. They grow and harvest the crops, teach the young, make the food and attend to the needs of everyone. No one here is without a job, unless they're too old or infirm to work. Qerhet is a perfect example of that. She's of noble birth, and as such she's one of the reasons Aten has never been discovered."

Grant eyed a piece of fruit before popping it into his mouth. "Explain."

Decard smiled slightly. "All the nobles in Aten are psis."

The statement made Kane's flesh crawl. "Psis, as in psi muties? A whole city of them?"

Decard shook his head. "No, only the noble class. Queen Nefron could explain it a lot better than I could, but from what Mavati has told me, during the first couple of years of unification, when the baronies were just being established, muties all across the Outlands were being hunted down and exterminated. That included a lot of doomies, telepaths and other psi muties. I guess somehow they were all attracted to Aten, and the ones who actually made it here were offered sanctuary."

The image of Baron Sharpe's doomseer adviser, Crawler, came to Kane's mind. He wondered if there was any chance that the mutant might know of Aten, and then he dismissed the thought. If that were the case, Sharpe's troops would have invaded long before.

"So," he ventured, "because of all the psi muties that came here, they were able to keep the city totally isolated and hidden from view?"

"That pretty much sums it up," Decard agreed. "The way I understand it, anyone who came into the city's territory was offered a chance to become a citizen, or they had their memories altered and were sent on their way. Over the past eighty years Nefron's people had encountered a few Magistrates and implanted memories of nothing but barren wastes around here. There probably hasn't been a Mag patrol out this way in thirty years or more."

Grant rubbed his temples as if in pain. "I still don't get it, though. If Qerhet is a noble, why is she serving us? Wouldn't you have other workers doing that?"

Decard smiled ruefully. "Yeah, you'd think so, wouldn't you? She actually chose the role for herself. She's not only a servant, but she's a loyal adviser to my wife and her best friend from childhood."

Kane sipped at the potent beverage again, realizing that Decard had been right. He was getting used to it. "You move fast, don't you?"

The young man stiffened slightly. "What do you mean?"

"You've only been in the city for what, about a year now? And you've married the daughter of the queen and apparently give orders to her sec men, the Incarnates. Pretty nice setup."

Decard stared Kane straight in the eyes. "I don't have any kind of setup going here. Just so happens that Mavati nursed me back to health after I was found out in the desert. Things just kind of clicked between us."

Kane found what he was looking for with his questioning. The young expatriate was clearly loyal to the queen and to the city, and not running a scam.

"How did she find you out in the desert?" DeFore asked.

Hesitantly, Decard answered, "It's a sort of complicated story. She wasn't looking for me."

"Who was she looking for?" Grant demanded.

"I wanted to wait until your friends got here, so I don't have to tell it more than once. They're a little late."

Grant's eyebrows knitted at the bridge of his nose. "What makes you think—" Comprehension dawned in his eyes. "I see. The oracles again?"

Decard nodded. "Exactly. I thought they'd be here by now. Qerhet told me she had been told they were on their way, but the oracles aren't always precise when the measurement of time is a factor."

Regarding the young man incredulously, DeFore asked, "If your oracles were so positive our friends would follow us, why couldn't we have just waited for them at the redoubt?"

"The way it's been explained to me," Decard declared, "is that until an action is taken by the subjects of a divination, only generalized guesses can be made. So, apparently your friends found out fairly quickly something was wrong and used the redoubt's gateway to come help."

Grant shook his head dubiously. "I find that a little hard to believe."

At the sound of the footfalls and murmuring voices outside the room, Decard grinned. His "Oh, really?" came out as a sardonic challenge.

The three outlanders hastily rose to their feet. Mavati swept regally through the doorway, followed by Brigid Baptiste, Domi and Lakesh. All of them looked perplexed and more than a little irritated, even though Brigid had perfected a poker face during her years as an archivist. She wore a formfitting shadow suit, while both Lakesh and Domi were rigged out in camous and ill-fitting flak jackets. The outfit looked so incongruous on Lakesh, Kane could not completely suppress a laugh, despite the tension.

Domi spoke first. "We figured you three needed some help. Got yourself into another shitty one-percenter situation again?"

Kane tilted his head toward the viand-laden table and grinned. "Doesn't it look like it?"

Spearing him with a frosty glare, Lakesh declared, "There's probably nothing more irritating on Earth than rushing to the rescue of endangered friends, only to find them breaking bread with their supposed captors."

"They're not prisoners," Mavati said, sidling around the table to stand beside Decard. "Neither are you, as I explained."

Grant noticed the three new arrivals were still armed. "No trouble, I take it?"

"None to speak of," Brigid replied. "Though we had a couple of bad minutes there after we opened the redoubt door and found a man with a jackal's head waiting for us."

"Nearly shot him afore he told us what was up," Domi chirped, making a gun out of the thumb and forefinger of her right hand.

Kane saw the frown crossing Mavati's face, so he quickly made introductions all around. Decard nodded to the three people in turn. "Brigid, Domi, Lakesh," he said. "I'm very pleased to meet you all."

"Why?" Lakesh asked with uncharacteristic bluntness.

"I've been asking him that myself," Grant commented dourly, "but he's been evasive. I can tell you, it has something to do with the presence of Erica van Sloan."

The reaction among the new arrivals was mixed. Brigid only blinked, Domi's upper lip curled over her teeth in a half sneer, half snarl and Lakesh's hand rose reflexively to touch the gray-threaded hair at his temples.

"What that bitch do here?" Domi shrilled angrily, reverting to the clipped mode of Outlands speech under sudden stress.

Decard gestured to the table and the cushions. "I was only waiting for everybody to arrive, so I could explain. There's a lot going on here that could impact the baronies...for both good *and* bad. It's pretty obvious the van Sloan woman and this imperator of hers are aware of it. If you'll take seats, please, Mavati and I will make you aware of it, too."

Chapter 15

The tale related by Decard with occasional interjections and clarifications by Mavati, was not as strange as some the Cerberus warriors had heard, but it was strange enough to rivet even Domi, whose attention span was notoriously limited.

The young man told the outlanders what he had learned of Mission Invictus, the redoubt in the desert and the project to create the perfect human specimen to thrive in a postnuke environment. They had succeeded, creating two life-forms, a male and a female. The male was named Alpha, the female Epsilon. Due to a side effect of the genetic recombination technique, there was a pigment change in the eyes, which turned them bright red.

The test subjects matured at an accelerated rate, but Epsilon died mysteriously. Alpha entered suspended animation for nearly a century. Upon reviving, he took the name Akhenaten and set about establishing the kingdom of Aten with the mind-controlled aid of a band of Farers who had arrived at the redoubt in order to loot it. He dominated them totally and took a Farer woman to wife, who bore him Nefron. A few years later, the woman died. Nefron blamed her father.

Sixteen years later, a group of wanderers arrived at the redoubt. Lured to Aten, they were ambushed and promptly captured. A woman with psionic abilities was among the group. She was chosen to become the bride of Akhenaten and the mother to a new race.

Over the years Akhenaten had developed a method of casting and molding through the application of natural softening and hardening agents. By utilizing it, he had expanded the city of Aten and seen to the construction of a pyramid. He believed that once the capstone, made of minerals with powerful piezo-electric properties, was put into place, his psionic abilities would become godlike.

The teenaged Nefron feared her father's ambition as much as she admired his other accomplishments. She wove a complicated web of plots, counterplots and deceptions that ended when the outlander woman Akhenaten had chosen as a bride killed him. Nefron had secretly built a mechanism into one of the pyramid's chambers that would cause it to collapse when triggered.

Nefron claimed the title of queen and the people of Aten accepted her unquestioningly. Over the following decade, she exerted a firm but just rule. She provided a high standard of living for her people. But even isolated as they were in the Barrens, Nefron was not completely ignorant of the events swirling in the outside world. When rumors of the Program of Unification reached her as fact, not unsubstantiated fears, she realized Aten was far too exposed and would eventually be discovered by baronial expeditionary forces.

The queen ordered the entire city dismantled. What could not be transported was buried in the shifting sea of sand. The rest, including its inhabitants, relocated to a canyon discovered some years before by the queen's father. There, using the stone-molding technique he had perfected, the entire city of Aten was rebuilt, including the black Sphinx meant to symbolize the dual nature of Akhenaten.

Within it was stored all of the scientific and medical equipment from the Mission Invictus redoubt, including the secrets of selective mutation, secrets that Nefron began using to improve the health of the citizenry and to insure their safety. Although Akhenaten's superhuman mental abilities were not something she had inherited, she set about making minute alterations in the genetic structure of Aten's nobility.

"You mean your queen deliberately created muties as Aten's ruling class?" Domi asked, her tone edged with distrust.

Mavati shrugged. "Helpful or harmful mutations often depend solely on the environment in which an organism lives. Here, the mutations were helpful."

"And what about the creatures who came out of the redoubt?" Grant demanded darkly. "Helpful or harmful?"

Brigid, in the process of reaching for a slice of fruit, cast Grant a quizzical glance. "What creatures?"

Tersely he told her about the cat and hawk-headed entities and how their retreat back into the installation had resulted in the malfunctioning door. During the story, Kane noticed how Decard shifted uncomfortably on the cushions.

"He called them a Horusian and a Bastian," Grant concluded, nodding toward the young man.

Lakesh grunted. "Obviously referencing Horus, the hawk-headed god, and Bast, the cat goddess. More of Nefron's mutations, I take it."

"Not exactly," Decard said uneasily. "More like Akhenaten's."

"Explain," Brigid requested, fixing a penetrating stare on the young man's face.

Decard shook his head in frustration. "I don't know if I can."

Mavati touched Decard's arm, saying softly, "I will explain. A century ago, Akhenaten determined to create an army to protect Aten."

"I got the impression that's what the Incarnates were supposed to be," Kane said.

"My grandfather used them as a template," Mavati replied, "only in this instance, he intended to cast them in the mold of the ancient Egyptian pantheon of gods, the Akhakhu. He created only a handful of them through genetic manipulation, speeding up their adaptations by some method I do not understand. My mother suspects the technique was actually ancient, perhaps of extraterrestrial origin, since Akhenaten created the pantheon in a vault hidden beneath the Sphinx in Giza."

Lakesh and Brigid exchanged quick, knowing glances as Mavati continued. "Akhenaten apparently was not pleased with the final result and had the Akhakhu placed in cryostasis. When my mother learned of their existence, she used the gateway to travel to the vault and freed them. She offered them full citizenship in Aten. At first they accepted…but then they turned against her."

"Why?" DeFore asked suspiciously.

Mavati opened her mouth to respond, then closed it again, shaking her head sadly. "The queen should be the one to reveal that to you. If she deems it part of the negotiations, she will tell you."

"Just what are we negotiating for?" Lakesh inquired.

Mavati cocked her head sideways, puzzled. "I thought you had realized by now that the imperator wishes to take possession of all the secrets of my grandfather's creation."

"We're not interested in a selective mutation process," Brigid stated.

"Nevertheless, you cannot have what you need to help Quavell and her unborn child without access to the Mission Invictus technology and methodology. If van Sloan is favored by my mother, then she will walk away with it all. You will then have to negotiate with her and her son, Sam."

"That won't happen," Kane said sharply. "Isn't there a council of nobles or elders we can appeal to? A king, maybe? Who is your father?"

A faint smile touched Mavati's full lips, but she didn't reply. After a moment, Lakesh said dryly, "I think if we ran a genetic test on both Nefron and Mavati, we'd find out they have completely identical DNA."

DeFore's eyes widened and she exclaimed, "You're a *clone* of Nefron, not her offspring!"

Kane stared at the girl, the meaning of the strong resemblance between Mavati and the queen rushing over him like cold water. "You're a copy of the queen?" he blurted.

Decard's expression locked into one of anger. "She was cloned from Nefron's cells and raised as her daughter. That doesn't make her a counterfeit!"

Lakesh interposed smoothly, "We know that, young man. I'm sure friend Kane was just surprised by the revelation."

Kane snorted. "Surprise is one way of putting it. Being fed up with all the mysteries in this place would be more accurate."

"Mysteries?" Domi echoed.

"Like why we're here in the first damn place," Kane retorted flatly.

Decard smiled, but it didn't reach his eyes. "We've been over that, Kane."

"Only through inference," DeFore shot back. "What's all this stuff about oracles foreseeing our arrival here, like we're fulfilling a prophecy or something?"

"In a way," Mavati said quietly, "you are. The oracles have foreseen that we of Aten cannot remain apart and isolated much longer from the outside world. Every day, events bring us closer to discovery. You and van Sloan represent two different paths Aten may walk."

"How did Erica find you?" Domi wanted to know.

"The one she calls Sam mind-touched the oracles," Mavati answered. "It is part of the duties of the oracles to cast about telepathically for those who share similar gifts. It is how my husband and the child Cassie came among us."

"Sam probably made contact through the Heart of the World," Lakesh said.

Mavati nodded. "I believe that was the means of initial communication, yes."

From his stronghold in Xian, China, Sam could manipulate the convergence of electromagnetic energies he called the Heart of the World. The Heart existed slightly out of phase with the third dimension, slightly beyond the human concept of space-time. From its central core extended a web of electromagnetic and geophysical energy that covered the entire planet. He was able to tap into it at will.

Grimacing in angry impatience, Grant growled, "So these oracles of yours knew we'd be arriving?"

Decard nodded. "Yeah. Van Sloan made them aware of all of you when she consented to have her mind scanned."

"And Queen Nefron ordered you to make sure that once we got here we couldn't leave." Kane didn't ask a question; he made a flat statement.

Decard nodded again, this time reluctantly. "Like you already figured out, I rigged the door."

"And you knew about the Horusian and Bastian showing up?" DeFore's tone was skeptical.

The young man frowned. "No…if the oracles knew about the Akhakhu gating in, they didn't tell me. I don't think they foresaw it. They're not infallible."

"The Akhakhu have been infiltrating Aten through the gateway for many months," Mavati said.

"Then why haven't you closed the transit line?" Brigid asked.

Mavati smiled at her almost pityingly. "If we had, then none of you would have been able to get here."

The outlanders stared at her for several seconds, surprised into speechlessness. Then Lakesh commented wryly, "Flawlessly logical."

The girl nodded regally. "I am honored. Thank you."

Mavati arose from the table, extending a hand to Decard. "Come, husband. We have revealed enough to our guests for the evening."

"Not nearly enough," countered Grant, rising also in a show of courtesy. His companions followed suit.

"Perhaps that is so," Mavati agreed. "But whatever

else you learn must be from Queen Nefron. She awaits you in the audience chamber tomorrow morning."

Decard swept a hand around the room. "When you're ready to sleep, you'll find plenty of bedrooms off this one. We'll talk more after you've had the chance to rest."

"Count on it," Kane snapped.

Decard's eyes flashed, either in apprehension or anger, but he didn't reply. Hand in hand, he and Mavati strolled out of the room through the arched doorway. The six people resettled themselves around the table. Domi propped her elbows on the top of it, resting her chin on her fists. She murmured, "Got a bad feeling about this place, girls."

"Join the club," Kane retorted, shifting position so he could rake Domi, Lakesh and Brigid with an accusatory stare. "And one reason why I have such a bad feeling is that Nefron now has the entire command staff of Cerberus in her hands. She can either let us go, or turn us over to Erica and Sam."

Lakesh's brow creased. "Do I detect a rebuke?"

"You've got to admit, it was tactically unwise to come after us through the gateway."

"The interphaser isn't finished yet," Brigid pointed out. "And if we came in the Mantas, we might not have been able to locate the city."

Brigid referred to the transatmospheric craft found on the Manitius Base and brought down to Cerberus. Powered by two different kinds of engines, a ramjet and solid-fuel pulse detonation air spikes, the Manta ships could fly in both a vacuum and in an atmosphere. The transatmospheric planes were not experimental craft, but examples of a technology that was mastered by a race when humanity still climbed trees to escape from saber-tooth tigers.

"We found the situation very strange," Lakesh stated brusquely. "We felt it best to investigate now, rather than take the chance of mourning your losses later."

Kane smiled bleakly. "I see your point. Well, we're swimming around in the stew now, so it's best to find out about all the other ingredients."

Brigid shook her head in exasperation at Kane's metaphor but said only, "It's apparent to me that this entire negotiation situation is something of a stalling maneuver, if not a dodge altogether."

"What do you mean?" Grant asked.

"I mean it's possible that Nefron has no intention of making a bargain of any kind with Sam, but she can't flat out refuse him without risking open hostility. He has the means to make it very unpleasant for her and her people."

Lakesh nodded. "True. There is far more going on here in Aten than what we've been allowed to see so far. Nefron seems much different from the schemer she was characterized as in historical documents."

"Maybe she's not the same Nefron," DeFore ventured. "How could she be and still look so young?"

Brigid shrugged dismissively. "With access to the

genetic manipulation technology of Mission Invictus, it would be a greater mystery if she didn't look young."

"How so?" DeFore challenged.

"Nefron could be employing a youth prolongation system that involves synthesizing telomeres."

Grant squinted toward her. "Telo-whats?"

"Telomeres are sections of DNA that cap chromosomes," DeFore explained. "They keep them intact, except during cell division. There are some types of enzymes that work as a telomere repair system, even when a cell divides."

"So?" Kane demanded.

"So," Brigid replied, "cells that don't lose telomeres are virtually immortal, capable of dividing indefinitely and remaining intact."

Lakesh tugged absently at his long nose. "Very interesting and very possible, all things considered. If such a mechanism is here in Aten, then by monopolizing it, Sam would have yet another fulcrum by which to force cooperation among the barons."

Brigid nodded. "Exactly."

"This is all speculation," DeFore announced crossly. "Until Mavati or even Erica decides to come clean with us, we're going to have to wait until our audience with the queen."

Kane consulted his wrist chron, turning the LCD face toward the flickering lamplight. "It can't happen soon enough for me."

Chapter 16

Decard led them down a corridor, wide and high, lighted by flickering tapers and lamps. It seemed to stretch the entire length of the black sphinx. A group of robed people waited by an archway and bowed their heads as Lakesh, Decard, Grant, Brigid and Kane passed by.

"The priesthood of Aten," Decard whispered.

"What god do they serve?" Brigid asked.

"A composite made up of Ptah and Tenen…a craft god and a creation god."

Kane did his best to swallow a yawn, but not because he found the young man's explanation boring.

None of the outlanders had slept very deeply, despite their hosts' assurances of safety. All of them had taken shifts standing guard until daybreak. A delicious breakfast served by Qerhet was a small consolation for a fitful night.

Decard joined them for the meal, wearing the traditional linen skirt and gold collar of Egyptian royalty. His wife, Mavati, had already departed to join the queen. He provided them with the bare bones of royal etiquette, which amounted mostly to not speaking unless spoken to. Domi and Reba DeFore had chosen to stay behind, just in case a rescue was called for.

As they passed the priests, they noticed one robed man standing apart from the others. Clad in a gold skullcap and a tabard of stiff red fabric, he didn't bow to the outlanders. Instead, his brown-eyed gaze was one of suspicion and hostility. His deeply seamed face held no particular expression as he watched the procession approach.

"High priest Opet," Decard side-mouthed. "He and his sect disagree with the queen about her policy of making contact with the outside. He's a fanatic isolationist."

Opet fell into step behind them. As the group walked through the archway, they passed a pair of Incarnates. The two animal-helmeted warriors paid no heed to the four people. They stood as still as granite statues, looking impeccable in their spotless gold-trimmed kilts and ram-headed helmets.

The walls and roof of the corridor were covered in brightly colored hieroglyphs. They were rendered with great artistry and each section of wall seemed to bear a single story. Kane stared at them as they passed, but not in wonder or curiosity. He committed to memory their location using certain illustrations as a reference guide.

Chambers opened off the corridor, and what the group of outlanders could see of their interiors gave an impression of an almost sensual luxury, with long, low divans of velvet and the gleam of precious metals and gems.

The procession made its way through a column-supported doorway, big and broad and magnificently carved in high relief were scenes of men and women riding in chariots. The corridor ended abruptly in an enormous cavern, a natural one where rock formations had been formed into fantastic shapes by the passage of aeons. Another pair of Incarnates stood at attention at the mouth of the cavern and they stepped aside, allowing the group to stride along a path of marble tiles sunk into the floor.

Light was provided by an inestimable number of brass lamps mounted on stone pedestals, made from stalagmites with the tops sheared off flat. The people followed the tiles to the audience chamber of Nefron, daughter of Akhenaten, ruler of Aten. Kane felt a distant quiver of surprise at its austerity.

Queen Nefron sat on a throne situated in the hollow center of the chamber. She wore a sheer white gown that left her arms bare. A high-crested white wooden crown with a small golden sun disk above the rim rested atop her head. It completely concealed her glossy black hair. She held the Nekhekh, the royal flail, at a forty-five-degree angle over her left breast. Many bejeweled rings winked on her long fingers. Mavati, dressed in a similar fashion, stood on her right side.

The throne itself was apparently carved—or

molded—from the same stone as the cavern, shaped to resemble a sitting man. It was modeled after the statues they had seen of Akhenaten, and so Nefron essentially ruled from the lap of her father. The symbolism was odd, but definitely effective. The throne was elevated about five feet above the floor by a miniature pyramid.

Erica van Sloan and her uniformed soldiers stood at the base of the pyramid. The troopers were armed, but so were Kane, Grant, Lakesh and Brigid. The outlanders had no grounds on which to lodge an objection. As it was, there were at least two score people in the chamber, from Incarnates to skull-capped priests to various officials and functionaries. Six blue-robed women wearing burnooselike headdresses stood in a little semicircle around the pyramid, their eyes downcast.

The atmosphere of the audience chamber felt electrically charged with anticipation. Nefron swept the outlanders with her chilling bloodred gaze and announced, "Brigid Baptiste, Grant, Kane and Prince Decard, I bid you welcome. Mohandas Lakesh Singh, Eric van Sloan, you may come forward."

Lakesh made a pointed effort not to so much as glance in Erica's direction, as he obeyed the queen's bidding. Erica didn't feel so restrained—she followed his progress with a smile of pure malice on her lips.

"I am told you have come here searching for a way to help a friend," Nefron said.

Lakesh nodded. "That's true, Your Highness. The medical knowledge you have here may save two lives."

"So my oracles have said."

Nefron fixed her gaze on Erica. "Tell me again why I should withhold my aid from these people."

Erica nodded deferentially. "Certainly, Your Highness. But I would prefer to speak of these matters with you privately, out of earshot of this man and his companions, who have declared war on my son. Lakesh will spout only lies about the imperator."

A faint smile creased Nefron's lips. She waved the flail toward the robed women. "They are the diviners, the most adept of Aten's sect of oracles. No lies shall be allowed to be spoken here, neither in public nor in private."

Opet suddenly spoke from behind them, in a strident tone full of angry resentment. "They are all strangers in our city, Your Majesty. We should trust one no more than another."

Nefron's eyes flicked toward the priest, then back toward Erica. "I am not fearful of strangers, Opet. Perhaps this imperator is part of a new force in the world. He may or may not be important to the future of Aten, and that is all I care about. After I have made my decision, we will know who is worthy of our trust and who is not."

The last few words were intended for Erica alone. The tall woman compressed her lips in a tight line as she smothered an angry protest. She inclined her head and began to speak of Sam the imperator, and the order he sought to bring to the chaos of the outside world. She told the queen of the boons her son had granted the Cerberus warriors, only to have them accept the gifts and spurn the imperator. They feared and hated him, rejecting his truths in favor of lies about personal freedom.

Kane gave the woman credit. She didn't speak complete falsehoods, but she presented Sam's point of view as a well-meaning victim of opportunistic hypocrites. She sounded very earnest, her moral outrage quite convincing. The woman would have continued with her tirade if Nefron had not interrupted. "Let me be clear about what you say. These people prefer chaos and madness to order?"

"They would not admit so, but they are corrupt, Your Highness." Erica cast the four outlanders a glare of barely veiled venom.

Nefron stared down at Lakesh. "Would you care to dispute these charges?"

"I do," Lakesh answered, "but there are several things that are disturbing me greatly, things I must make you aware of."

Nefron opened her mouth to respond, but Lakesh held up one hand to stop her. "Please, allow me to speak my own thoughts, rather than hear their interpretations from you or your diviners."

Nefron nodded her head in acknowledgment of his request, clasping her hands before her in a traditional Hindu gesture of respect. "Forgive me, it's a habit."

"Thank you, my queen," Lakesh said, smiling at the simple gesture. "I am very concerned about the ramifications of your kingdom reaching any kind of accord with Erica van Sloan. Do you have any idea what sort of creature her imperator is?"

"I've told them all they needed to know," Erica said haughtily.

"'Told them?'" Lakesh echoed incredulously, glancing toward her, then back to Nefron. "Due to your formidable telepathic talents, I was certain that you garnered all the information you needed about him from Erica's own mind."

Nefron shook her head and looked directly at Erica although she addressed Lakesh. "There is something strange about the structure of the imperial mother's mind…I can only catch glimpses of her surface thoughts when they dwell on her son. She is, quite honestly, an enigma to me, and that has me more than a little intrigued."

Lakesh recalled what he knew about Erica van Sloan, and he couldn't think of anything that indicated she was even slightly psionically endowed. Then he realized the telepathic screen was due to the cybernetic implants in her brain, the superconducting quantum interface device, or SQUID.

As a brilliant predark cyberneticist, Erica van Sloan had perfected the SQUID implant as an interface between mechanical-electric and organic. They were only one-hundredth of a micron across and drew power from the electromagnetic field generated by the neuronic energy of the brain itself. And now Sam controlled the SQUID.

Lakesh saw Nefron stiffening and he understood that she was reading his thoughts even as they formed in his mind. She asked, "Will you allow my diviners to enter your mind and relay your memories among all of us who can share them? Imparting information in this way will be a good deal faster than verbal communication."

Erica took a step toward the throne, her expression registering fear and anger. "Your Highness, I must protest! This man's thoughts regarding my son would be of a highly subjective nature, even his memories!"

Nefron glared at Erica. "Silence!" she hissed.

A shiver of fear played up and down Lakesh's spine. He felt certain Nefron could read his thoughts without trouble, and despite his own mental discipline, he was sure that she could bash her way through any barriers he might attempt to erect to keep his private thoughts hidden from her.

He nodded reluctantly. "Yes, but I ask you one favor."

Nefron tilted her head in a curious manner. "What is it?"

"Please, just focus on Sam the imperator. My personal thoughts should remain just that."

"As you wish. To make it easier, simply bring Sam into the forefront of your thoughts." Nefron turned. "Cassandra, please come forward."

A small robed figure shuffled hesitantly from the group of diviners. She was a girl-child, but her big eyes held a solemn, sad wisdom. Decard whispered with pride evident in his voice, "That's Cassie, the kid I told you about."

"Search his mind, Cassandra," Nefron instructed, "and share what you find."

Lakesh saw the queen, Mavati and all of the diviners bowing their heads and closing their eyes. Shutting his own eyes, Lakesh visualized an image of Sam as he was when he last saw him, in the temple of Shakti in Assam—a young man of medium height, but exceptionally lean of build. He was dressed in an impeccably tailored white linen suit, but he exuded as ominous a flair as if he were dressed in funeral black.

His head was long and his face high-planed with prominent cheek- and brow-bones. The chin was small but sharp. His hair was a lusterless silvery gray and looked very thin, even sparse in some places, but it swept across his high forehead and left temple in a dramatic style. His ears were very small and delicately shaped, nestled close to the skull. A pair of dark, curve-lensed sunglasses masked his eyes. His thin lips were creased in a superior smile.

After building Sam's appearance in his mind, Lakesh concentrated on recollections of their prior encounters. He could almost feel the ghostly mental fingers of Cassie creeping along his neural pathways, following the twists and turns as each linked memory touched upon another containing information on the enigma that was Sam the imperator.

Then, as gently as a lover's caress, the insubstantial fingers withdrew from his mind and he opened his eyes. He saw the diviners still standing motionless with their heads bent. They were completely absorbed in what his mind had revealed. He wondered how long the process had taken.

Nefron answered his unspoken question. "Only a matter of a few seconds."

"He means us no harm, Your Highness," Cassie said.

Lakesh nodded. "Now do you know exactly what Sam has in store for you and the rest of the world?"

"You lie, Lakesh," Erica bit out.

Nefron sat silent for a long time, brooding. Finally, she turned toward Erica and said, "There is one thing that puzzles me about your son. You are afraid of him, and of what he is becoming. You feel a great deal of love, as well as fear when you think of Sam. Why is that?"

Erica tilted her chin at a defiant angle. "If you know as much as you are claiming, then why are we even bothering to discuss this? You could quite easily choose which side you wish to join and be done with it."

The queen bowed her head ever so slightly. "That is true. But the fact that I can't read your intentions as well as I can those of Lakesh makes me less than willing to trust you."

"That may be so," Erica replied coldly. "Let us assume for the sake of argument that my son is the ruthless conqueror Lakesh and these others make him out to be. By joining us, we will offer Aten untold power in exchange for your loyalties. Aten would be stronger, more powerful than all of the baronies combined. And again, if Sam *is* who Lakesh believes he is, by allying yourself with him, not only would your power spread across this nation, but the rest of the world, as well."

She gestured toward Lakesh. "What does he have to offer?"

Lakesh didn't hesitate. "Freedom, more than these people have ever had in the past. Your Highness, under Sam you would ultimately answer to him, and the citizens of Aten would be subservient to his every whim."

The queen's expression remained neutral. "We have all the freedom that we could hope for. We fear no baron, no Roamers, no raiders."

Lakesh mulled that over for a moment, chewing his lower lip. "You think that you might be enjoying freedom, but consider this—you are still in hiding. Does hiding in a canyon qualify as freedom?"

"To us, yes," Nefron retorted. "We are waiting until the time is right to join the rest of the world, to announce our presence. The arrival of not only Erica van Sloan, but your people, as well, may be a portent. For good or ill, I am not sure."

Shrugging, Lakesh said, "I would strongly disagree with you on the freedom aspect, Your Majesty. To me, you're nothing more than a bird in a gilded cage. A prisoner in a beautiful home, with the illusion of freedom."

Nefron regarded him curiously. "I cannot glimpse the future, but my diviners can. Cassandra, what do you see if we strike a bargain with either of the factions represented here?"

Cassandra didn't close her eyes this time, but her gaze became distant and vague, fixed on some faraway point. The girl suddenly drew in a sharp breath, then let it out again, blinking repeatedly.

"What do you see?" Nefron demanded.

"Blood," the child answered in a voice barely above a whisper. "Much blood will be spilled if we ally ourselves with either the man Lakesh, or the woman van Sloan. Death will come to the holy city of Aten…death from within and then from without."

Opet spoke, a hard-edged burst of hatred. "Then all of the outsiders must die."

Lakesh stiffened, casting a surreptitious glance over his shoulder at Kane. He passed the questioning glance on to Brigid and Grant, who nodded almost imperceptibly in response. Kane and Grant began tensing their wrist tendons in preparation of unleathering their Sin Eaters. The hall became so still Kane fancied he could hear every breath that was drawn, every beat of a heart.

A pain-filled grunt broke the silence, and Kane spun toward the direction of the sound. One of Erica's troopers was bent over almost double, squeezing his helmeted head with both hands. Erica gaped at him, too surprised to speak.

The man straightened as suddenly as if he had been jerked erect by an invisible string. He looked around the cavern, his narrowed eyes traveling over the gathered people, pausing only briefly on Grant, Lakesh and Brigid, then they froze on Kane's face.

The trooper whipped up his SIG-AMT, training the barrel on a direct line with Kane. A rattling roar filled the hall, a short tongue of flame flickering from the bore.

Chapter 17

Erica van Sloan delivered a graceful high kick to the barrel of the subgun, and the stream of slugs went high, bouncing and ricocheting from the roof of the cavern. Kane felt rather than heard their passage as they thumped the air inches over the top of his head. Rock chips sprinkled down. The acoustics of the audience hall magnified the staccato hammering of the SIG-AMT, turning the reports into a series of overlapping thunderclaps.

Kane dodged to the side, moving with a swiftness that surprised even him. He heard Nefron and Mavati both crying out in shocked outrage. Grant and Brigid instinctively lunged away from each other, so as not to present conveniently grouped targets. Sin Eaters snapped out of Kane's and Grant's power holsters, slapping firmly into their hands. Both weapons swung toward the imperial trooper who stood gaping open-mouthed at his weapon as if he had no idea what it was.

Erica snatched it from his hands and tossed it away, her eyes fixed on Kane's face. She shouted, "No! He's not responsible!"

Screams of fear and anger filled the cavern as the people began a panicky run toward the exit. The diviners backed away from the throne, and Decard bounded forward to snatch Cassandra up in his arms. Lakesh extended a hand toward Nefron. "Your Highness, come down from there! You're not safe!"

A quintet of Incarnates jogged toward the throne, *metauh* rods held out before them like spears. Kane met Brigid's eye and she shook her head in confusion, letting him know she had no more idea of what was going on than he did.

An explosive boom compressed Kane's eardrums, and he glimpsed Brigid wincing in reaction to it. An Incarnate spun on his toes, his upper left shoulder flying away in a gout of blood and mangled tissue. He dropped his *metauh* rod and clapped a hand over the ghastly wound as he fell to his knees. The screams of terror increased in number and volume.

Kane wheeled in the direction from which the shot had come—and froze, momentarily paralyzed by the nightmare face leering at him from around the side of a stalagmite.

The face was inhumanly narrow, and the entire head looked very small in proportion to the rest of the body. It was covered by a downy growth of dark feathers. Instead of a nose and mouth, a cruelly hooked bronze-hued beak jutted out. The eyes on either side of it burned as molten yellow as a falcon's, but with a hatred too bright even for the hunting bird.

The creature's body was small and slender, muscularly compact. The wings springing from the shoulders were as darkly feathered as the head, but the span was far too short to allow for true flight. The genetic mutation had not given the creature the gift of flying like the Horus hawk. Instead, it was only a malformed imitation of the magnificent sun god of myth.

The Horusian's arms clasped a heavy rifle of the same make as the one recovered out in the desert. The bore centered on him, looking like a hollow, cyclopean eye. Kane depressed the Sin Eater's trigger stud and three rounds tore through the narrow Horus head, blowing the back of its skull out amid a scattering of feathers.

Even as it fell, a bellow of outrage filled the cavern, then it was answered from another point. Kane tried to fix the positions of his friends among the milling throng in the cavern. One of the priests blundered into him and went on without pausing. The tumult in the cavern grew louder as those inside fought their way toward the door.

Then a great, darkly furred thing with a broad muzzle and very long arms sprang toward the throne, swinging clenched fists at the Incarnates who raced to intercept it. One of the blows bowled a lion-helmeted man off his feet. Kane heard bones break.

The creature howled and Kane realized it dimly resembled a baboon, but one the size of a man. Although its body was completely covered by a coat of stiff black hair, it also wore a kiltlike loincloth. Belly slipping sideways, Kane realized that the genetically altered Akhakhu were loose in the audience chamber. He knew the timing wasn't a coincidence, not with the queen, the priesthood, the outsiders and the nobility all present in the same place. It was a coup, pure and simple.

The baboon creature's black lips writhed back over foam-flecked yellow fangs as the Incarnates converged, little flares of light bursting from the V prongs of their *metauh* rods.

The baboon creature howled again, but this time its cry held a quavering note of pain. Propelled by inhumanly long arms, the creature bounded swiftly away from the Incarnates, snatched up one of the lamps from its pedestal and flung it at its tormentors. Flaming oil splashed, spread and exploded into smoke and flame. Two of the Incarnates reeled away, beating at the skeins of fire that ignited on their kilts. The baboon creature lunged away into a wedge of murk.

The hammering of autofire rose above the shouts and screams. Squinting through the billowing smoke, Kane saw Erica running through the crowd, followed by two of her men. The other two were engaged in a firefight, but he couldn't see against whom.

Brigid rushed over to Kane, pushing the running, milling people out of her way. She double-fisted the Iver Johnson TP-9 autopistol she favored. Shouting so she could be heard over the mingled cries of terror, she demanded, "Where's Lakesh?"

Kane glanced toward the elevated throne, but didn't see Lakesh or the queen. He caught a very brief glimpse of Decard, still holding Cassie, rushing hand in hand with Mavati across the cavern to a shadow-shrouded point. He assumed they knew where they were going.

The staccato roar of guns firing on full automatic slapped at their ears again, and a stream of slugs tore long gouges in the surface of a stalagmite.

Brigid winced, crouching. "Who's doing all the shooting?"

"I don't know," Kane snapped. "But we need to get the hell out of here and let the Incarnates deal with—"

A half dozen black-skull-capped men, stripped down to breechclouts with their limbs wrapped in linen bandages, charged out from between a pair of out-croppings. They gripped skeletal-looking S&W M-76 subguns and they fired indiscriminately, short sprays of flame erupting from the slender barrels. The shell casings twinkled in the light provided by the flames and the lamps.

Kane wrestled Brigid down as bullets thumped through the air above them. Two of the Incarnates spasmed as the rounds sewed bloody little dots across their broad chests. They fell backward into screaming, tangle-footed sprawls. The baboon creature lifted its voice in a high-pitched shriek of malevolent triumph. As the echoes of the screech bounced from the walls and ceiling, Brigid said breathlessly, "I don't think we can count on them."

Kane didn't bother to respond. From his prone position he took hasty aim and fired a burst at the four skull-capped men. At the same time he heard Grant open up with his own Sin Eater. A sleet storm of rounds pounded into one man's shoulders, chest and neck. He gurgled out a cry of pain and collapsed to the floor.

The three survivors opened fire. One of Aten's nobles spun on his toes, the top of his shaved skull floating away in a red mist.

Grant returned the fire with his Sin Eater, the 9 mm rounds driving through the side of an attacker's head, opening up his cranium like a ripe melon struck with a hammer. The man collapsed, his feet kicking spasmodically.

More bandaged men with black skull caps came bounding into the cavern. The audience chamber of Aten erupted with gunfire, screams and shouts. The Incarnates and the weapon-wielding men fired wildly, almost blindly in any direction.

Kane and Brigid stayed low, crawling to the cover of a cluster of stalagmites. They prayed Grant was doing the same. The two imperial troopers raced to join them, but a burst from a subgun punched through the midnight-blue helmet of one of the soldiers. He dropped dead without a sound. His companion managed to make it to cover.

Across from their position, a pair of the black-capped attackers lay down suppressing fire with the subguns. Kane was forced to pull back when a massed fusillade blew fist-sized chunks of stone out of the stalagmite he and Brigid crouched behind. "It's getting messy," she declared grimly, pointing with her gun barrel.

Turning to the right, he saw several of the Incarnates engaged in hand-to-hand combat with the new assailants. The din from the stuttering subguns was almost deafening, but they could still hear the shouts of pain and curses coming from all around. He didn't see Grant, but he heard the unmistakable cracking reports of a Sin Eater.

Kane rose to a crouch, with his back against the stone column, his Sin Eater held high. Carefully, he peered around it. Instantly the rock exploded under the impact of another full-auto burst, scouring his face with sharp bits of stone and grit. Brigid gazed at him with weary exasperation, but she knew better than to admonish him. If nothing else, he had fixed the position of at least two of the blastermen.

Kane switched to the other side of the stalagmite. He eased down to one knee and took a deep breath. Then, swiftly, he reached out around the column and kept the trigger stud of his Sin Eater depressed, hosing the area down with a steady 9 mm spray. He pulled back just as quickly, as several rounds struck his shelter, dangerously close to his hand.

He returned to the other side of the column as the

skull-capped men concentrated their fire on the side. As he had expected, the two men had exposed themselves to return the fire, to keep him pinned down. Kane put a triburst into each man, dropping them.

Movement attracted his attention. Kane saw Grant executing a run-dodge across the cavern. As he watched, he saw an imperial trooper, the one Erica had disarmed, move into the open and raise his SIG-AMT, training it on Grant. The expression on the man's face was one of torment, as if he were in great pain. The barrel of the weapon quivered as he brought it into line with Grant.

Brigid Baptiste didn't hesitate for a second. She squeezed the trigger of her pistol. The weapon thundered, a single bullet punching the soldier through the upper chest. Staggering backward, his finger constricted on the trigger and held it down, emptying the entire magazine in a thundering drumroll and whine of ricochets.

Grant threw himself against an eight-foot-tall stalagmite, doing his best to mold his big form against the column. "Thanks!" he shouted over the din of the ongoing battle.

Both factions of the combatants abandoned their positions and rushed forward, meeting one another almost in the dead center of the cavern. The field of combat wasn't designed for mutual advantage. There were only winners and losers, the living and the dead. It was the code by which Kane and Grant both lived, how they were trained as Magistrates. The subguns chattered and the *metauh* rods flared and sizzled.

Animal-headed figures fell and writhed around gun-shot wounds. Black-skull-capped men convulsed, rolling madly across the cavern floor. More Incarnates were falling and staying down than the linen-wrapped attackers.

Kane realized that the only chance he, Grant and Brigid had of leaving the cavern alive was to join the melee and force the enemy to disengage from the Incarnates and take them on. It wasn't a prospect he looked forward to, but it was also clear that the black-skull-capped attackers were quickly gaining the upper hand over the Incarnates. He and his friends had already chosen sides, and he doubted they would be treated as neutrals if the attackers were victorious.

Catching Grant's eye, he made hand signals, indicating what he had in mind. The big man scowled, but nodded. Kane started to edge away from the stalagmite, but Brigid grabbed his left forearm. "What are you going to do?" she demanded.

Impatiently, not removing his gaze from the milling combat, Kane retorted, "Try to tip the scales a little so we won't end up as either POWs or confirmed kills."

She moved up beside him. "I'm going with you."

He glanced toward her, noting the hard glints of worry in her emerald eyes. "I'd prefer you didn't. Stay out of sight, be our ace if things start to go sour."

"And then what?"

A corner of his mouth quirked in a wry smile. "I'll leave that to your discretion, but I think I can speak for Grant in this...we'd very much appreciate a rescue of some kind."

Brigid gazed at him searchingly for a silent second, then nodded. "Understood."

Kane eased out from cover, Grant shadowing his movements. Almost immediately, four of the linen-wrapped figures converged on Grant. Kicking himself into a spring, Kane raced to intercept them.

He had crossed less than half the distance, a matter of perhaps ten yards, when a blinding pain shot through his right leg. It didn't seem to be there and he fell heavily, barely able to catch himself on his elbows. He looked down, too shocked to do otherwise, expecting to see blood flowing from the ragged stump of where his leg had once been attached...but there was no sign of damage anywhere.

Just as he laboriously realized he was stunned, a blow connected with his jaw and knocked him onto his back. Starbursts flared behind his eyes. He didn't lose consciousness, but he instantly forgot about the pain in his leg. Another blow struck his Sin Eater.

Dimly, he understood he had been struck, just behind the knee. His mind felt as if it were coated with soggy cotton wadding. Through the blurred haze of his vision, he watched the baboon creature shamble toward him. A heavy wooden bludgeon was gripped in its right fist, and Kane realized it had delivered the blow to his leg. The creature's muzzle wrinkled in a sneer as it raised the club. "Time to die, outlander." Although its pronunciation was slurred due to the structure of its mouth, Kane understood the creature perfectly.

The baboon creature brought down the club in a whipping arc, the knotty end of it on a direct line with his head. Kane thought he heard Brigid cry out his name. As if someone had removed the cotton that had been clouding Kane's perceptions, his mind cleared. Despite the pain in his leg, he moved with the speed of a striking cobra, rolling to one side as the cudgel smashed into the stone floor.

Coming out of the roll, Kane stayed low and depressed the firing stud of his Sin Eater. Nothing happened, which he had feared. The blow from the club had been delivered with just enough force to knock the firing pin askew.

The baboon creature swung his bludgeon. With his adversary's much longer reach, Kane knew he couldn't backpedal out of range, so he saw only one option. He threw up his right arm to block the blow. The wood connected solidly with the power holster, which cushioned the impact, but pain still streaked up and down his forearm. The impact sent him staggering.

Man and baboon creature slowly circled each other. The creature made a few halfhearted feints toward him, narrowly missing Kane with the wooden club. The human eyes in the beast face burned with hatred and with a sinking sensation in the pit of his stomach, Kane realized he couldn't appeal to his human reason, if any remained inside the malformed head.

It lashed out with the club again, and Kane slid to the left, biting back a cry of pain as his injured leg twinged. The muscles were already stiffening, slowing his reflexes and reaction time. Suddenly, his adversary jerked as if he had heard some strange noise—which with the near deafening cacophony of battle, Kane figured was almost impossible.

Lowering its club, the creature glanced first to right, then to left and back at Kane. Its eyes widened in wonder. Its lips peeled back from its teeth in a grin. Then bloody foam surged forth past its fangs. Gurgling, it slowly pitched forward onto its face, the grin still fixed on its muzzle. Kane saw the crimson bubbling up from the wound in the back of its skull.

Massaging his throbbing forearm, he saw Brigid step out from cover, hefting her autopistol, face pale and pinched with fear. He husked out, "Thanks. That's the kind of ace I like to see played."

She shook her head. "I didn't play it."

"Then who—?" Cold realization washed over him and made his flesh crawl. He looked wildly around and saw who and what he feared. Erica van Sloan stood atop a rock about seventy feet away, with one of the SIG-AMTs on her shoulder. She flashed him a mocking grin and then leaped down, out of sight.

Kane set his teeth on a groan of frustration and

Brigid murmured bleakly, "You can bet she'll be call-ing in that marker as soon as possible."

Kane didn't dispute her. He was too busy watching Grant in the middle of the whirling, eddying mass of skull-capped and animal-headed men. He moved through the combat like a phantom black panther, shooting and clubbing with his Sin Eater.

The attackers began a slow retreat, dropping out of the melee one by one, then in twos. Then, as if obey-ing a prearranged signal, all of them that were still am-bulatory spilled out across the smoky cavern in a run. Only a few of the Incarnates were in any condition to pursue, and they declined, letting their enemies with-draw from the field of battle.

Calmly, Grant picked off a pair of the black-capped men, dropping them with a single shot apiece to their backs. The cavern fell silent, broken only by the moans of pain from the wounded and the heavy breathing of the combatants.

"We've got to find Lakesh," Brigid announced, cast-ing her gaze all over the cavern.

"He's fine, never fear," Mavati said, seemingly to appear out of nowhere and causing both people to jump. "As is the queen."

"What the fuck just happened?" Kane demanded an-grily. "Who were those sons of bitches?"

The girl shook her head sadly. "It appears that the coup we've been fearing has finally started."

Grant stalked over to them. "Where the fuck did you

and Decard disappear to, Mavati? We could've used some more help out there."

Her eyes turned cold, and she stared defiantly up into Grant's face. "My mother's safety is paramount to us. We went with her and your friend Lakesh to protect her, just in case you and the other defenders couldn't beat off the attackers."

Kane rubbed his arm, then his leg. "Why is it," he muttered bleakly, "that whenever we show up somewhere, a revolution begins?"

Chapter 18

After leaving the Sphinx, they were forced to shoulder their way through a large crowd of citizens who were being held back by a group of armed Incarnates. The shouted demands for information were almost deafening. Not since the overthrow of Nefron's father more than a century before had such violence touched the city-state of Aten.

"Where is Erica?" Kane asked once they had gotten past the crowd. "It was one of her men who started this, after all."

Mavati slowed her pace so she could walk beside Kane. "I'm sure the queen knows where to find her. Besides, her soldier was not acting of his own free will."

Kane put his hand on Mavati's shoulder, forcing her to halt. "How can you be so sure of that?"

"Come on, Kane, you should have figured that out by now," Brigid declared with a dour smile.

Grant glanced toward her, then back to Mavati. "Enlighten us," he said.

"His mind was controlled," Mavati said. "You already know that many of the citizens of Aten possess psionic abilities to one degree or another. There were a number of nobles in the audience chamber today."

"So any one of them could have been responsible?" Kane demanded.

Mavati shook her head. "Theoretically, yes. But there are many possibilities."

Grant glowered down at her. "And Erica could be part of them. She's smart, and she's Sam's puppet. The bitch could have easily staged the whole thing in order to take out your queen."

Mavati tilted her head slightly and stared up at Grant through critical eyes. "Do you actually believe that's likely?"

"We're in a city filled with psi muties," Grant retorted. "My definition of what's likely and what isn't has changed a little bit."

It was clear his words disturbed the young woman, but she composed herself. "My mother will get to the bottom of it soon enough. There is no way that Erica could hide such blatant treachery from her or from Cassie. The truth will come out, one way or another."

"Where is your mother?" Kane asked. "Where are you taking us?"

Mavati paused for a thoughtful moment before answering, "I believe you would call it a safehouse."

They continued walking through a residential neighborhood and reached a plain, single-story building. There were the usual flowerbeds present, and a pair of small palm trees stood like sentries on either side of the doorway. Mavati pushed open the wooden door and motioned for her three companions to enter.

To their mild surprise, they found themselves in a Spartanly furnished sitting room. Nefron and Lakesh were present. She sat in a simple wooden chair, while he paced anxiously to and fro before her. When the four people came in, his face lit up with relief. Erica van Sloan stood there, as well, arms folded across her breasts. Her eyebrow crooked at a challenging angle when she caught sight of Kane. He angled his own, silently daring her to claim she had saved his life.

"I'm delighted to see you all," Lakesh said. "Even though Her Highness kept assuring me you were all right, I was still worried."

"You do that too often," Nefron observed dryly. "It'll age you before your time. I should know."

The informal banter between the two people made Kane feel slightly uncomfortable, for a reason he couldn't quite identify. Addressing Nefron, he stated, "It seems that our arrival triggered Cassie's portent."

Nefron sighed sadly. "The insurrectionists."

Kane nodded grimly.

"The queen has told me that my man was under some form of telepathic control," Erica stated. Her violet eyes flicked over to Brigid. "Sam won't be happy when he hears he's lost a man, but I'm sure he'll understand you had no choice."

Brigid's lips worked as if she were on the verge of spitting at the woman. With an icy sarcasm, she said,

"You have no idea how happy I am to hear that. I'm positive he'll bawl his eyes out when he hears that one of his 'one size fits all' drones was killed."

Erica shook her head pityingly. "How little you understand him."

She turned to Nefron. "She has just demonstrated what I've been talking about, Your Highness—"

"Enough," Nefron broke in sharply. "There are other matters concerning us this day. We've known that an uprising like this was in the making for a very long time."

"You knew?" Lakesh asked incredulously. "Then why didn't you do something about it beforehand?"

Nefron tilted her head back, staring into his face. "You're a very intelligent man. You tell me why."

Her straightforwardness took him back a bit. Blinking, he exchanged swift glances with Brigid, Grant and Kane before saying slowly, "Like you, the insurrectionists have people who can mask or hide their thoughts and plans from your oracles. Perhaps they even have allies among your oracles."

Queen Nefron smiled, but there was no warmth in it. "Exactly."

"What do these insurrectionists want?" Grant demanded.

Mavati lifted a shoulder in a shrug of resignation. "What do insurrectionists always want? A change in the status quo, where their wants take precedence over anyone else's needs."

"Whatever their demands," Kane pointed out, "they're apparently in league with the Akhakhu mutants."

"Actually," Nefron replied, "it's more the other way around. The Akhakhu enlisted support from a small handful of dissidents here in Aten."

"Why?" Brigid asked.

For a long, stretched-out tick of time Nefron and Mavati exchanged searching glances. The resemblance between the two women was so strong, they might have been mirror images of one another. Then Nefron sighed. "The Amkihiu."

Lakesh slitted his eyes. "The what?"

"Essentially, it's a word describing the souls of the blessed who have been fortunate enough to obtain admission into the boat of the sun god Ra, as he crosses the night heavens. It's the belief in a form of ascension to a higher plane of existence."

"What's that got to do with a bunch of muties?" Grant asked suspiciously.

"Aten has many things it wishes to forget about in its history," Mavati answered, her tone edged with pain. "The Akhakhu and their belief that they will ascend to a state matching those of the actual gods is one of them."

Nefron's full lips compressed as if she tasted something very unpleasant. "When my father created them, he was not at all pleased with the final result. He considered them failures, monstrosities. But he didn't express his disgust to them…quite the opposite, in fact. Due to his advanced powers of mental manipulation, he convinced them they were avatars of his new order, the first generation of godlings, and he was their deity. Their Ra, so to speak."

Lakesh regarded the two women gravely. "I think I can guess the rest. They willingly entered stasis, fully believing your father would resurrect them when the time for gods and goddesses had come around again. The Akhakhu were less than thrilled when you did the actual reviving instead of your father. I imagine they were downright upset when you finally informed them they had not been birthed by a god, but spewed from Petrie dishes full of recombinant DNA."

Nefron nodded. "When all else is scraped away, yes. That is fundamentally what happened. They tried to live among us here, but could not. Nor could they come to terms with the truth of their existence."

"What could the dissidents possibly get out of working with the Akhakhu?" Erica asked.

"An Aten more to their liking," Mavati answered. "One that is closer to the standard established by the original Akhenaten over three thousand years ago…a revival of the old, old Egyptian ways."

"That's ridiculous," Brigid snapped. "No one really has a solid idea of what the 'old, old Egyptian ways' actually were. Even before the nukecaust, the secrets of that civilization hadn't been fully revealed, not even the exact method by which the pyramids were built was known."

"Nevertheless," Nefron declared, her voice rising, "it is what they believe. And I must deal with it." Her eyes narrowed and she fixed her crimson gaze first on Lakesh, then on Erica van Sloan. "And unfortunately, you must deal with it, too."

Mavati ran her hands through her hair, smoothing it with short, agitated motions. "Our entire way of life is about to change. Your arrival seemed to be the final push that they needed to mount an all-out attack."

"Let me guess," Kane grated. "You want us to help you hunt down whoever started this, don't you?"

The queen tilted her head once. "Yes. If you will help my people in this task, we will give you the equipment you need to help Quavell and the unborn child."

Erica stepped forward, and sounding scandalized, she exclaimed, "Your Highness, you can't be serious! If you ally yourself with Sam, we can have troopers in here within a day! They'll protect you and end any and all threats to your rule."

"Right," Grant drawled. "That's just what Aten wants…a permanent garrison of foreign soldiers. That'll restore the queen's popularity."

Nefron leaned forward. "At this time, I am not interested in allying my people with either Cerberus or Sam."

Lakesh glared at the queen. "Then why are we even discussing this right now, if you've already made up your mind?"

"If you succeed in the mission of tracking down the Akhakhu and their collaborators, I will give you the equipment and data you need for the hybrid. We will be open to trade with you and the others whom you trust."

Erica opened her mouth to voice a protest, but Nefron raised an imperious hand.

"We will also trade with the imperator. However, if in the future open hostilities break out between your two groups, we will remain neutral, no matter what."

Kane nodded. "Understandable. But I hope *you* understand that before we risk our asses to clean up a mess left over from your old man's reign, you show us proof you can deliver the goods."

Lakesh swung his head toward him, eyes shining with anger and shame. "Kane, how dare you question Her Highness?"

Kane met his outraged stare with one of wide-eyed innocence. "What? Her Highness wants us to get involved in a local political conflict. I want an idea of what we'll get out of it."

"You suggested that Her Majesty's word was not to be trusted," Mavati said coldly.

Kane's face locked in a hard, tight mask. "Did I? My diplomacy fails me when blackmail is used as a negotiating tool, regardless of the circumstances. Let me remind everyone, we didn't ask to come here. The situation was set up so we had no choice. The queen's word will be honored—I'm certain of that. Once we see what she's giving her word about."

Nefron at first appeared to be deeply offended, but then an abashed smile creased her lips. "You are a man of honor yourself, Kane. I won't presume to debate you on this matter."

Still smiling, Nefron stood and walked over to a low table by the far wall. Pulling open a small drawer, she withdrew a compact disc. She tossed the disc to Lakesh, who barely managed to catch it.

His face a mask of confusion, he asked, "What is this?"

"It contains all the files that we recovered from the medical database of the redoubt. It seems that the woman who created my father knew far more about selective mutation, the pantropic sciences and gene therapy than most of her contemporaries. The healer DeFore brought with her a small computing machine you call a laptop. It should be able to access the files on the disc."

Lakesh studied the disc in his hand. "Thank you. I'm a little surprised that you would be so willing to part with this, since it more than likely contains not just the inner workings of Mission Invictus, but all of Overproject Excalibur's researches."

Nefron simply shrugged. "I already have copied the information on it. And it's encrypted."

"Would you care to give me some of the highlights of what I'm going to find here?" Lakesh asked. "Once it's decrypted, that is?"

Nefron nodded graciously. "I would be happy to. Once you and your people agree to my terms."

"None of us are interested in making more muties," Grant rumbled. "So if the data on the disc is mainly about that, you'll have to offer something else."

"There's no need to offer me anything else, Your Highness," Erica said smoothly. "I await your command."

Kane snorted in derision. "You wouldn't fool a croupy Dreg with that routine, Erica. So drop it before we all lose our appetites for the next year."

She whirled on him, teeth bared. "Who do you think you're talking to, Kane? I saved your life less than an hour ago, you turncoat thug."

"I wondered how long it would take you to bring that up." Kane smirked. "You shot that poor deformed bastard so the queen wouldn't suspect you or Sam of having a hand in the uprising. I just happened to be standing there. It could have been anybody."

Erica planted her fists on her hips. "Do you really think I had anything do with the attempted coup?"

"That's not up to me to decide," Kane countered. He shot Nefron a challenging stare. "Is it, Your Highness?"

"You have a lot of anger and resentment, Kane," Queen Nefron said calmly, unperturbed by the heat of the argument. "In your mind I can see concern about the hybrid, but more so about the baby she carries. You're not so much worried about its paternity, but what Sam wants to do with it. You feel he means it harm."

Brigid gestured angrily at Erica. "She was involved

in abducting Quavell only a few months ago. All of us feel that Sam means the baby harm. Forcing us to work with van Sloan is not the action of a friend."

Nefron shook her head in exasperation. "You want a simple solution to this problem. I'm afraid there isn't one this time around. Aten needs your help, and I am going to use the medical data and technology you need as leverage to get it. I'm sorry, but that's the way it's going to have to be."

Lakesh murmured, not unsympathetically, "Uneasy lies the head that wears a crown."

Kane stared at Nefron, the sudden anger leaving. Although he knew that she was genuinely sorry for using him and his friends in such a manner, it didn't take away the resentment. "What about the Incarnates?" he asked.

"They will help you. My oracles are hunting for the citizens responsible for aiding and abetting the Akhakhu at this very moment. It is doubtful that those involved will be able to shield their thoughts for long. There will be three teams, led by you, Grant and Decard."

"You're purposely splitting us up," Grant growled.

"By no means," Nefron said sternly. "You, Decard and Kane have the most experience in such activities, even more so than my Incarnates."

"So," Lakesh ventured, "once your oracles acquire some solid information, we'll be tracking down the perpetrators?"

"We, but not you," Kane told the scientist. "You're not going."

Lakesh's face turned several shades darker. "Why not? I have as much right to be with you on this hunt as Brigid."

"I would prefer it if you would stay and talk with me, Dr. Singh," Nefron said. "Once you have reviewed the data on the disc, we will have a great deal to discuss."

"I don't like this," Brigid declared matter-of-factly, locking stares with Erica van Sloan. "She's probably keeping Sam up-to-date second by second."

"If we want the equipment we need to help Quavell, then we have no choice but to work alongside her," Kane said.

Brigid's eyebrows rose, then lowered. "You can't possibly trust her."

Kane showed his teeth in a hard, humorless grin. "I don't know what would give you that idea. I trust her so much that one of my conditions for agreeing to this hunt is that Erica be on my team. But before I do that, I want some proof that Aten can deliver its end of the bargain."

Mavati and Nefron engaged in a brief, whispered conference. Mavati straightened and announced, "I will show you the proof. Come with me."

Chapter 19

Acceding to a request from Kane, a messenger went to fetch Reba DeFore and Domi from Decard's home. Erica opted to meet to discuss tactics with her soldiers, while Mavati led the group of outlanders through the streets of Aten. There were more people out and about than any of them had seen previously. Frightened children clung to the sheer dresses of their mothers, while the men talked in low, grim tones, eyeing them suspiciously as they passed by.

Word had leaked out of the attempted coup and almost everyone was armed, carrying one form of weapon or another. Everything from sickles used in harvests, to swords with strangely curved blades, spears, pole arms and even axes.

"Looks like your people are preparing for war," Grant said to Mavati.

She nodded in misery, but said nothing. Lakesh, Brigid, Domi, DeFore, Kane and Grant followed the girl down a narrow twisting lane, until they reached a long, sprawling building. Its facade was unadorned except for a small caduceus, the ancient intertwined snake symbol of medicine.

"What is this place?" Domi asked, eyeing the building uneasily.

"The hospital of Aten," Mavati answered.

The interior was almost as plain as the exterior, with bare, whitewashed walls and exceptionally clean floors. The air smelled strongly of antiseptic. There were several wooden stools situated on the floor, as well as three benches lined up against each of the walls. A single desk sat by another doorway at the opposite end of the room.

A woman, dressed in a comfortable-looking tan, sleeveless shift, sat at the desk, writing on a piece of parchment. Her long black hair was streaked with threads of gray, but it flowed evenly across her shoulders and back. Her slanted eyes were shaded by blue makeup, and her thin lips were pursed in thought. She looked up and smiled at Mavati. "Yes, my princess?"

"Our guests would like a look at our medical facilities," Mavati said.

The woman frowned slightly in consternation. "Why, may I ask?"

"It is the wish of the queen, Dr. Ninghal."

The women stood and opened a door behind the desk. She beckoned to them and the visitors joined her, walking down a long corridor. Unlike the lobby, both walls were decorated in hieroglyphic style, depicting men and women performing various medical procedures, many of them holding what was clearly high-tech, modern tools.

Doorways were on both sides of the corridor, some closed off from the rest of the building by wood, others by simple curtains of beads. Peering through the beads, Kane could see that several of the rooms were occupied by people who had suffered injuries during the battle at the audience chamber.

The woman led them down the corridor and stopped at the second-to-last wooden door on the left. She held the door open for them and waited. Mavati waved them toward the doorway. "There is the proof you seek."

They stepped in, and DeFore uttered a murmur of surprise as her eyes swept over the heavy trestle tables loaded with a complicated network of glass tubes, pipettes, beakers and flasks. They recognized a fermentation tank, a blood-purification system, microscopes and centrifuges from the Cerberus infirmary, but there was much no one but DeFore and perhaps Lakesh could identify.

The medic moved through the labyrinth of medical technology, exclaiming over several items. "My God...three different kinds of bioreactors...oligonucleotide probes...autoclaves...even omni-gene cell analysis systems. This is cutting-edge apparatus, things I have only read about!"

"There is more," Mavati declared. "Much, much more."

Turning, she fixed a level gaze on Kane's face. "Are you satisfied now?"

Kane refused to answer her directly. "Reba, what do you think? Can this stuff help Quavell?"

DeFore laughed, swiveling her head toward him, her brown eyes alight. "Kane, with this kind of equipment and the proper chemicals, like gluten hydrosylate, I could help anybody."

Mavati indicated the disc Lakesh held in his hand. "That contains a comprehensive inventory of all medicines we have available."

Kane nodded brusquely. "Now we know what we'll receive in return for hunting down and killing strangers."

Mavati's eyes widened. "We are not sending you out to assassinate our own people, Kane!"

"What if they leave us no choice but to kill them?" Brigid asked.

"We can only hope you'll do everything you can to find another option," Mavati replied coldly.

Kane grunted and crossed his arms and then turned away from Mavati. Aware of Brigid's gaze upon him he said quietly, "This is blackmail by any other name. But it's the only choice we have, Baptiste."

Brigid placed her hand on his shoulder, and Kane felt himself gathering strength from the simple gesture. "I know, Kane. No matter what happens, you always do what's best, not just for yourself, but for everyone."

RATHER THAN RETURN to the safehouse, Mavati arranged for an escort of Incarnates to take the outlanders back to the home she shared with Decard, while she rejoined her mother.

Decard was waiting for them, his face a tight, grim mask, as Qerhet helped him don his Magistrate armor. Erica and her two troopers were there, as well, helping themselves to the food laid out on the table.

"The queen has gone back to the Sphinx to consult the oracles," Decard told them without preamble. "Once they get a line on the bastards behind this, they'll let us know."

Lakesh nodded distractedly, tapping the disc against his chin. Addressing DeFore, he asked, "Do you have your laptop handy, Doctor?"

DeFore cocked her head at a quizzical angle. "Nefron said the disc was encrypted."

An impish smile creased Lakesh's lips. He said nothing, but DeFore nodded in sudden comprehension and turned toward the doorway. "I'll get it."

Grant sampled a sweetmeat from the table. "I wish we had some kind of idea of the opposition," he groused. "How many of these muties we may be up against."

"Hopefully," Decard said, wincing as he sealed a seam on his breastplate, "the oracles can answer that question."

"Too bad they didn't have answers about when a coup would be pulled," Domi observed with a snide snicker.

Decard nodded in embarrassment. "I know. But

whoever is the ringleader of the insurrectionists must be able to shield not only his thoughts, but those of others."

"That's a pretty formidable ability," Kane stated. "Probably beats out all the other telepaths we've run into over the years."

Brigid ran a hand through her mane of hair. "There could be a much simpler explanation."

"What do you mean?" Erica asked.

Waving away the question, Brigid said, "Let's settle the logistics of this little undertaking while we have the time."

Kane regarded Erica and her troopers with a chilly smile. "Erica, Domi and one of your imperial joy-boys will go with me."

"Keep your enemies closer," Grant muttered.

"Something like that," Kane said genially. He turned toward Lakesh. "You and Reba will be sitting this one out."

"I won't be," Brigid declared.

Erica smiled disdainfully. "Has it occurred to any of you that this whole insurrection business might be the queen's way of getting rid of some political rivals, while leaving her hands clean?"

Voice sharp with anger, Decard snapped, "That's absurd and an insult to your hostess."

Kane turned toward him. "Did your IQ drop a dozen points since you've been living here? Regardless of her motivations, you're as much a pawn of the queen as we are." He hooked a thumb toward Erica. "We both have our reasons for being here, and the queen is taking full advantage of them."

Erica bristled. "If anyone is being taken advantage of, it's her. Sam won't leave me here. If I don't return, he'll send troops to find me. If Nefron angers the imperator, she'll have a lot more to worry about than a few dissidents." Her eyes narrowed as she speared Kane with a gimlet-hard stare. "So don't get any ideas about killing me and putting the blame on the insurrectionists."

Kane shook his head wearily. Erica's paranoia and fanatic devotion to Sam grated on his nerves, even though he expected nothing less. He refused to dignify her warning with a response, but Lakesh was not so restrained. He snapped angrily, "Just make sure you don't have similar notions, Erica."

Erica arched an eyebrow at him, a smug-smile crossing her face. "I only do what Sam asks of me, ever and always. Mohandas, it's not too late for you and the others to join our cause. We're your only protection against the barons when they inevitably come to smoke you and your crew out of your little mountaintop hideaway. Your future lies with us."

"I have it on very good authority that it doesn't," Lakesh retorted. "And I know why."

"And you're that sure of yourself?" Erica challenged.

"Oh, yes. Very much so, indeed."

"How?" The woman's voice was heavy with a mocking skepticism.

Lakesh smiled lopsidedly, as DeFore came in carrying the laptop. "For the time being, that will be my—*our*—secret."

Erica's superior smile faltered and Kane repressed one of his own, amused by Lakesh's enigmatic references to a recent event, when they had received a message from the future. The communication had laid out, in a very shocking manner, what would befall the Cerberus personnel if they allied themselves with Sam and became part of what he called "The Great Plan."

Although the Cerberus warriors knew the path to take and the steps to avoid so as to minimize such a future coming to pass, no one in the redoubt felt particularly comfortable about an imperator controlling the villes instead of a group of hybrid barons. According to the intel provided by Quavell, very few barons felt good about it, either.

The ancient Roman Empire was governed by a senate, but ruled by an emperor, sometimes known as an imperator. This person served as the final arbiter in matters pertaining to government. The villes acted interdependently, unified in name only. The arrival of Sam, the so-called imperator, changed all of that.

All of them, barons and Cerberus exiles alike, had believed the barons were under the sway of the Archon Directorate, a mysterious race that had influenced human affairs for thousands of years. Allegedly, the sinister thread linking all of humankind's darkest hours led back to a nonhuman presence, that conspired to control humanity through political chaos, staged wars, famines, plagues and natural disasters. The nuclear apocalypse of 2001 was all part of the Archon Directorate's strategy. With the destruction of social structures and severe depopulation, the Archons established the nine barons and distributed predark technology among them to consolidate their power over Earth and its disenfranchised, spiritually beaten human inhabitants.

But over the past couple of years, all of them had learned that the elaborate back story was all a ruse, bits of truth mixed in with outrageous fiction. The Archon Directorate didn't exist, except as a vast cover story, created in the twentieth century and grown larger with each succeeding generation. The only so-called Archon on Earth was Balam, the last of an extinct race that had once shared the planet with humankind. All of the barons believed that they acted as the plenipotentiaries of the Archons, or they had until the destruction of the Archuleta Mesa installation.

After the destruction of the mesa installation, the barons held an emergency council that dealt with only one topic—the survival of their people. Baron Cobalt, whom Lakesh had once served as a high adviser, put forth a proposal that would not only save the hybrids, but elevate him to a new position of power.

During the council, Baron Cobalt proposed to establish a new central ruling consortium. In effect, the barons would become viceroys, plenipotentiaries in their own territories. They were accustomed to acting as the viceroys of the Archon Directorate, so the actual proposal didn't offend them.

Although each of the fortress-cities with its individual, allegedly immortal god-king was supposed to be interdependent, the baronies still operated on insular principles. Cooperation among them was grudging, despite their shared goal of a unified world. They perceived humanity in general as either servants or as living storage vessels for transplanted organs and fresh genetic material.

The barons were far less in favor of Baron Cobalt's proposal than his intent to be recognized as the imperator. However, they really didn't have much of a choice. After the destruction of the medical facilities in the mesa, the barons were left without access to the ectogenesis techniques of fetal development outside the womb, so not only was the baronial oligarchy in danger of extinction, but so was the entire hybrid race.

Baron Cobalt presented his fellow barons with a way to stave off extinction by occupying Area 51, with the spoken assumption of taking responsibility to sustain his race, but only if he was elevated to a position of the highest authority.

Area 51 was the predark unclassified code name for a training area on Nellis Air Force base. It was also known as Groom Lake, but most predarkers preferred to call it "Dreamland." Contained in the dry lake bed was a vast installation, extending deep into the desert floor. Only a few of the buildings were aboveground. Area 51 was more than just a military installation; it served as an international base operated by a consortium from many countries. Baron Cobalt proposed that a consortium of barons, which in turn would be overseen by him, supervise its operation.

Since Area 51's history was intertwined with rumors of alien involvement, Baron Cobalt had used its medical facilities as a substitute for those destroyed in New Mexico. No one could be sure if the aliens referred to by the predark conspiracy theorists were the Archons, but more than likely they were, inasmuch as the equipment that still existed was already designed to be compatible with hybrid metabolisms.

In any event, Baron Cobalt reactivated the installation, turning it into a processing and treatment center, without having to rebuild it from scratch, and transferred from the Dulce facility the human and hybrid personnel who had survived the destruction there.

Still and all, the medical treatments that addressed the congenital autoimmune system deficiencies of the hybrids were not enough to insure the continued survival of the race. The necessary equipment and raw material to implement procreation had yet to be installed. Baron Cobalt had unilaterally decided that the conventional means of conception was the only option to keep the hybrid race alive.

When Baron Cobalt dangled the medical treatments before his fellow barons like a carrot on a stick, rather than share them freely, war was the inevitable result—particularly after Sam, supported by none other than Balam, hijacked not only Cobalt's plan, but also the title of imperator.

Qerhet, still in the process of helping Decard put on the body armor, suddenly stiffened, drawing in a sharp breath. Closing her eyes, she pressed the fingertips of her right hand against her forehead. Her lips stirred slightly, as if she were whispering to someone only she could see.

"What's going on?" Domi demanded, hand reaching for her Combat Master.

Decard shushed her. "She must be in telepathic communication with Mavati. They have a rapport that way."

Lowering her hand and opening her eyes, Qerhet announced flatly, "The queen summons the hunting parties to the audience chamber. The prey has been located."

Chapter 20

Long before they reached the audience chamber, they heard the murmur of voices echoing down the corridor, like the sound of rushing water. A crowd gathered below the throne, clotting around the base of the pyramid like swarming bees. Incarnates drew their ranks tighter, the V prongs of the *metauh* rods pointing outward.

Nefron and Mavati were back at their places, regarding the people milling around the cavern with a combination of haughty disdain and impatience. Cassie stood on the left side of the throne. As Kane, Grant, Brigid, Domi, Decard, Erica and her two troopers entered, the distinct elements became evident in the crowd. They seemed not to mingle. Foremost around the pyramid, doing most of the shouting, were the priests. Standing farther back and appearing subdued in comparison, were the nobles.

Over the babble of many voices, they heard snatches of argument—some said Aten ought to shut itself away in its hidden valley and tunnels. Others wrangled about baronial forces, whether they would learn of the city if the strangers were allowed to leave, whether or not Aten should strike first, whether or not both those issues were pointless, because the queen would make the final decision. Men and women screamed at each other.

The crowd parted as the group approached. Kane kept his eyes fixed on the throne, neither looking right nor left. He was glad that before leaving Decard's home, he had taken two of the weapons Lakesh had brought from the Cerberus armory, the carbine and the .45-caliber automatic.

When the outlanders had assembled around the throne, Queen Nefron held up her hands to silence the crowd, her bloodred gaze traveling over their faces one by one. "There are those in the kingdom of Aten who think that because I keep our glorious city hidden from the rest of the world, that I am weak, and unfit to rule."

A muttering of resentful agreement arose from a number of the gathered people. Nefron paused for a few seconds and then continued. "Then there are those of you who feel we should be even more isolated than we are at present and put all strangers to death who stumble across traces of our existence."

The answering murmurs were fewer in number, but no less vehement. Nefron declared, "Aten has shaped us. We have a set of laws we live by. If we were in another place, we would not be the same people and we would have a different set of laws. The dissenters who would like to see us rise up and challenge the might of the barons directly, to take our place as the rulers of the Outlands, have forgotten that.

"Those who believe we should retreat even further have forgotten our laws, as well. This is not a matter of right or wrong. It is a matter of abiding by our laws. If we do not, we are no longer Aten."

From the crowd, a voice called, "You're negotiating with two outlander factions...how do we know that by doing so you are not turning Aten into something else? An outpost of this so-called imperator?"

The queen's face remained impassive, although the crimson hue of her eyes seemed to deepen. "The Outlands and the imperator mean little to me one way or the other. But I tell you this—I am not turning over control of our kingdom-city. We will never bow before the imperator or his representative. They, like our other guests—" she waved a hand toward the Cerberus exiles "—are here because we have something they want. If we can work out a mutual agreement, then for the first time since the death of my father, Aten will willingly open its doors to the outside. But only to those we choose."

Kane and Grant exchanged confused glances. The insurrectionists and the Akhakhu clearly wanted to wrest control from Nefron so that they could directly challenge the baronies and another group who wanted to keep the city separate from the rest of the world. Now Queen Nefron was talking about doing that very thing, in a limited fashion. She walked a fine line.

"But before such an action can be undertaken, much less discussed in an open forum, the kingdom must be made secure," Nefron stated. "And to that end, the insurrectionists and their allies who brought violence into my audience hall will be apprehended and neutralized."

Staring out over the crowd, Nefron announced, "With the exception of our guests and others who will be directly involved in my counterinsurgency operation, everyone else must leave my chambers. Spread the word among my subjects, among the citizens of Aten—the first blow against my rule has been struck, but I will strike the second and final one. If those of you here like not my rule, then come and take my crown. You will have to fight and die for it."

More than a few angry comments reached Kane's ears as the assembled crowd milled out of the cavern. It was clear that many of the people weren't happy with what the queen had planned, and a substantial number might hold sympathetic views toward the insurrectionists.

He glanced up as Queen Nefron watched the crowd file out of the huge chamber. She appeared to be remote and grimly determined. As if sensing his eyes upon her, the queen looked directly at him and nodded ever so slightly.

Kane returned the nod. Grant shifted his feet slightly, and Domi just looked on, paying full attention to what was happening around them. It took a great

deal of willpower for Kane not to actually growl, as
Erica moved over to stand next to him. Her troopers
made as if to follow, but a simple wave of Erica's hand
caused them to stay where they were.

After the audience hall had emptied, Nefron said
flatly, "That did not go as well as I hoped, but better
than it could have."

"What have your oracles learned?" Brigid asked.

"The insurrectionists have separated into several
groups," Nefron answered, "and they're trying to consolidate their forces for an impending counterattack.
Because their plan to control the imperator's soldiers
didn't go as smoothly as they had hoped, they feel that
they must act now, while they perceive that I am still
reeling from the initial onslaught."

As Nefron spoke, Kane noticed several people approaching from the far side of the cavern. He stiffened,
ready to defend not only himself, but his companions,
as well. Then he realized that Queen Nefron was also
watching them, appearing totally unconcerned. They
were men in warrior harness, brandishing swords,
bows and quivers of arrows. To Kane's surprise, he saw
that the man in the lead was the high priest Opet. Without his robes, he looked like a soldier by trade, wide
in the shoulder, rangy and muscular. Old scars crisscrossed his torso. He gave Kane a strangely penetrating look as he and his companions took up position at
the base of the pyramid.

"Kane, you and Erica will lead a small squad consisting of several of my own warriors," Nefron announced. "Opet, you will act as guide."

"As you wish, my queen," Opet said, bowing his head.

Clearing his throat, Kane said, "Your Highness, I'm not trying to stir up a controversy, but isn't old high priest Opet here opposed to Aten playing host to outsiders? Wasn't he suggesting all of us be put to death only a couple of hours ago?"

Opet's lips creased in a haughty smile. "I spilled blood for Aten long before I was a priest, outlander. I may disagree with the queen's policy and let my dissatisfaction be known, but I am loyal to the kingdom she has ruled all my life. Ever and always. From what I understand about you, that kind of loyalty is alien."

Kane felt anger and shame rushing warmth to the back of his neck, and his hand tightened on the stock of the carbine.

Grant interjected loudly, "How many of the insurrectionists are we dealing with? How many of the Akhakhu?"

Nefron leaned toward Cassandra, and several minutes passed as the queen conferred with the girl. Nefron shook her head in frustration. "The minds of the Akhakhu are very different, and neither I nor any of the oracles can receive more than flashes of their thoughts, flickers of intent. They are very angry, however, and will not surrender."

"If your father created them," Brigid pointed out, "surely you would have an idea of the different kinds."

"He created pairs of each," Nefron responded matter-of-factly. "So they could mate. Two Horusians, two Bastians, two Khemuians and two Thothians, one of whom—" she nodded toward Erica "—you so skillfully dispatched."

Erica smiled pridefully. "Thank you. It was a rather remarkable shot."

Lines of anger creased Nefron's brow. "I wasn't complimenting you. If you had not murdered him, he would have been a valuable source of information."

Erica's flush of pride became one of anger. "Killing in battle isn't murder, Your Highness."

"Killing is murder, just like guzzling is drinking or eating devouring," Mavati put in.

"In any event," Nefron went on, "the remaining members of the Akhakhu have been in the city for a long time, hiding in the catacombs. No doubt the Bastian and the Horusian who arrived at the redoubt yesterday planned on joining their comrades here, where the final phase of the insurrection would be put into play."

"What about the humans who are allied with them?" Grant demanded.

"We've put several of them in custody," Nefron answered. "Unfortunately, the handful who have offered the Akhakhu help cannot identify a ringleader as such."

"Are they hiding their thoughts from you, from your oracles?" Brigid wanted to know.

Cassandra smiled and Nefron all but laughed. "They can try," the queen stated, "but it will avail them nothing…not when the diviners, Cassie in particular, sift through their minds. No, their memories of whoever has given them their orders were altered or completely erased by the ringleader himself. Whoever it was, their psionic powers are exceptionally advanced."

Uneasily, Kane asked, "How do we know the ringleader won't just telepathically command us to forget about hunting down the Akhakhu? Or force us to kill each other?"

"That's a damn good question," Domi said. "What kind of weapons do they have? Who supplied them?"

"That we have never been able to determine," Mavati answered. "Despite our best efforts."

Domi's face contorted into a suspicious scowl. "I don't get this. You live in a city full of psi muties, but you don't know what other psi muties are up to?"

"And that's an equally damn good question," Kane rejoined. Questions piled on top of each other inside his head. As a Mag, he hadn't been faced with deep thinking on a regular basis. Baron Cobalt had laid down the laws, and Mags made sure they were enforced. Still, he didn't put all of his questions into words.

Nefron sighed wearily and massaged her temples. "The nature of telepathic ability is very specific and very highly trained here. Those born with the ability have long since learned to always keep their mental shielding in place, to avoid a constant barrage of thoughts from those around them. So, if one psi wishes to contact another, they have to deliberately make the effort to mentally reach out, in order to transmit or receive input from another mind."

Mavati picked up the thread. "That scan can vary from a superficial surface level to a precise plucking of one small bit of information from a whirlwind of mental impulses, to a highly detailed examination of the individual's innermost thoughts, history and basic nature, right down to feelings and memories that they themselves may no longer be consciously aware of. While a superficial scan is something the most untrained of our citizens can perform with only the barest amount of effort, a more detailed scan requires deep concentration."

"As you already are aware," Nefron said, "such a powerful and unique ability could easily give us access to the private thoughts and personal secrets of others, but our own honor code, ingrained from birth, prevents us from violating another being's privacy, unless absolutely necessary."

"Wouldn't you say this situation qualifies as necessary?" Grant asked dubiously.

"The people here have never used their telepathic abilities to harm one another," Decard said defensively. "It's a testament to the trust the citizens share among themselves that most of them feel entirely comfortable here, without fear that their neighbor will be looking into their minds. To anybody who has been here awhile, the notion that the citizens would violate each other like that is too absurd to take seriously."

Mavati smiled fondly down at her husband, but the outlanders weren't so easily mollified.

Brigid said contemplatively, "The exact physical basis of the telepathic ability is unclear, though it's theorized that it involves the reading of electronic impulses that course through a living mind during thought, and that leave behind after images as memories and personality indicators."

"That was my father's theory, as well," Nefron agreed. "He considered the ability not so much a power, as added sensory receptivity for which the precise scientific explanation has not yet been uncovered. What is known is that the ability appears to be inheritable."

She patted Cassandra's shoulder. "In Cassie's case, neither of her parents was a telepath, but apparently some of her ancestors were said to have had some trace of the ability. Likewise most of Aten's children manifest a very rudimentary telepathic ability, having fairly clear mental links with one another, and occasionally being able to catch a thought or emotion from someone else. As it is, I feel the telepathic ability is a primitive one, a throwback."

Brigid nodded. "If telepathic ability took root in our ancestors, it would have been so valuable that it is surprising not to find it fully developed in modern humans."

"A counterargument might be that telepathy is present to a greater extent in animals," put in Erica van

Sloan, "and that, as in the case of the olfactory sense, humans lost their telepathic abilities. The reason could be that, following the emergence of a sophisticated spoken language, people had less need to rely on a purely mental and much less precise method of conveying thoughts."

"When do we move out?" Kane demanded, before anyone else could continue the discussion.

Opet took it upon himself to answer. "I suggest as soon as possible. We must attack while our enemies are still weak and trying to consolidate their forces."

"The main group has retreated to the catacombs, where our departed are laid to rest," Nefron said. "They feel that our own people will be reluctant to pursue them into the necropolis."

Kane chewed his lower lip before responding. "We need a map of the catacombs, then we can move in from several sides, and all at once, to close off any possible means of escape."

Decard nodded. "I'll talk to our scribes and get some maps. They'll be accurate, unless..." His voice trailed off.

Grant eyed the young man. "Unless the insurrectionists have made their own changes in the catacombs, right? Digging new tunnels?"

"Right," Decard agreed. "Although, I don't think they could have made major excavations. Someone would have spotted them and reported it."

Opet spoke up. "Not necessarily." As all eyes turned toward him, he said, "The leader of our enemies might have wiped the memories of anyone that stumbled upon their lair."

Kane thought that over for a few seconds, then shrugged. "Get the maps," Kane told the young man. "We'll have to take our chances and hope for the best."

"Follow me," Decard said.

Before he did the young man's bidding, Kane looked over at Erica van Sloan. "Are your people ready to follow my orders?"

"They'll listen to me," the dark-haired woman said cryptically.

Kane slitted his eyes. "That's a little vague."

"It'll have to do," Erica retorted. "But I intend to cooperate."

Kane stepped to one side and waved his arm toward Decard. "After you, imperial mama."

The woman's eyes glinted hard for just a second, then she sauntered past him, putting a little extra sway to her hips as she moved. Her pair of soldiers followed her, keeping close behind her. Kane didn't really fault them, since the view was very pleasant.

"Kane," Grant called out as he walked past.

He stopped and looked over at his partner. "Yeah?"

Grant indicated himself, Domi and Brigid with a sweep of his hand. "We all need to talk before you head out."

"Count on it," Kane said. With that, the outlanders followed Decard and all of the others involved in the hunt out of the audience chamber.

Chapter 21

Decard and Opet led Kane, Grant, Brigid, Domi and Erica into an adjacent chamber. Like the audience hall, the chamber was a cavern, but of much smaller dimensions. The walls were covered by colorful murals. In the center of the room rested a large wooden table, the legs of which were beautifully crafted to resemble those of a horse.

As the outlanders reached the table, they noticed that its surface bore carvings that depicted various Egyptian religious symbols, such as the eye of Ra. A dozen elegant chairs circled the table. Kane ran his hand over the symbols and was surprised that the table felt perfectly smooth under his touch, yet each image was deeply ingrained in the wood. He realized that the entire wooden surface was covered in some sort of transparent varnish.

Decard removed a sheaf of parchment from a shelf and took a seat at one end of the table. Opet sat down directly across from him. The others followed suit, and Grant almost growled when Erica van Sloan sat next to him. She met his scowl with a smug smile. Grant glared at her, but kept his mouth shut.

Decard spread out the maps of the catacombs. Kane leaned forward, studying them carefully. The parchment was covered by countless lines, arrows and color-coded squares. The map was marked with many of the same glyphs he had seen covering the walls of the city.

"Your map makers don't do things half-assed, do they?" Kane asked absently.

Leaning back in his seat, Opet put his feet on the table. "Why would they? We have all the time in the world. Our artisans take great pride in the work they do."

Kane ignored the priest and let his eyes wander over the layout. With a forefinger, Brigid traced a single long tunnel that led to an octagonal chamber and then continued on to two more similarly shaped rooms. The tunnel leading past the third room showed numerous side tunnels leading to smaller chambers and even more tunnels. It was a virtual maze.

"So, this tunnel leads to what, a preparation chamber?" Brigid asked, running her finger along the lines.

Decard nodded. "Yeah. There are a series of chambers, each one is dedicated to one of the steps of mummification."

"What about these?" Grant pointed at the numerous tunnels that branched off after the third chamber.

"They're the crypts, where the bodies are kept."

Kane nodded. "I'll bet you that's where we'll find your rebels."

He questioned Decard and Opet about several features he had noted on the map, all the while studiously ignoring Erica, even though he knew she was paying close attention as they discussed the route they would take to the catacombs. Domi remained silent for the most part, only occasionally asking for clarification.

"So, this is where we're going to split up, then?" Domi asked, tapping a point on the map where an intersection appeared, a little past the preparation chambers. Catacombs and tunnels branched off from it, but they did finally converge in a single large chamber, at the very edge of the map.

"Seems reasonable," Erica said.

Domi sneered. "Somehow I don't think we'll be lucky enough to catch them there."

Kane shook his head. "No way they would be stupid enough to hole up in that spot. So, we're going to have to leave people at the entrance, to prevent them from getting past us and out."

Leaning back in the chair, he looked toward Opet. "Seems pretty straightforward. Are you sure your people can be trusted?"

The priest smiled condescendingly. "They can be trusted to do their job. Can you and yours?"

Kane felt himself bristle at the arrogance, but he didn't allow himself to react with anger. "I think so. I guess we'll both find out, won't we?"

Opet's smile widened. Standing, he clapped his hands once. "We have the honor of biting the head off the asp. Without it, the body will wither."

For a second, Kane almost asked how he knew that, but he kept the question unspoken. He knew the answer. He sighed, feeling both tired and somewhat impatient.

As if sensing his discomfiture, Opet grinned. "We'll go as soon as you give the word, Kane."

Kane looked over at Erica. "Are you and your troopers ready?"

She nodded. "And willing."

Kane's head turned toward Decard. "You ready?"

Decard shrugged. "I just want to get this over with, so we can get back to enjoying life."

Standing, Kane placed his hands on his hips and stretched his back, feeling the muscles move under his flesh. "All right, let's do it. But I want to confer with my people first."

Suspicion flashed in Erica's eyes, but she said nothing. She and her troopers crossed the cavern to stand by the entrance. Opet regarded Kane, Grant, Domi and Brigid with an expressionless face, then joined the others. He gestured to them and they followed him out.

"I don't like Opet, or trust him," Grant said, crossing his arms over his chest.

Brigid smiled wryly. "You think any of us do? He's got the attitude of a baron."

"Yeah, and maybe their tendency toward treachery," Grant replied.

"What are you getting at?" Domi asked, looking at

the big man curiously. "You think he may have something to do with the insurrectionists?"

Grant nodded, his perpetual scowl firmly back in
place. "I do. Kane, you're going to be working with
Opet and van Sloan, so watch your ass."

"Always," Kane said simply.

The outlanders left the chamber, and Opet led the
way back through the main audience chamber. Kane
eyed the priest's back as he followed him, wondering
if he had overheard the conversation. Then he realized
that considering the sheer number of telepaths that
resided in the city, his thoughts were already being
conveyed to Nefron.

They followed Opet out of the Sphinx and into the
streets of Aten. Opet led the party out of the main part
of the city, toward the extreme end of the canyon. The
farther down they went, the more the homes gave way
to shops and storehouses and finally even they tapered
off, leaving just barren stone. It opened into a field of
upthrust rocks, all of them of similar size and shape,
approximately six feet tall and quarried flat on facing
sides. They were arranged in a double row with an
aisle about eight feet wide between them. The aisle
ended at the mouth of a dark tunnel punched into the
canyon wall. Kane turned and looked at Decard, the
angle of his eyebrows requesting an explanation.

Before the young man could speak, Opet said
haughtily, "The stones mark the boundary of the city.
From here on, the main tunnel leads to the mummifi-

cation chamber and the catacombs, our necropolis. So show the proper respect."

Arrogance was a quality that Kane had never much cared for, and he found himself disliking Opet all that much more. Looking over at Grant, he could read the same thoughts on the big man's face. Brigid, as usual, wore her poker face, but her eyes snapped green sparks of repressed anger.

"Have you ever been there before?" Kane asked Decard.

The young man shuddered almost imperceptibly. "Yeah, a couple of times. I guess I wanted to see everything, and after what Mavati told me about the way they dispose of their dead, I had to check it out myself."

Kane addressed the assembled group, hefting the carbine. "We're about to enter dark territory people, so get your weapons ready. Stay on triple red."

Without so much as glancing at Opet, Kane turned to the rest of the group. "Decard, you're with me. Opet, you follow, but stay at least a good thirty yards behind. Grant, stay with him. Domi and Baptiste, you fall back about ten yards. Erica, I want you and your drones to follow about three yards behind them."

"We're bringing up the rear?" Erica demanded in an outraged tone.

"We can't afford anyone sneaking up on us. Look at it as a show of my trust in you. Just keep the noise to a minimum."

Erica's eyebrows knitted at the bridge of her nose.

She grunted. "Do you think we're a bunch of amateurs?"

"As a matter of fact," Kane retorted, before turning his back on her, "I do."

Facing the tunnel mouth, he took a deep breath and entered the necropolis of Aten.

UPON HIS ARRIVAL in Aten, one thing that Kane had noticed was the overall cleanliness of the city. That devotion to neatness extended even underground. There was a distinct lack of dust and debris along the floor of the tunnel as he walked along its course, keeping close to the left-hand wall. The rock floor pitched slightly downward and was worn smooth, either by tools or the passage of many feet over many years.

The silence of the tomb hung as thick as dust, but the air was breathable. The passageway was dark, but not black, the gloom alleviated by flickering bronze lamps set in wall sconces every dozen or so yards. He quickly realized the map's depiction of the tunnel was slightly misleading—it didn't run straight, but meandered to the right. Moving quickly and with the stealth learned from years of being a point man, he quickly reached the first intersection and came to a halt. He could barely hear Decard's footfalls as he crept along beside him.

Kane saw a glimmer of faint light to the right and turning in that direction he saw a broad arch. Side by side, he and Decard moved to the entrance of the mummification chamber. Kane waved a hand, indicating that those behind them should stop.

Peering through the gloom, Kane saw distorted shadows dancing along the floor and walls of the tunnel. For an apprehensive half second, Kane thought that the chamber was occupied, and then he realized that the light was shed from torches. He half expected to see a dozen armed insurrectionists, but the tunnel remained empty.

Creeping forward, walking heel-to-toe as always in a potential killzone, Kane kept his gaze on the chamber beyond the stone arch. He started to make out details of the chamber itself. Directly in front of him, in the dead center of the chamber, stood a black stone slab, massive and somber. Even by the dim illumination, Kane saw the body-shaped indentation in the top of the slab. Several large urns and jugs lay around the base of the slab, as well as a wooden table holding tall stacks of bleached linen.

Stealthily, he crept into the room. Kane saw only one exit from the chamber. He motioned with his hand for the rest of the people to join him. They spread out across the chamber, looking around alertly.

"This is the Ibu," Dooard said. "It's the place of purification."

Kane nodded. "Go on," he said.

Opet interjected, "Here the dead are brought, the bodies washed carefully. Originally, the embalmers used palm wine and then rinsed it with water from the

Nile. But since this isn't Egypt, we use wine that is grown locally and water from the underground river."

"It's really quite fascinating," Brigid murmured. She came up to the stone slab and ran her hand over the indentation. "I remember reading that after they cleansed the body, they then removed all of the internal organs except the heart."

"That's right," Opet agreed. "Since the entrails are the first part of the body to rot, they have to be removed quickly to avoid bloating."

Interested in spite of himself, Kane asked, "Why did they leave the heart, then?"

Opet smiled almost cruelly. "The ancient ones believed that the heart was the originating source of intelligence and emotions, not the brain. So they used a long hooked needle and inserted it through the sinus passage in order to pull the brains out."

Domi didn't try to repress her utterance of disgust. As Opet spoke, Kane let his eyes wander over the walls. He noticed that the hieroglyphs depicted exactly what the priest talked about. Not only was the room used for preparation, but also the exact instructions on what to do were displayed, so that anyone could follow them with relative ease.

"The stomach, liver, intestines were carefully washed, as well," Opet continued, "and then packed in natron, a natural salt used to dry out the organs."

"Sounds a lot easier than just burying the body, doesn't it?" Grant asked sarcastically.

Kane threw him a sour smile. "Let's move it."

Taking the point again, Kane moved across the chamber and out into the adjoining passageway. The distance to the next chamber was less than thirty yards, but he approached it cautiously. This room was approximately the same size as the last one, but instead of a single stone slab in the center of the room, the walls were perforated with alcoves, three to a side.

Like the first chamber, it was roughly octagonal in shape. Less than a third of the alcoves contained anything. The rest contained tall, vaguely humanoid shapes, shrouded in gauze. The fabric appeared to be covered in a white, granulated powder. Kane saw four clay jars inside the alcoves.

As he had done before entering the purification chamber, Kane carefully scanned it, looking for any sign of occupation. When he was satisfied that the chamber held only shadows and the shrouded bodies, he stepped in, beckoning for the others to join him.

"This is the chamber where the bodies are dried out," Opet declared, reaching out to touch the linen swathings. A little cloud of powder puffed up under his touch. "The wrappings are saturated with natron, and the body cavities are stuffed with it, as well. We leave them here for forty days, until all moisture is dried from their bodies."

"What's with the jars?" Grant asked, gesturing with the barrel of his Sin Eater.

"Those are canopic jars, containing the organs that

were removed. Each one represents one of our gods." Opet gestured to one of the vessels. "That one is Imsety…it holds the liver."

Noticing that both Erica van Sloan and Domi grimaced, Opet pointed to the other jars, seeming to take a boyish relish in their reactions. "That's Hapy, and this jar contains the lungs. And the next one, the jackal-headed one, is Duamutef. It holds the stomach."

"And that one?" asked a blank-faced Brigid, pointing to a jar topped by a falcon-headed lid.

"That's Qebehsenuef, where the intestines are stored."

Kane spotted a smaller jar, one that seemed to be fabricated of metal instead of clay like the others. The whole container bore the outline of a pregnant woman. "Why is that one so different?"

Opet actually looked uncomfortable as he replied, "That's Isis, the goddess of fertility. That hermetically sealed jar contains a sample of the dead person's genetic code."

Raising an eyebrow, Brigid asked, "Genetic material? Is Nefron planning on cloning these people?"

The priest shrugged. "We keep it for posterity's sake. Perhaps one day it will be very useful to a member of the deceased one's family."

Brigid nodded. "That makes a certain amount of sense. The donor cells are forced into hibernation and the hibernation brings about a genetic reprogramming of the cell, switching the adult cells back to an embryonic state."

"What good would that do?" Domi asked.

"Conceivably, scientists here in Aten could take a normal unfertilized egg from a woman and remove the DNA from it. Taking the DNA-empty egg, they would immerse it in a solution with the reprogrammed donor cell...an electric current is passed through the donor and the egg cell, fusing them together. The new cell is then planted into a surrogate mother. The baby that results. is genetically identical to the donor." Brigid glanced over at Decard. "I wouldn't be too surprised to learn that was the method of Mavati's birth."

Although Decard didn't answer, Kane found the information fascinating. He half chuckled, realizing just how much of Baptiste's influence had rubbed off on him over the past couple of years. He turned toward the exit and left the chamber.

The tunnel stretched for thirty yards and opened up into a third chamber. As with the first one entered, there was a single large stone slab rising from the floor. Several jars stood atop it. Tall shelves were bracketed to the stone wall, each one filled to capacity with rolls of fresh linen.

"I'd guess this is where the mummified remains are wrapped," Kane said to Opet as they entered.

The priest nodded. "First oil is rubbed into the skin to keep it from breaking. The corpses are filled with sawdust, leaves and linen, so as to maintain a lifelike appearance...at least for the first few decades."

Kane looked at the murals on the walls and saw the

steps that Opet had described. He even noticed how the corpses were wrapped, the first image showing the head and neck being wrapped first, then each finger and toe. The arms and legs were wrapped separately, and finally the torso. The illustrations showed strangely shaped amulets placed inside the wrappings. The next image showed the arms and legs being tied together, with a scroll held between the hands. The final image showed the wrapped body taken by mourners into a crypt for its final rest.

Impulsively, Kane stepped up to the slab and lifted the lid from one of the jars. A strong, sweet odor wafted out from the opening, and he saw it was filled with thick oil. Replacing the lid, he crossed the chamber and looked through the door and down the adjoining tunnel. As had all the other stretches, it appeared deserted.

He glanced over his shoulder at the people in the chamber. "So far so good."

"That could change," Decard said flatly.

"In fact," Opet declared confidently, "I know it will, sooner before later."

Grant glowered at him. "You'd almost think you were psychic or something."

Chapter 22

Turning, Kane fixed his gaze on Opet's face. "You'd think they would have tried to ambush us by now, or that we would have found some trace that they were here in the first place."

Opet's face registered irritation. "What do you expect, Kane? The insurgents aren't stupid, and staging an attack against as well armed a force as we are, even with a psionic leg up on our plans, wouldn't have much chance of succeeding. No, they'll be waiting for us in the crypts—there can be no doubt about that."

Kane considered Opet's words and said, "Considering how extensive the maps showed the catacombs are, I'm tempted to break our group into smaller bodies, so that we can cover more ground, but that would mean reducing our fighting capability."

Decard and Opet nodded in agreement. The young man asked, "Want us to stay in position?"

Kane sighed wearily, aware of the mocking stare Erica had fixed on him. "Yeah, at least for now."

Kane took the point again. He paused only long enough to make sure the others took up their assigned positions. As he eased into the passageway, he immediately noticed that the stretch ahead wasn't as well lit. There weren't as many brass lamps as he had seen before, and there was a visible increase in the amount of dust and debris on the floor. He stopped and knelt on one knee. A number of people had passed through the tunnel, judging by the scuff marks and blurred footprints in the dust, but he had no way of knowing how long ago it had been. He called Domi up and she examined the tracks with a critical eye.

"'Bout ten people came this way," she said quietly.

"How long ago?" Kane asked.

She took a pinch of dust between thumb and forefinger and let it sift down. "Not long. An hour at the most. Maybe less."

With a word of thanks, Kane continued down the passageway. Domi returned to her position. About sixty yards down the corridor they came to an X intersection. He wasn't sure which way to go, but as he had done many times in the past, he decided to trust in his instinct to guide him. He turned back to Decard, whispering, "Everybody wait here. Stand guard at all the tunnels."

"What are you going to do?" Grant demanded, the lionlike rumble of his voice softened to a hoarse whisper.

"I'll scout ahead a little ways. I'll only be gone a minute."

Kane moved slowly down the left-hand tunnel. Although he didn't possess Brigid's eidetic gifts of memory, he recalled from the maps that the entrance to the crypt complex lay ahead. Just as he came within sight of the square-cut doorway, he heard soft footfalls behind him.

Glancing over his shoulder, he saw Decard moving up swiftly. "Grant sent me ahead," he whispered. "He figured you might need your six watched."

Kane tamped down the surge of irritation and only nodded. Together, they continued into the first of the chambers. It held an oddly shaped eight-branched candelabra in which black candles burned with guttering flames. The illumination barely penetrated the near total darkness, as if not to disturb the eternal slumber of those interred in the tomb. Unable to fully adjust to the gloom, Kane donned his night-vision glasses. The built-in light-intensification feature of the lenses allowed him to see clearly in deep shadow for approximately ten feet, as long as there was some kind of light source.

The red-tinted visor of Decard's Mag-issue helmet served several functions—it protected the eyes from foreign particles, and the electrochemical polymer was connected to a passive night sight that intensified ambient light to permit one-color night vision. The tiny image enhancer sensor mounted on the forehead of the helmet didn't emit detectable rays. The limits of its range were only twenty-five feet, even on a fairly clear night with strong moonlight.

Kane saw eight large oblong cavities dug into each of the walls. Each cavity held a tall, carved sarcophagus of red-and-black-lacquered wood. On the lids of every case, graven in ivory, was the countenance of the occupant. Curiosity got the better of the former Magistrate and he approached the nearest one.

A series of tiny pictographs and hieroglyphs was neatly inscribed in the stone at the base of each niche, depicting the life and important events of those interred. A shelf was built into the cavity above the mummy case, holding four canopic jars.

The sarcophagus itself was a thing of beauty. The image on the lid presented what he assumed to be a very close approximation of the person within it, right down to the color of the eyes, as they had appeared in the prime of their life. Once again, Kane was deeply impressed by the awe-inspiring artistic talent possessed by the citizens of the city.

Apparently their talents at housekeeping were restricted to the streets above. Layers of dust covered everything, which indicated the age of the burial chamber. He realized this chamber was probably the first of the crypts to be constructed.

Motioning for Decard to take the opposite side of the chamber, Kane made his way along the wall until he reached the hallway connecting the next series of crypts. The lighting didn't improve. As they approached the next burial chamber, a nauseating stench clogged his nostrils.

Fingering his nose, Decard whispered hoarsely, "Goddamn, somebody's embalming technique needs work."

Kane placed a finger to his lips, annoyed that the younger magistrate had broken the silence. But he couldn't deny the odor was of old death—dusty, musty and putrid all at once.

Suddenly, from within the burial chamber, he caught a brief flicker of movement, and he raised the carbine. Decard spied the shifting of shadows, too, and snapped up his Sin Eater.

Even with the light amplification that his glasses provided, Kane could just barely make out the figure at the end of the tunnel. He assumed one of the insurrectionists had shown himself, but the form moved toward them slowly, listing from side to side, almost as if it were shambling.

He heard a rustling, scraping sound accompanying the figure's approach, then a faint noise as of wood creaking. Whirling, Kane saw the lid of a sarcophagus slowly rising, pushed up from within. The stench of putrefaction increased almost exponentially, and even as he watched, his autorifle raised, gnarled brown fingers curled around the edge of the lid.

Flesh crawling with revulsion and a mounting horror, Kane felt rooted in the mire of a nightmare. The ripping sound of Decard's Sin Eater on full-auto broke the spell of terror threatening to engulf Kane's mind. He whipped his head around, as Decard fired a steady burst at the approaching figure. By the strobing flame licking from the pistol's bore, Kane saw a withered, wizened shape with dried, dark limbs like dead wood, showing through moldering, ragged bandages.

The figure shambling from the burial chamber was a mummy, and Kane's reason recoiled from the sight, his breath seizing in his lungs. The fusillade tore strips from the animated cadaver's body, the impacts turning it this way and that, but still it shuffled forward.

Teeth bared, eyes wide and wild as he kept the trigger stud depressed, Decard grated, "This is not fucking happening! This is *not* fucking happening!"

The mummy staggered under the 9 mm hammer blows, and it fell backward, arms and legs twitching. Kane returned his attention to the creature pushing its way out of the mummy case. His mind did a pirouette of insanity. The bandages had come loose from around its head, revealing leathery flesh, drawn drum-tight over the contours of the skull. A bright red, malevolent light gleamed inside the empty sockets, sending a stream of mad fear through Kane. Its jaws open and closed in a sickening, silent pantomime of speech.

He squeezed the trigger of the carbine, holding it down, firing through the entire magazine, blasting out waves of ear-shattering sound. The skull of the creature flew apart under the barrage and two of the canopic jars in the niche behind it shattered, amid sprays of clay and desiccated viscera.

"This is not fucking happening!" Decard's groaning, profane mantra penetrated Kane's own haze of terror. "This *can't* be fucking happening!"

Looking down the passageway, Kane saw the mummy Decard had fired upon staggering back to its feet, hooking its fleshless, clawlike fingers into the wall and hoisting itself erect. Slowly, with jerky movements, as if responding to the tug of invisible puppet strings, the cadaver advanced upon Kane and Decard.

Kane could only stare, unable to blink or breathe or even think. At the fringes of his awareness he heard the scraping creak of more mummy case lids opening. He watched as all of the sarcophagi opened, the bandaged corpses rising from their resting places. He felt as if the blood in his veins had congealed into icy mud.

Kane dropped the carbine with a loud clatter and drew the Colt automatic. Holding it in a two-handed grasp, he squeezed off single shots, carefully placing the rounds through the skulls of the mummies, although he had no idea how he could possibly kill something that was already dead.

Decard continued to fire his Sin Eater, blowing away half of the mummy's skull. No blood poured from the wound, and pieces of cranial bone clattered against the floor and walls.

He put his back to Kane as the withered corpses shambled toward them in a hideous mockery of life and movement. Shifting his aim downward, Kane fired a round at a mummy's knee joint. Dried flesh and bone shattered, the knee literally disappearing in a mushroom explosion of dust, rags and fragments of ancient cartilage and scraps of leathery skin.

The mummy fell forward as its leg collapsed, but it still continued to crawl toward him, using its arms and remaining leg to propel it along the tunnel floor. Kane fired directly into its face, the .45-caliber wrecking ball shearing away its jawbone. Teeth rattled off into the shadows like a handful of parched corn kernels.

Following his lead, Decard aimed for the knee and elbow joints on another of the walking corpses. He squeezed off four shots in rapid succession. A mummy was bowled off its feet, as a shinbone splintered under the autofire. It fell to the ground, flopping helplessly as it tried to rise again.

Kane fired on another mummy, shattering its spine completely. Its torso folded in half like a jackknife, its head dangling between its legs. Despite the cold sweat of terror beading his brow, he was able to think a bit more clearly. Returning rationality pushed away the fog of unreasoning horror. Although the gunfire was effective, the results were too slow. He knew he had to come up with a faster method of disposing of the cadavers, without burning through all of their ammunition.

Burning…

Kane's gaze darted to the candelabra and with the thought came motion. He lunged forward, back into the burial chamber, elbowing a cadaver aside. He heard ribs crunch under the impact. The clawlike hand of another mummy reached for his face, and his cheek was scratched by split black fingernails.

A bandaged creature lurched directly into his path, arms outflung as if inviting an embrace. Kane ducked beneath it and grabbed the candelabra. Even through the gloves of his shadow suit, he felt the heat of the brass. A brown, gnarled hand darted for his throat and he spun out of reach, touching the flame of a candle to a dangling scrap of bandage.

The ancient, oil-treated linen instantly caught fire, like dry tinder. Tongues of flame engulfed its body, leaping from limb to limb. In a matter of seconds, the animated corpse burned as brightly as a torch. Even though the mummy was burning up, it still took several shambling steps, its unnatural mimicry of life keeping it on the move. Kane kicked it against one of its brethren.

The bandages of the other creature caught fire with an explosive pop. Both of the mummies collapsed, arms entwined in a mass of roaring flame. The heat seared Kane's face and he backed away. As if striking out in defiance, one of the cadavers lashed out at Kane with an arm, its bony fingers closing around his right ankle. Kane stomped on the wrist with his left foot, putting all of his weight down. The forearm snapped like a broken stick, and he kicked the severed hand away.

He touched a candle to another mummy's wrappings, and almost immediately the fire spread over the creature's body, consuming it in a blaze of blue-and-orange flame. Decard hurled the final shambling corpse against it. Both figures were completely consumed, falling apart before their eyes, the glowing embers of blackened bones scattering over the floor. The two men fanned the smoky air away from their faces and coughed at the acrid stench.

The pounding of running feet echoed loudly in the chamber as Grant rushed into the room, eyes and Sin Eater questing for a target. He skidded to a clumsy halt as his gaze took in the scene of blazing carnage. "You've got to be kidding!" he blurted.

Kane kicked at a heap of embers and repressed another cough. "Do you see anybody laughing?"

Grant stood there, staring through the smoke at the flickering coals, too stunned to speak. Opet, Brigid, Domi and Erica van Sloan and her troopers rushed into the chamber. Even Opet gaped dumbfounded at the pyres. He was about to speak when Kane whipped about, and strode to the first mummy that shuffled down the tunnel toward him and Decard. Despite the damage inflicted upon it, the cadaver still crawled across the floor, dragging its crippled legs behind it.

The mummy clawed at him, but Kane sidestepped and dropped a candle on the creature's linen-wrapped back. As with the others, flames enveloped it swiftly, consuming the cadaver, reducing it to coal and ash. Thick, cloying smoke hung heavily in the air, impairing both respiration and vision.

"Let's get out of here," Grant said, wiping his watering eyes. He coughed rackingly.

All of them traversed the tunnel, anxious to get out of range of the smoke and the stench of burned oil, flesh and cloth. The next burial chamber was identical to the first, but it had two exits, one on the opposite wall and another to their right. One of the sarcophagi hung open. It was empty.

"Guess that's where your friend came from," Kane said to Decard.

When Opet entered, he turned to face the priest. "Is this something that happens often?"

"I had no idea that they would desecrate our dead like that," Opet said defensively.

Kane raised one eyebrow and Domi asked querulously, "Your people can do that, Opet? Bring the dead back to life?"

"No," Opet answered grimly. "Of course not. We can't raise the dead—there is no way. The only way that could have happened is if the insurrectionists have someone, or several people with telekinetic ability."

"Telekewhat ability?" Grant rumbled, looking confused.

"Telekinesis or psychokinesis," Brigid stated. "The ability to move things with the energy of the mind, moving objects from one place to another without using physical contact. It also means reshaping objects using the mind's energies, such as bending a spoon, or key, by just holding it and focusing. Psychokinesis comes from the Greek word *psyche,* meaning 'life' or 'soul,' and *kinesis,* meaning 'to move.'"

Kane looked from left to right, and then ran his hand across his face, wiping away a layer of sweat and ash. "It would be safe to assume that the insurrectionists do have people with that ability, then."

He turned toward Erica. "I want you and your blastermen to spread out along this tunnel." He pointed down the passageway on the right. "If there's going to be a pincer maneuver, it'll come from there."

The violet-eyed woman nodded to him, then to her soldiers. They went through the doorway without hesitation or argument.

"What about us?" Decard asked. "What are we going to do?" The young man's lips were ashen and sweat glistened on his cheeks. The barrel of his Sin Eater trembled ever so slightly.

Kane opened his mouth to speak, but a deep rumble, like that of an approaching locomotive, cut off his words. It grew in volume, vibrating deep in the bones of those gathered. The room seemed to heave around them.

Kane looked up at the ceiling of the chamber. A cascade of dust spilled from a widening network of cracks. Chunks of stone and earth pelted down from above.

Everyone rushed for the doorway as the ceiling crumbled. Large slabs of rock fell and clouds of dust arose, blinding eyes and filling lungs. As Kane tried to run, a down-rushing avalanche of stone and loose earth engulfed him.

Chapter 23

Grant, Domi, Brigid, Decard and Opet stood on the other side of the settling rock pile, staring at it in near disbelief. As far as they could see through the pall of dust, the entire ceiling had collapsed. The shuddering crash of tumbling stone slowly faded.

"Goddammit!" Grant roared, plunging his hands into the pile of dirt. "How the fuck are we supposed to get through this shit?"

Opet stepped up to the doorway, his hands on his hips. "It's going to take a while for them to get here, but I can summon a crew and start clearing this out of the way."

"Summon them how?" Domi demanded impatiently. When she saw Opet close his eyes and his brow crease in concentration, she said simply, "Oh."

"Kane could be hurt," Brigid said worriedly as she stepped up to the stone-clogged doorway. Behind her, Erica van Sloan and the two soldiers stood silently, watching and waiting.

Feeling both helpless and enraged, Grant whirled, looking for someone to take his anger out on. Unfortunately, one of Erica's troopers stood within arm's reach. Grant grabbed the startled man and threw him bodily at the mound of dirt and stone. "Start digging, asshole," he snarled.

The other soldier standing with Erica raised his weapons threateningly, but the raven-tressed woman motioned for him to put down the subgun.

Grant glared at her, expecting to see anger contorting her face, but to his surprise, he saw instead sympathy in her violet eyes. He took a deep breath, forcing the rage and frustration down, letting his intellect overrule his passion.

"Help him," Erica instructed, gesturing for the trooper to step up to the doorway. The soldier's lips twisted as if he wanted to spit, but he shouldered his weapon and pushed past Grant. He and his companion pulled at the stones and debris, clearing away as much as they could.

Grant found that he couldn't bring himself to actually thank the woman, so he nodded to her in acknowledgment. She smiled slightly. "You might not believe this, but I would not take any pleasure in Kane's death. Or yours for that matter."

Both Domi and Brigid made sounds that sounded like simultaneous snorts, but they kept their comments to themselves.

"A crew with the appropriate tools should be here in about ten minutes," Opet announced.

Decard shouldered between the pair of imperial

troopers. "That might be nine minutes too long." He began digging with his gauntleted hands, small stones clattering to the tunnel floor.

Grant pointedly looked at Opet and then at the rock pile. "What are you waiting for then?"

"You actually expect me to help?" Opet asked incredulously.

Grant moved over to the men who were already hard at work, trying their best to clear away the detritus from the chamber door. Decard and the troopers wrestled with a large chunk of rock, trying to pull it through the archway. Kneeling before the rock, Grant took several deep breaths, then wrapped his arms around the stone and pulled with all his might. The tendons on his neck and head stood out in stark relief as he strained to move the massive piece of rock. Slowly but surely, with dirt sliding from around it, he began to pull it free.

Decard wormed his way next to the huge man in order to help.

"You're just going to get in the way," Grant said through gritted teeth, straining at the rock.

"And you're just going to rupture something," Opet said, joining him and standing on the opposite side of the doorway, facing the young man.

The priest knelt before the stone and placed his hands beneath it, motioning with his head that Decard should do the same. Working in unison, straining until their muscles bulged and sweat poured down their faces, the three of them worked the stone free amid a small avalanche of dust, dirt and loose gravel.

"One down," Grant half gasped, massaging his aching hands and forearms.

"Yeah," Decard agreed gloomily. "Only a couple hundred more to go."

THE STENCH of decomposing meat, the nostril-abrading odor of smoke and even the faint tang of urine invaded Kane's nostrils. He tried to crawl away from it, wishing his sense of smell was as impaired as his vision at the moment. He could see only a few inches in front of him.

Coughing loudly, Kane swung out his arm, and felt the impact of his hand against fur-covered flesh. With a start, he caught sight of a large rat scurrying away from his path. That simple act sent waves of nausea through his stomach, threatening to purge all the food he had eaten over the past day. He squeezed his eyes shut, feeling the sickness subside.

He remained on all fours, crouching on the rough floor for several long minutes, trying to recover his equilibrium. His head throbbed in time to the beating of his heart. Lifting his hand, he gingerly touched the back of his skull. He could feel a lump where one of the hybrid horde had managed to club him with the sonic wands they carried.

He heard a faint scuff and scutter, as of footsteps in the distance. "Anyone there?" he called out, his voice hoarse and just barely above a whisper.

The words echoed hollowly off the walls. Against his better judgment, Kane opened his eyes once again. This time he didn't suffer from an onslaught of sickness and his vision had improved.

He found himself looking down a long, smoke-and-haze-filled corridor. Chunks of stone and broken equipment littered the corridor from end to end, as far as his eyes could see. Light flickered feebly from several neon ceiling strips, casting grotesque shadows and shapes across the walls and floor.

"What the hell?" he husked out, pulling himself slowly and painfully to his feet.

Only minutes before he, Baptiste, Grant and Domi had entered the Archuleta Mesa facility. Originally, their intent was to prevent the hybrids from sending out the Aurora aircraft to harvest internal organs and genetic matter from some isolated outlander ville. But something unexpected had happened. When Grant shot down the Aurora with a rocket launcher, it triggered a blast of near atomic proportions. Instead of leaving, the Cerberus warriors had decided to forge ahead into the facility and search for survivors, to see exactly the range of damage inflicted.

He remembered the brief battle with the tunneling machine and the elfin hybrid female who piloted it. He couldn't bring himself to kill her, and despite the past hour of crawling through rubble and finding nothing but corpses, somehow he hoped to find other survivors.

Instead, they encountered a small squad of hybrids,

most of whom were suffering from some sort of injury. He had tried to talk to them, but they attacked with their deadly infrasound wands. He had no choice but to fight. The last thing he remembered was hearing Grant call out a warning to him. Then blackness overcame his senses.

Glancing down at his right forearm, Kane noticed how his Sin Eater hung loosely from its holster. On impulse, he flexed his wrist tendons, but the blaster refused to respond to the actuators. He saw a deep dent on the barrel extending all the way into the frame and with a sinking sensation in the pit of his belly, he realized there was no way he could hope to fire the weapon. The odds were high it would blow up in his face the second he touched the firing stud.

Knowing the weapon was useless to him, he pulled the Velcro straps and opened the tabs, allowing the pistol to fall to the floor. Reaching down, he felt along his right boot where his fourteen-inch-long combat knife was scabbarded. The sheath was there, but it held nothing, not even an impression of the tungsten-steel blade. For some reason, Kane wasn't all that disquieted by the lack of weaponry.

Kane crept along the corridor, walking heel to toe, studying his surroundings as he went. He walked for nearly fifty yards without seeing any other doors or exits. The air in the facility was stifling hot, as of many fires raging unchecked. After a few minutes, he came across a doorway. The metal-sheathed door was bent nearly in half, bulging outward as if an unimaginably violent force had smashed into it from the other side. The wall was badly discolored, showing scorch marks and soot.

Peering beyond the maimed door, he looked into a chamber. The exact dimensions of the room were impossible to determine, as it was nearly pitch-black inside. The only illumination filtered in from the corridor. Still, he was able to make out blackened and still smoldering objects.

An intense fire had raged in the large room in the fairly recent past. As he was about to turn away, he noticed a misshapen lump on the floor, several feet inside the room, lying at the very edge of the light.

Something about the shape of the object tugged at his subconscious. Stepping back from the doubled-up door, Kane searched the corridor. With all the debris strewed about, he didn't have to look long to find what he needed. He retrieved a sturdy piece of wood, about two feet in length, but studded with rusty nails. The makeshift club would have to suffice as a weapon until he rejoined his friends or managed to find something more suitable. Rummaging through his pockets, he found and pulled out his Nighthawk microlight and turned it on.

Looking back into the chamber, he shone light around the door. The five-thousand-minicandlepower beam was sufficient for him to make out not only the object on the floor, but also the size of the room. It appeared to be a laboratory of sorts, as he could discern the remains of at least a dozen trestle tables, although most of them had been reduced to kindling. The smoke was a bit thicker in the room, but it wasn't intolerable.

The object on the floor lay amid a pile of broken and half-melted glass. It was clearly a corpse, curled in a fetal position. Kane carefully squeezed around the twisted door and crossed the few yards to the corpse. Kneeling, he glimpsed a glimmer of dark silver beneath the body. He gently turned the corpse over by its shoulders.

Even with the damage inflicted by the intense heat, the domed cranium of a hybrid was very recognizable. The silvery glint that had originally caught his attention was the remains of the one-piece metallic-weave jumpsuit normally worn by the hybrids as something of a uniform. It had protected the body from being consumed by the flames. In its arms rested the corpse of an infant, either killed by the heat or the concussive force that had thundered through the installation.

Standing and brushing off his hands against the leg of his whipcord pants, Kane shook his head sadly and whispered faintly, "We didn't mean for this to happen."

He moved around the laboratory, looking for another way out. He found a secondary exit on the rear wall, but the ceiling had collapsed on the other side, blocking his way entirely. With the exception of burned-out cupboards and storage cabinets, he found nothing of use.

Reentering the corridor, Kane continued to follow it. He passed by several more large rooms, in similar condition to the laboratory. He was forced to skirt one section entirely, as a fire raged out of control. The sprinkler system in this part of the facility had either malfunctioned entirely or the water in the pipes was spent. As he walked, Kane saw at least half a dozen corpses, all of them hybrids, judging by their slender, gracile builds and large skulls. Of Grant, Brigid and Domi, he saw no sign. That alone provided him with some comfort.

After what seemed like several miles, but in reality was only a hundred or so yards, the corridor dead-ended at a pair of metal doors with a push bar. Knowing he had nothing to lose, Kane leaned into the bar and gave it a gentle push. The screech of metal against metal tore through the silent corridor, but the door swung inward.

As he stepped through the door, Kane's stomach lurched sideways. Before him spread a cavernous ovoid chamber, crammed with catwalks, lifts and Y-shaped power-induction pylons. Here the damage was almost total. He saw small, graceful figures scattered about, their bodies frozen in twisted, broken poses. The facility sprinklers had been activated in this particular section, and steam mixed in liberally with the smoke from the now extinguished fires.

He walked over to the railing of a catwalk and looked down. He seemed to be about six stories above the lower level, and he suddenly found it difficult to re-member where he and the others had entered the mesa installation. He found himself wishing he could find a living hybrid, so that he could at least interrogate him or her. At the very least, they could show him the way out.

Going strictly on the memory of his first visit more than a year before, Kane ran along the walkway, head-ing toward the section of the sprawling facility that held the mat-trans jump chamber. If he could make it to the gateway unit, providing it still functioned, he could jump back to Cerberus and enlist the help of Bry or one of the others.

Passing the entrance to another corridor, Kane paused. Searching his memory, he knew that some-where down that particular passageway lay the cryo-genic facility that housed the remains of his father. He told himself that certainly the man—or whatever might have been left of him—had perished during his first visit to Dulce complex, when he had set off the incen-diaries.

The desire for closure won out over cold reason. Kane pushed open the door and ran through the debris-cluttered tunnel. In far less time than he expected, he reached the cryonic section, which held in stasis the men and women who had been deemed worthy of do-nating their genetic material to the hybridization pro-gram.

He saw near total destruction. The upright stasis

units that housed the bodies of those men and women were dark and devoid of power and of life. Absently he noted how much they resembled Egyptian-style sarcophagi. The charnel-house stench had long ago faded into a mere suggestion of what it had originally been. Still, even through the cloying odor of smoke and superheated metal, he could still detect the unmistakable scent of death.

A pang of guilt stabbed at his heart. Had there been a chance that he could have saved his father? And if he had, would it have made any difference? Like a burst dam, Kane's mind flooded with questions and regrets. He stood there, trying to gain control of a riot of wild feelings threatening to overwhelm him. His reasoning abilities crawled their way up through the morass of confused emotions and thoughts. Kane violently shook his head, and straining with all his considerable will, fought back the onslaught of crippling guilt.

Heeling around to flee the room, he almost collided with a man who stood directly behind him. Biting back a startled cry, he instinctively flexed the tendons in his wrist in an attempt to unleather a Sin Eater that was no longer there.

He stared face-to-face, eye-to-eye with his father.

"Hello, son," the elder Kane said almost casually.

Kane stood there, stunned into immobility by the sight before him. The man was indeed his father, but not quite the broad-shouldered, iron-faced warrior he remembered. The build and height were basically the same, but the elder Kane was wearing the ragged remains of denim coveralls, and he appeared almost emaciated, the bones of his face jutting sharply, his eyes burning deep in the sunken sockets.

Kane managed to make his mind and vocal cords work in tandem. "Dad?"

The man nodded. His hair was long and wild, shot through with gray. "It really is me, son."

"How can you be here? Alive? I set off explosives over a year ago."

The elder Kane shook his head sadly. "You succeeded in destroying most of those who were held in stasis with me." He gestured to the units. "There have been many times since that day when I wished you had killed me with the rest."

Kane's eyes never left the older man's face as he spoke. "How *did* you survive, Dad?"

Shrugging, the elder Kane gave him a halfhearted grin. "Luck of the Kanes, I guess. After you blew this section, I found myself lying in a pool of my own blood and the fluids from the stasis unit. The hybrids, the new humans as they prefer to be called, were fighting the fires, and somehow I found the strength to crawl out of the room, without them seeing me."

"How did you know I was the one who blew the chamber?" Kane asked in sudden suspicion, his eyes narrowing.

"I overheard the hybrids talking. Seems that you,

and your partner Grant, were responsible for my freedom…and a lot of dead new humans, too."

Kane nodded thoughtfully. "But that was over a year ago. How did you manage to keep yourself hidden all this time? And how did you survive the crash of the Aurora into the fusion reactor?"

"It wasn't as hard as you might think. This place is huge and understaffed. I was able to hide from the hybrids using the maintenance tunnels and air vents. I survived on what food and water I scavenged from around the place."

Kane bit his lower lip as he digested what his father was telling him. "Why didn't you try to escape?"

The elder Kane shrugged. "Where would I go? There was no way I could have survived the desert, and the gateway was too well guarded."

A sudden wave of anger flowed through Kane. "That's bullshit and you know it. You were trained as a Magistrate. You had a hell of a lot more years experience than I did. Getting out of the base and surviving would have been a simple matter to a man like you."

Unperturbed by his son's outburst, the elder Kane shrugged. "Once again…and go where? Back to Cobaltville? Not likely. And even if I could have reached an outlander settlement, once the people there discovered who and what I was, they would have killed me."

"I can't see how that would have been much worse than living here like an animal," Kane half shouted, taking several steps toward the man. "You could've tried to get word to Cerberus, to Lakesh. We would have come for you. Look at you now—you're a disgrace to everything that we stood for!"

"And what was that?" the elder Kane retorted with as much anger. "You turned your back on everything we stood for! You pissed on it. And here you are judging me, as if you actually think you've earned the right."

Kane tried to soften the hard edge of anger in his voice. "I have earned it, Dad. Many times over. If you'd ever made it back to Cerberus, you'd know that."

"I know a lot more than you realize, son," the elder Kane said with a grim smile. "A *hell* of a lot more."

Chapter 24

Opet suddenly swayed as if faint. He reached out for the wall to steady himself. Sweat pebbled his face and his lungs labored. Concerned, Brigid asked, "Are you all right?"

The priest nodded absently. "I'm not accustomed to this kind of exertion."

"None of us are," Grant grunted, working his stiff fingers. "Where the hell is this crew of yours? Shouldn't they have been here by now?"

Opet smiled wryly. "They might've taken a wrong turn in the maze. I'll take one of the secondary tunnels and try to get a line on their progress."

"You're not worried about running into the insurrectionists?" Domi challenged.

Opet shook his head. "I don't sense them in the vicinity. I should be safe enough." His face, if not his tone, registered a degree of doubt.

"I didn't think that accounted for much," Erica said, slapping dust from the sleeves of her tunic. "If they have people among them who can animate corpses, hiding their thoughts from you wouldn't be all that difficult, would it?"

Opet regarded her sternly. "It's a different application of abilities. Wait here. I'll be back as soon as I can."

Turning smartly on his heel, he marched down the corridor and quickly out of sight in the murk. Grant looked after him with slitted, suspicious eyes. Lowly, he said to Brigid, "Maybe it would be a good idea to go with him…make sure he doesn't get lost."

She cast him a swift, penetrating gaze, then nodded curtly. "Maybe I'd better."

Brigid strode quickly after Opet, calling, "Wait up! I'll keep you company."

If the priest replied, none of them heard it. Grant returned his attention to the rock- and earth-clogged burial chamber. Musingly, he said, "You'd assume Opet could just send a thought transmission that the work crew could follow. If he could sense the insurrectionists around, he should be able to summon laborers."

"He can't detect the minds of those muties, right?" Domi asked dubiously. "So he's got limits."

"That's true, but if there are regular citizens with the Akhakhu, Opet ought to be able to sense their minds," Decard commented. "As far as I know, there's not a range limit on psionic abilities…they've got to be around. How else were they able to reanimate the mummies?"

Erica sidled closer. "I agree. Minds that can make

dead bodies into puppets wouldn't have much trouble triggering a cave-in. The timing of that was a little too convenient, if you ask me."

Grant started to snap, "Nobody did," but a new sound reached his ears—the protracted grate of stone against stone. All of them heard the noise at the same time and spun toward it, gazing down the tunnel. A slab of rock wall turned on hidden pivots. For what seemed like a very long time, the slab kept turning, revolving, crunching and creaking.

Then, an ape-thing, a cat-creature and a ram-headed monster, followed by three bandaged men in black skullcaps, rushed into the tunnel, howling like devils booted up from Hell.

"WHY DO YOU THINK I was brought into the Trust?" the elder Kane demanded. "Because Baron Cobalt *trusted* me."

Kane stood, staring at his father without speaking. He had never been at such a loss for words. To be a Magistrate was to follow a patrilineal tradition; Magistrates assumed the duties and positions of their fathers before them. Mags didn't have given names, each one taking the surname of the father, as though the first Magistrate to bear the name were the same man as the last.

As Magistrates, the courses their lives followed had been charted before their births. They were destined to live, fight and die, usually violently, as they fulfilled their oaths to impose order upon chaos. Kane's life had taken another course, but he learned later he was only following the secret path laid down by his father. Or so he had thought.

"Why did you do it, son?" the older man asked.

Kane took a deep breath. "I did it because I had no choice. And because I did it, humanity now has a choice…or at least the chance of one. We won't have to be slaves to the barons or the hybrids any longer. Humanity can reclaim this planet."

The elder Kane snorted. "Humanity doesn't deserve this planet. Look at what we did to it. We were destroying the world before the skydark, breeding faster than flies. Humanity had to be culled, controlled. If the nukecaust hadn't come, we would've just wiped out our species by some other means. It was inevitable. Now we have to atone for what we did. Slavery to a higher form of life is humankind's penance. We've earned no better."

Kane snarled out a laugh. "Listen to yourself—you sound like a textbook definition of the baronial doctrine of unity."

"I don't know how I could have sired such a fool," the elder Kane said, his voice barely above a whisper. He glared at his son, rage building in his haggard features. "After seeing you and listening to you, I wish that you *had* killed me when you blew up the cryo section. All you've done is return chaos to a country that was finally dragging itself free of it."

Kane stared hard at the older man, his mind reeling. As reluctant as he was to acknowledge it, in some ways, his father might be right. But he wasn't going to admit it.

A cold, triumphant smile spread across his face as he looked at his father. "You know what, Dad? I can't argue with you about the chaos. But if I had the chance to do it all over again, I would. Me, Brigid, Grant—everyone in Cerberus has made a difference, more so than all the Mags who ever lived, ever did."

Sighing, the older man sat down on the edge of one of the destroyed stasis tubes. He leaned forward, placed his elbows on his knees and stared at the floor. Wearily he said, "I almost believe you, son. But there is no way that a handful of people can make any difference in the world. I'm living proof of that."

Kane gazed steadily at his father, feeling anger and compassion toward the man. He didn't want to leave him all alone in the facility, no matter what the man might feel about Kane's decision to join Cerberus. He wanted the chance to get to know his father, as he never had when the elder Kane was still in Cobaltville.

"Arguing about this is getting us nowhere," Kane said, offering his hand to his father. "I need to find the people I came here with, and then we can go to the mat-trans and gate out of here, back to Cerberus. We'll get you cleaned up and fed—"

The elder Kane grabbed the offered hand and pulled himself to his feet, and in the same motion, brought up

his right hand, slashing with his long, dirt-caked fingernails across the side of Kane's face. A white-hot
flare of pain brought tears to Kane's eyes, and he instantly let go of his father's hand and staggered back.

His own hand shot up to his face, and when he
pulled it back, he was shocked to see scarlet gleaming
on the tips of his fingers. He could feel the blood running down his cheek. Rarely had anyone managed to
catch him as flat-footed as this.

"Only one of us is going to leave this place alive,"
the elder Kane growled, holding a jagged chunk of
glass in his hand before him. He crouched low, in the
classic knife-fighting stance, the makeshift weapon
held before him. He smiled. "And, son—it's not going
to be you."

Kane hefted his nail-studded length of wood. The
thought of using it against his father awakened nausea
in the pit of his belly, and he tossed it aside. The older
man moved toward him, waving the splinter of glass
back and forth. He slashed at him with it, aiming low.

Kane was barely able to sidestep the attack. For a
man with such a sickly and wasted appearance, his father possessed the speed and agility of a Magistrate half
his age. He felt the tip of the glass dagger drag along
the left side of his shirt, parting the tough khaki as if it
were so much tissue paper.

Before his father could withdraw, Kane brought
down his elbow, smashing it into the man's forearm.
The blow almost missed, but the impact was sufficient

to throw the older man off balance for a second. Kane took advantage of that second, driving a hammer blow with his left fist against the back of his father's head.

The blow landed solidly and drove the elder Kane off his feet. He slammed into the debris-covered floor face first. The makeshift dagger flew from his hand. Turning off his emotions, Kane delivered a vicious kick to the ribs, lifting his opponent right off the floor and rolling him over a half dozen times before he came to a face-up stop, against the far wall near the exit.

His face and upper torso were a scarlet latticework of cuts and gashes, blood flowing freely from the open wounds covering him. He stared up at Kane, one lifeless eye a ruined, gelid mass, a chunk of glass embedded deeply into the eye socket.

Remorse and horror filled Kane like a cup, and blindly he stumbled toward the doorway. A hand shot out and closed like a vise around his ankle. Shocked into immobility, he saw his father, looking uninjured, grinning up at him savagely. Faintly, Kane said, "I thought you were dead."

"I am," the man said, pulling up on Kane's leg. "I thought you'd figured that out by now."

Kane landed hard on his back with a whoof of expelled air. The elder Kane bounced to his feet and laughed. "You ought to see the look on your face, boy. It's classic."

Slowly, Kane climbed to his feet, letting his battle instincts take over. He backed away from his father, putting a good dozen feet between the two of them. As he moved, he never took his eyes from the man's face.

With a whoop of malicious triumph, the elder Kane rushed forward. Kane stood his ground and met the charge head-on. Wrapping his arms around his torso, his father bodily lifted him off the floor and carried him straight through the open doorway into the corridor beyond. There he continued running, pile-driving Kane into the metal-sheathed wall behind him.

Agony blazed in Kane's body as the air was forced out of his lungs. He felt his rib cage cracking beneath the inhumanly powerful pressure that his father exerted. White spirals of light burst behind his eyes. In desperation, Kane brought up both his hands, cupped them and slapped them as hard as he could over both of the man's ears.

The twin concussions forced his father to loosen his grip slightly, but he cinched down again, forcing a grunt of pain from Kane's lips. Agony shot up and down his spine. The older man jammed the crown of his head against Kane's chin, forcing his upper body to bend over the encircling, pinioning arms. He knew his father's homicidal fury could break his back.

Cupping his hands, Kane smashed them over the man's ears again, using every iota of his strength. The elder Kane shrieked in agony as his eardrums imploded under the concussive pressure from the blows. His grip loosened and Kane fought his way out of the murderous embrace. His father stumbled a few paces away, clasping his head between his hands, gasping in shock.

Ribs and back throbbing, Kane bounded forward. He rained a flurry of blows on his father, pounding the older man in the midriff several times. Each blow forced the elder Kane farther back into the cryogenic suspension room. Physical pain fueled Kane's rage as he delivered jabs, right and left hooks, and side-fisted hammer blows to his father's face.

His flattened nose streamed blood, mixing with that flowing from his split lips. Kane delivered a snap kick to the pit of his opponent's stomach. He doubled over. Grabbing the back of his neck, Kane held his father's head in position and brought up his knee with as much force as he could muster. He not only felt, but also heard, the sickening crunch of bone as the elder Kane's jawbone shattered. The man dropped limply on his face and made no movement afterward, not even a twitch of fingers. Kane stood, catching his breath, glaring down at the motionless man. The kill-rage drained out of him, leaving him weary. He leaned against a cryo unit for a moment, hanging his head and panting.

Pushing himself erect, Kane painfully stepped out of the chamber and looked down the corridor, kneading the hot wire that felt as if it were boring into the small of his back. His head hurt abominably, as well, a pressure seeming to build in his forehead.

The pain grew worse as Kane quickly retraced his steps. His skull felt as if it were on the verge of flying apart. When he pushed open the double doors, his point man sense screamed loudly, overwhelming the fiery throb. Pivoting on his heel, he saw his father swinging the nail-studded length of wood at his head.

Kane shifted aside and avoided having his cranial bone perforated, but the club slammed into his left shoulder. The force of the blow nearly knocked him to his knees. The older man followed through with a straight-leg kick to the chest. The impact sent him slamming hard against the top rail of the catwalk and he toppled over it, arms flailing.

Somehow, he managed to grab the bottom crossbar. Kane hung there, his arms feeling as if they were about to tear free from their sockets. His whole body felt awash in waves of pain as he looked up at his father's unmarked face smiling genially down at him. He waited for the man to stamp on his fingers, or use the spiked club to maim and blind him.

A vision of Brigid flashed unbidden into his mind. Kane thought about all the things he wanted to tell her, to share with her, and now he would never have the chance. And then the memory was replaced by the elfin features of Quavell.

Quavell, he thought. Who is Quavell?

A maelstrom of confusion drove away the clouds of fear and pain. For the briefest of moments, his sight blurred and his surroundings shifted. Instead of looking down at a wreckage-strewed floor far below, he saw hard-packed earth only a couple of feet from his face.

The pressure in his skull abated. Then, as quickly as the vision had appeared, it was gone.

Feeling his grip weakening, Kane began to swing his body back and forth, trying to build up enough momentum to kick one leg up and over the edge of the catwalk. He was barely able to accomplish it. His father watched his struggles with an amused, almost affectionate smile on his face.

With one leg secure, and his hands still tightly gripped around the railing, Kane slowly heaved himself up, back onto the catwalk. His father allowed him to do so, not interfering or even speaking. Panting in pain and from the exertion, Kane leaned his weight on the top rail. Rivulets of sweat slid down his face and filmed his body, soaking into the fabric of his clothing.

The elder Kane casually slapped the makeshift club against his palm. "Almost lost you there, didn't I, son?"

"That would've been a pity." Kane's eyes, stinging with sweat, searched the vicinity for anything he could use as a weapon. "Same way you lost Mom, probably."

The smile left his father's face. Growling, he rushed forward, bringing up the spiked club. Leaning his weight against the railing, Kane lashed out with both legs, his feet connecting solidly with his father's chest. He staggered against the opposite rail and nearly went over it. He dropped the club and caught himself.

Shoving himself away from the railing, the elder Kane said, "Not bad, boy, not bad at all. You surprise me. I guess they trained you a hell of a lot better at the academy than I ever imagined."

The words struck Kane as strange. His father had years of experience on him. His eyes narrowed and once again, his surroundings seemed to flicker. The catwalk was abruptly replaced by rough-hewn stone, and instead of seeing his father before him, he caught a microsecond's glimpse of a bald, dark-skinned man. Then his father stood before him again, and the pain in his head increased.

The older man's eyes narrowed suspiciously. He snatched the club from the catwalk and swung it at Kane's head. He ducked the almost clumsy blow and backpedaled as quickly as he could. "Pretty pathetic, old man," he said with a taunting smile. "About what I would expect from a slagjacker in Tartarus, not a hard-contact Mag."

His vision blurred for an instant and when it cleared, he saw a dimly lit, stone-walled chamber. The pain in his head disappeared entirely. Kane bounded forward, his right hand lashing out to grab his father's wrist, his left driving deep into the man's solar plexus.

Except, it wasn't his father he had struck. The man's craggy face contorted in shock and pain as the wind was driven forcibly from his lungs. The club fell from his hand as Kane maintained his grip, squeezing his wrist with all of his strength.

Opet struggled, snarling in hatred, and his eyes flashed. Kane stared, astounded, wondering if he was hallucinating. Then the pain in his head returned, triple-fold. It felt as if molten lead were being poured into his brain. The sudden agony completely overwhelmed his ability to think, to move or even to scream. All around him, the tunnel strobed, flickering between the image of the decimated Dulce facility and the catacombs deep within the canyon of Aten.

Agony washed over every nerve ending, every cell like a torrent of lava, and he knew he was dying, the man before him was peeling away his mind, layer by layer.

Opet gently pushed Kane to his knees with his free hand. "You should never have come to Aten, outlander. You and the rest of your people are going to die."

Kane's head pounded as if pickaxes chopped away at the bone on the inside of his skull, and he knew Opet spoke the truth.

Chapter 25

All of the attackers swarming into the tunnel were armed with swords that resembled machetes with flat, oversize blades. The lamplight winked dully on the steel edges. Grant shouted a wordless warning, and it was met with a blood-chilling yowl from the cat-man.

He drove the point of his sword straight into the slant-eyed face of an imperial trooper. The man's visage dissolved in a crimson smear of ruined flesh.

Grant swept Domi to one side, his Sin Eater springing into his hand. He depressed the trigger stud, but it didn't budge, as if it had been welded in place. Squeezing with all his exceptional strength, the stud bit deep into his index finger, but it didn't depress.

Decard blurted, "Something's wrong with my blaster—"

Voice high and wild with fear and confusion, Domi struggled with her own pistol, clenching her teeth as she tried to fire it. "Mine, too! It's jammed!"

Erica's voice cut above the babble of voices and the animalistic growls of the creatures advancing on them.

"Telekinetic influence!" she cried, backing away from the ram-man. "Must be!"

Relaxing his wrist tendons, letting the heavy weapon slide snugly back into place along his forearm, Grant snapped to Decard and Domi, "Blades!"

The five attackers spread out across the width of the passageway. Domi drew her hunting knife with the nine-inch-long serrated blade, and Decard unsheathed his Mag-issue combat dagger. The tunnel was no place for a fight of any kind, much less one where razor-keen weapons fell like butcher's cleavers.

Grant took two steps forward and feinted as if to grapple the nearest of the human attackers, then he shifted position. He snatched at the baboon-man's machete. The feint didn't work out as well as he had hoped.

The Akhakhu's reflexes were a shade faster than a human's, and he had sufficient time to bring his deadly blade in a sweeping downward strike, but it failed to connect. Grant sidestepped and the razored edge just kissed the fabric of his sleeve.

Decard stepped up beside him and the two men grappled with him, trying to force his arms to his sides, opening him up completely to either of the two Akhakhu's weapons. Decard allowed himself to fall back, pulling the two men toward each other. They were forced to release his arms, or they would have collided.

The other two attackers weren't deterred. As Grant

regained his footing, the ram-headed man charged in, sweeping his sword in a figure-eight pattern before him, the flat of it striking Decard's knife and wrenching it from his hand. At the same time, the cat-man bounded between Grant and Decard, lunging for either Domi or Erica van Sloan.

Domi tucked and shoulder-rolled forward. The cat-man leaped straight up to avoid being clipped at ankle level. As he did, the albino slashed upward with her knife. The creature screamed in agony, clapping furred hands to his right leg, where the tendons had been severed. A geyser of scarlet spewed from between his fingers.

The felinoid fell onto his side, clawing at his maimed leg and screeching madly. Erica kicked him hard under the chin, closing his jaws with a loud clack. Consciousness went out of his eyes with the suddenness of a candle being blown out.

One of the skull-capped men took several steps backward and stared directly at Grant through half-closed eyes. As if someone had turned a dial in his body, the strength began to seep from his arms, replaced by a cold numbness. Grant heard himself mutter, "What the hell?"

Triumph glinted out of the dark eyes of the baboon-man. He shambled swiftly toward Grant, raising his sword over his head for a skull-splitting stroke. Domi's arm and wrist snapped out in perfect coordination of hand and eye. The knife smacked into the man's chest, the blade sinking into his clavicle. The impact drove him backward a few paces. His eyes popped open in pained surprise.

The numbness in Grant's arms suddenly disappeared. Snorting like a crazed bull, Grant rushed forward, meeting the baboon-man with a resounding crash, the machete blade striking the rock wall amid a little shower of sparks. The arms of both men automatically clasped each other, Grant's hand holding at bay the blade straining to decapitate him.

Grant gazed into the mad black eyes of the baboon-man and could smell his feral breath. They locked for a long moment in a quivering embrace, bracing themselves on spraddled legs.

Grant realized he had made a grave tactical error. The baboon-man was much stronger and more than his match in a strength-versus-strength contest. On impulse, Grant snaked a foot around his opponent's left knee, pulling forward with a hooked ankle. It cost him his balance, but the baboon-man's knee buckled at the joint.

Releasing his grip on Grant, the Akhakhu tried to catch himself and spring back. Grant maintained his grasp on the mutant man's forearm, using the elbow of his freed arm as a battering ram, whipping it forward, slamming it solidly into the hollow of his throat.

A gush of thick saliva foamed from the baboon-man's muzzle as he wrenched himself loose and threw himself backward, away from Grant. Snapping at air, the Akhakhu swung his sword in a flat, backhand arc. Grant nimbly skipped backward, then threw himself forward, shouldering the baboon-man down the tunnel, half lifting him from his feet. In the process, they bull-dozed right into the other skull-capped man.

The creature fell, dragging Grant with him, with the human insurrectionist crushed beneath their combined weight. He uttered a single squall of pain. They grappled savagely, rolling across the tunnel floor. The beast-man's canine teeth snapped for his face.

A hard, thin object chopped lengthwise across Grant's lower back, the force of the blow sending shivers of pain through his torso, very nearly smashing all the wind out of him. The baboon-man flung him aside and scrambled to his feet. Fighting off the instinct to curl into a wheezing, gasping ball, Grant wondered if his spine was severed.

The ram-man stood over him, both hands gripping a sword, and he lifted it for another downward stroke. Only his shadow suit had saved Grant from being cleaved in two, but his head was unprotected and the next chopping stroke of the sword would split his cranium like a melon. The ram-headed Akhakhu scuttled close, sword angled over his right shoulder, positioning himself for a decapitation. He laughed, an animal, guttural sound like the bleating of a goat.

The triumphant bleat suddenly became a gargling cry of pain. A blue-rimmed hole appeared magically above his right eyebrow and the back of his head broke apart. Through the pounding of blood in his ears, Grant heard that single, telling shot.

The ram-man fell backward, sword blade chiming against the stone. Grant turned to see Decard aiming his Sin Eater. "*Now* it works!" he exclaimed in a stunned, wondering voice.

The baboon-man blinked foolishly, his eyes darting from Grant to Decard to Domi. He sucked in a long, wet breath, braced his legs and said, in a hoarse, husky whisper, "*Shit.*"

Grant's Sin Eater sprang from the holster into his hand. The firing stud depressed under the pressure of his index finger. He caught only a fragmented impression of the surviving Akhakhu's distorted face flying apart—an eyeball bursting in a gelatinous spray, the fang-filled jawbones dissolving in eruption of bone splinters and liquid tendrils of crimson. Both Decard and Domi opened fire at will. The thunderous echoes of the triple fusillade rolled and rang.

The baboon-man careened away from the steel-jacketed barrage, body jerking and twitching under the multiple impacts. His bare, callused feet slid and rasped on the stone floor as the bullets directed him into the open portal in the tunnel. Heels catching on the edge, he fell unceremoniously onto his back, legs kicking spasmodically.

Domi rushed over to Grant and helped him climb to his feet. He regarded her with mild surprise and grunted words of thanks. Erica announced calmly,

"The two men were the psychokinetics. When their brain functions ceased, so did their influence over the firearms."

Grant squinted through the flat planes of smoke hanging in the air of the passageway. "I figured that out myself, Erica. And there's something else I just figured out, too."

Decard regarded him curiously. "What's that?"

Nudging the body of the skull-capped man who had been crushed against the tunnel floor, Grant answered quietly, "It wasn't a work crew Opet summoned. It was these bastards. And I sent Brigid off with him."

WITHOUT WARNING, the darkness enfolding Kane's mind changed. An even darker spot opened up in the space he considered to be facing him. He felt himself sucked toward it on gentle eddies. A cold ball formed in his stomach, not true fear, but a warning nonetheless. Instinct told him that if he entered that spot, only bad things would happen. However, he had no control over his own movement.

Then brightness entered the dark, chasing it away in peeled shadows. A woman's hand, followed by a slender arm clad in a sleeve of some shimmering material, thrust out of the darkness. For some reason, Kane thought a sword should be gripped in her hand.

A distant female voice breathed, "Kane, it's not time to leave yet. You're not finished."

With a titanic effort, Kane reached out for the hand,

grasping it tightly. The warmth flooded his body, chased away the deep cold that had frozen him from his bone marrow down to his very soul. The hand pulled, drawing him from the cloying darkness. He heard himself whisper, *"Anam-chara."*

The fear in him was suddenly, abruptly replaced by a torrent of rage.

"Lie down and die, Kane," he heard Opet say. "There's no shame in it. You've been bested."

The darkness receded and he squinted up at Opet, who towered above him, smiling down with an expression of smug malice. The priest stood on widebraced legs, his chest out.

"Go ahead," he urged. "Let's get this over with. Lie down and die."

"You first, asshole," Kane snarled, and delivered a swift uppercut. His fist tore right through the man's kilt and pulverized his testicles. As if a switch had been flicked to the off position, the pain in his head disappeared. He felt his heart begin to beat regularly and the blood flowed again through his veins.

Kane clutched Opet's testicles, squeezing as hard as he could. The priest howled in pain, but Kane maintained the hold. He had learned it many years before at the Magistrate academy. His martial-arts instructor called it Monkey Steals the Peach.

Standing, Kane didn't relax his grip on the man's privates. Opet's scream climbed to a high-pitched wail of pure agony, as Kane literally lifted the man off his feet. Only when he felt the tender flesh begin to tear from his opponent's body did he open his hand. By then, high priest Opet had passed out.

As he stood over him, breathing hard, a strange tickling sensation began at the back of Kane's head and rapidly grew more insistent. Some instinct told him he shouldn't fight the sensation, so he gave in to it. Then, with a shimmer, as of water passing over a dusty pane of glass, he saw Nefron in his mind's eye, as clearly as if she were standing before him. He not only saw her, but also heard her voice.

Well done, Kane, well done indeed. Opet's abilities were only slightly less powerful than my own. Perhaps there was no substantial difference between them now, since I trained him myself over a period of many years.

Kane looked down at the man at his feet, still seeing Nefron's face superimposed over the body. "He was the instigator of the insurrection?"

Yes, and now that he's been defeated, his followers will give up.

Drawing in a deep breath, Kane asked, "You knew it was him all along, didn't you? But you were afraid if you confronted him directly, you'd spark an outright revolution in Aten. That's why you wanted outsiders involved…as pawns and scapegoats, if necessary."

Nefron's amused voice caressed his mind. *I won't admit or deny those charges, Kane. But know this—if Opet's faction had succeeded in taking power in Aten, many people would have died. Not just here, but in the outside world, as well.*

Kane took a deep breath and looked around the chamber. He could see another exit from the antechamber he had jumped into when the roof caved in. "So the struggle was all in my mind?"

And heart and soul, as well.

"What about the others? My friends?"

They are fine, never fear. They are close by. You can rejoin them whenever you wish.

Instead of leaving the chamber, Kane slowly sat down, leaning against the rock wall. He felt completely drained, thoroughly enervated. Hoarsely, he said, "I'm so tired."

Nefron replied breezily. *Of course. The kind of combat you've engaged in is exceptionally taxing, even for those experienced in it. Take your time…you're safe now.*

"So you helped me defeat Opet?"

He sensed Nefron's sudden surge of puzzlement. *Why do you ask that?*

"Because a woman extended her hand to me…pulled me out of the darkness…"

That wasn't me, Kane.

"Then who—?"

"Kane!" He heard the swift scuff and scutter of running footsteps. Before he could rise, Brigid Baptiste appeared in the doorway, disheveled and out of breath. Her penetrating emerald gaze swept over the unconscious Opet on the floor, then fixed upon Kane's face.

"He was the ringleader, wasn't he?"

Kane only nodded, realizing with a distant sense of surprise that Nefron's image had vanished from his mind. Brigid approached him cautiously, eyeing him. "Are you all right? Are you hurt?"

He shook his head. "No. Yes. I don't know."

Brigid carefully eased down beside him. "Do you need medical attention?"

He hung his head. "I don't think so, Baptiste."

She laid a hand on the back of his neck. "Do you want to tell me what happened to you after the cave-in?"

Kane gusted out a heavy sigh. "Opet got into my mind and used some of my memories against me."

"How so?" Brigid asked quietly.

"I was back in the Dulce facility, just after we had accidentally destroyed it. I found—" Kane stopped speaking.

"Found what?" Brigid asked, but already she was reviewing the possibilities in her mind. She thought she might know already what Kane was referring to.

The destruction of the Archuleta Mesa installation had wrought profound changes over the small band of exiles in Cerberus, some more so than others, as in Domi's case. Before the incident, the albino girl's hatred for the hybrids had bordered on the pathological, but after the short period of time she had been a captive in the Area 51 facility, and had learned about the infant deaths, her attitude had drastically changed. She had even forged a strong bond of friendship with Quavell, which had grown even stronger after Domi, Brigid and Shizuka had fought Sam's forces together at Mount Uluru in Australia.

Kane, too, seemed somehow different after his time there. Lifting his head and staring at the senseless Opet, Kane declared matter-of-factly, "I saw my father."

The simple statement hit Brigid with the power of a sledgehammer. Kane almost never talked about his father. The last time he had even mentioned him was right after the destruction of the Dulce facility. However, she knew he had never really gotten a chance to know the man.

"Kane—" She started to reply, but he held up his hand.

"It's all right, really, Baptiste, I guess he's been on my mind for a long time. I know that he probably died when I firebombed the cryostasis section a couple of years ago. I tried not to think about it…but maybe there was a chance we could have saved him."

Brigid nodded in understanding. "We both know there's no percentage in dwelling on maybes or might-have-beens. You did what you figured was right at the time. You always do what you think is right, even if the consequences aren't easy to live with."

For several long seconds Kane stared at her, not quite sure if he should take offense at what she had said. He knew that at least once, his impulsive actions had caused her a great deal of pain, and although it was forgiven, he suspected that it would never be forgotten.

"So, what happened when you met him in your mind? Did you talk?"

Kane hesitated, then decided to open up to Brigid, unlike so many times in the past. "We talked a little…while we tried to kill each other."

Brigid's stolid expression didn't register surprise or dismay. She only smiled encouragingly. As he spoke, she listened quietly, not interrupting or asking any questions.

Finally, Kane took a deep breath and blew it out through his nose. He rubbed the heels of his hands over his stinging eyes. "That's it. When I finally broke through Opet's mental control and realized what was going on, I put an end to it."

Brigid laid her hand on his. "Kane, it didn't really happen. It was all just an illusion, that bastard playing on your misplaced guilt. I know the memories can't be easy to deal with, but you've got to always remind yourself, it didn't happen. Your father really didn't try to kill you, it was only images Opet fed into your mind." She squeezed his hand as hard as she could.

Kane chewed the inside of his cheek, mulling over her statements. At length he said, "Okay, I'll be fine." His chest heaved as he sighed. "Like a lot of other things that have happened to me, it's just going to take some time, time to come to terms with all of this. It felt like I was trapped in the facility for hours."

Brigid nodded contemplatively. "By my calculations, I doubt you were under Opet's influence for more than ten minutes, if that. It was evidently quite a struggle for Opet to maintain his control over you… that's why he left us, to attend to you directly. If I hadn't been following him, we might never have found this hidden passage."

"And if you hadn't found it," Kane said quietly, "I might not have found my way out of the nightmare Opet had forced me into."

She cocked her head at him quizzically. "I don't understand."

He smiled wanly. "Never mind, Baptiste."

Their eyes locked, but neither one spoke. The sudden, peremptory clearing of a throat caught both people's attention. Together, they turned, Kane tensing his body like a bowstring. He relaxed when he saw Decard standing in the doorway, a knowing smile on his face.

"Hope I'm not interrupting anything, but we've still got an insurrectionist leader to locate."

Brigid waved grandly to the prone, unconscious form of Opet. "Not any longer. Compliments of Kane."

Decard squinted in the direction of her wave. "Opet?"

"None other," Kane replied smoothly. "After today, if his sect has a choir, he'll be able to join the soprano section."

The young man looked startled and then curious, but apparently decided not to ask for details. Kane really couldn't blame him.

Chapter 26

Kane stood before a smiling Nefron. He was back in the audience chamber surrounded by a huge gathering of citizens. Word had spread through the city like wildfire about the defeat of the insurrection. Beside him stood Grant, Domi, Brigid, DeFore, Lakesh and Decard.

In the hours since the final battle in the catacombs, Erica van Sloan had slipped out of the city, barely stopping long enough to give her regards to the queen. Kane felt relief that the woman hadn't tried to talk to him or congratulate him. He knew that sometime in the near future, the Cerberus warriors would encounter Erica and Sam again, and it would more than likely not be as allies, even of convenience.

The queen of Aten stood and held up her hands to silence the crowd. "Citizens of Aten, you may rest easy. Thanks to the efforts of our new friends in our city, my reign is secure once again."

An uproarious cheer engulfed the assembled outlanders. Kane felt distinctly uncomfortable. He wasn't used to so much attention or approval. In his years as a Magistrate, once he had donned the armor and the badge of his office, he had become a faceless component of a powerful machine, and had ceased to be an individual. In his work with Cerberus, he and his friends had only rarely been appreciated. Resented and occasionally even feared among those they had helped, they'd never met such overwhelming approbation.

Nefron waited until the cheers ebbed away before continuing to speak. "This incident, as unfortunate as it has been, also marks a new, more hopeful chapter in the history of our kingdom." She paused for dramatic effect, then announced, "After today, we will no longer hide ourselves from the rest of the world. We will open our arms and hearts to the other villes, offering what assistance we can, in exchange for whatever they may be able to offer us in return. If the baronies wish to treat us honestly and openly, we will reciprocate. But if they bring violence to our city, then I have been assured we may count on the aid of the imperator."

Kane felt shock and a sinking sensation in the pit of his stomach. He exchanged swift, grim glances with Brigid, Lakesh and Grant. He knew he should have realized that Erica van Sloan would not have simply left Aten with only dead troopers to show Sam. She had wrangled an agreement from the queen in return for fighting the insurrectionists.

Kane couldn't really fault Nefron for making such a deal. Even with the power of the insurgents broken, there were factions among the citizenry who still opposed Aten coming out of hiding after a century. No doubt if another uprising threatened the throne, Nefron could call on imperial forces to help her put it down. Sam had the resources to protect Aten, and Cerberus didn't.

The queen continued to speak to the gathering for nearly half an hour, outlining her vision of how the future would change the city, how trade would begin with the nearest of the Outland settlements. But at the end of her speech, she also warned that the transition period wouldn't be an easy time, and the wrong tactic could lead to a possible conflict with one or more of the nine baronies.

When she was done, she blessed those gathered and turned away from the crowd, leaving the throne. In small groups, the gathered people exited the chamber, filtering out slowly, talking excitedly among themselves. As the crowd passed by, they patted Grant's and Kane's shoulders and kissed the hands of Brigid and Domi.

Grant looked over at Kane, his lips creased in a wry smile. "And I thought that some of the lectures Lakesh gave us were dull."

Lakesh glared at Grant and then couldn't help but chuckle when Domi slugged the big man on the arm. "Show him a little bit of respect," she scolded. "The queen was lots more dull."

Grant's perpetual scowl returned, but his eyes twinkled. "I stand corrected."

"So," DeFore asked, "now what?"

"I guess we wait," Lakesh answered. "It's the queen's turn to fulfill her side of the bargain."

"If she decides to keep her word," Grant said, crossing his arms over his massive chest.

Decard overheard, and spots of red appeared on his cheeks. "The queen is a woman who would never go back on her word, unlike some Mags that I've known."

If Grant was bothered by the young man's defense of the queen, he didn't show it. He looked down at Decard dispassionately. "If you say so."

Sensing a potentially violent encounter brewing, Kane stepped between the two men, shooting a warning glance at his longtime friend and partner, and placing one hand on Decard's shoulder. "We'll wait for word from the queen."

Lakesh cleared his throat, glancing into the faces of all the people from Cerberus. "I'm very proud of all of you, you know. You put your lives on the line once again."

Kane shrugged uncomfortably. "We did what had to be done, no more, and no less."

In a surprising gesture, DeFore slipped her arms around Kane's waist, stood up on tiptoes and kissed him tenderly on the lips. "I'm sure that both Quavell and the baby will thank you for it. And so do I."

Domi giggled, and Grant actually broke into a tired smile, as well. Mavati came around the base of the pyramid and approached the gathered group. "Her Highness will see you now."

She led them into an adjoining chamber and they found Nefron sitting comfortably on a padded bench, looking as regal as always. She remained seated, even after they had entered. Two Incarnates stood on either side of the entrance, *metauh* rods held crosswise across their chests.

Without preamble, Nefron declared, "You've done me a great service, and I will give you the medical equipment and supplies that you need."

Lakesh bowed his head, folding his hands before him. "Thank you, Your Majesty."

"That's a lot of stuff for us to lug across the desert to the redoubt," Kane said doubtfully.

Nefron shook her head. "I've already had the equipment collected and crated. A caravan is waiting for you to join it."

"There are some perishable drugs we can use, but we'd be putting them at risk by carting them across the desert, even after dark," DeFore said hesitantly.

"Perhaps one of us can gate back to Cerberus, or contact Philboyd and have them bring a Manta here," Lakesh said. "The drugs that are at risk could be easily and swiftly transported back to Montana."

Brigid nodded in agreement. "Maybe that would be for the best, besides, it would mean sticking around here for a little longer."

Domi shrugged. "I wouldn't mind."

Glancing over at Grant, Kane saw that the man was not enamored of the idea. He was impatient to get back to Shizuka. He said, "Using a TAV isn't a bad idea. We can properly refrigerate the drugs and fly them back to Cerberus in pretty short order." Addressing Grant, he said, "And I can drop you off at New Edo, if you want."

He noticed Domi bristling slightly, although after all this time, the outlander girl had seemed to come to terms with the relationship between Grant and the leader of the samurai. He knew that she was still hurt, but she had retreated into Lakesh's arms, and she seemed to be quite content with that.

"What are you going to do with the insurrectionists?" Lakesh asked.

The queen met his stare evenly, unblinkingly. "They will be dealt with in a manner that befits their crimes." The tone of voice Nefron used made it very clear that Lakesh should not press for more information. Wisely, he nodded in respectful acknowledgment.

"All of you are more than welcome to stay here for as long as you wish," Nefron said quietly.

Rising from the bench, she strode among the group, kissing each one ritualistically on the forehead, even though both Grant and Kane had to bend their knees for her to perform that action.

"And when you leave," she said, "know that you may return any time you wish. I consider you citizens of the kingdom-city of Aten and accord you all rights and benefits."

"Does that come with an old-age pension?" Lakesh asked, smiling.

Nefron nodded gravely. "It does indeed. One I hope you will take advantage of, if the time ever comes."

Epilogue

The terrain around the Archuleta Mesa looked as dead as the most bleached-out pumice plains Kane had seen on the Moon, or the endless desert wastes on Mars. The coarse dry sands had been baked for centuries in the unremitting blaze of the sun.

The thorny scrub brush crowning the rocky hills was the only sign the New Mexican Outlands had ever harbored even rudimentary life. Huge boulders of limestone thrust up from the desert floor, like the grave markers of long-dead giants.

As it had done for thousands upon thousands of years, the gargantuan rock formation stood a silent vigil, a tombstone looming over the crypts of dead aeons.

The glaring yellow orb of the sun had already dropped halfway behind the mesa, while the other half was draped by a thick stratum of fleecy clouds.

Kane sat in the cockpit of the Manta, staring out over the seemingly endless terrain that overlay the now abandoned Dulce complex. To the untrained eye, it appeared as if there had never been any signs of habita-

tion in this remote, desolate locale. Animal life and
nocturnal predators began to stir. Far overhead, a lone
eagle soared majestically, riding the thermals still rising off the sands from far below.

Kane removed his helmet and opened the canopy.
The hot desert air invaded the climate-controlled cockpit, causing beads of perspiration to form on the exposed skin of his face. He didn't wipe it away, since he
had sweated a lot over the past couple of days. It had
taken only a few short hours to load up the necessary
medical supplies into the Manta's small, hermetically
sealed cargo hold and deliver them to Cerberus.

Brigid had opted to stay behind in the redoubt and
help inventory the material when Kane announced that
he was going to take the Manta once again for a short
flight.

He could still picture the knowing, compassionate
expression on her face as she wished him clear skies
and swift sailing. There were times that he could have
sworn she was telepathic, much like the citizens of the
great city they had just left. When he asked if she
wanted to come along, she had only smiled and said,
"This is something you have to do on your own, Kane."

Kane climbed out of the cockpit, jumped the last
couple of feet to the desert floor and walked in the general direction of the Archuleta Mesa. He glanced back
at the metal-sheathed craft that held the general shape
and configuration of a flattened javelin head, not much
more than a wedge with wings.

The resemblance of the ship's contours to that of a sea-going manta ray was more than superficial resemblance, particularly with its pair of extended, down-and-incurving wings. The wingspan was around twenty yards and the fuselage fifteen. An ace-of-spades-shaped rudder tipped a short tail assembly.

The hull appeared to be made of a burnished bronze alloy. Covering almost the entire surface were intricate geometric designs, deeply inscribed into the metal itself. There were interlocking, swirling glyphs, the cup-and-spiral symbols, even elaborate cuneiform markings. The hull was smooth, with barely perceptible seams where the metal plates joined.

The craft had no external apparatus at all, no ailerons, no fins and no airfoils. The cockpit was almost invisible, little more than an elongated symmetrical oval hump in the exact center of the sleek topside fuselage.

The eagle flying overhead cried out mournfully, as it glided higher and higher into the fading light, lamenting the realization that neither Kane nor the Manta ship was suitable prey for it and perhaps a nest full of hatchlings.

Trudging over the sandy surface, Kane topped a rise and quickly located what he had been looking for, nearly a quarter mile to the east. To the naked eye, there was nothing to see but a broad depression in the surface of the desert, a sinking of the bedrock perhaps. But Kane knew the depression marked gigantic doors that had once opened to a hidden underground hangar. From there the hybrids, doing the bidding of the barons, dispatched the Aurora stealth craft to collect human organic material in order to prolong the barons' lives.

After the crash of the Aurora, the twisted wreckage had been painstakingly removed, and the most visible signs erased, lest it attract the attention of the wandering nomads or Roamers who might be able to find their way through it into the installation itself.

It took Kane several minutes to walk up to the lip of the depression. When he reached it, he noticed that even though it had been just a little over a year since the destruction of the facility, the desert had already done its best to bury all signs of it. Kneeling, Kane scooped up a handful of sand and let it sift through his gloved fingers, forming a tiny mound at his feet.

He glanced up at the mesa, its long shadow inching across the barren ground toward him. The significance of the ancient rock formation was not lost on him. In most ways, the Archuleta Mesa represented a mile marker on the journey of his life. His service as a warrior in the cause of human freedom, instead of human slavery, had begun in the labyrinth beneath the enormous monolith of stone. His father's life had ended upon the same day his new one began.

Kane reflected that his second visit had truly turned the mesa into a tombstone, looming over the mass grave of thousands. But out of that inadvertent act of devastation and near-genocide had grown the beginning of a new life, perhaps even a new life-form, the child carried by Quavell.

Again, the eagle's cry echoed through the diminishing light, and much to his surprise, the magnificent bird landed on the opposite side of the depression. It stood perched on top of a boulder protruding through the sand.

Kane stood, and from the slit pocket of his shadow suit, he removed a small, flat object and held it in his hand, allowing the last remaining rays of sunlight to play over its smooth, polished surface. It was the badge of the Magistrates, the symbol of baronial power, of unity. He, Grant and his father had worn ones like it for many years.

Glancing over at the bird, and then at the sunken ground before him, he said softly, "Dad, I'm sorry that we never had a chance to really get to know each other. If I'd known of the work you were doing with Cerberus, maybe I could have saved you. Maybe by taking up that work for myself, I did save you, in a way. I guess I'll never really know."

Kane turned the badge over in his hand, running his fingers over the nine embossed spokes of the wheel surrounding the representation of the scales of justice. "We all make decisions," he said in a whisper. "Some of them are good, most are bad, seems like. I've made a lot of decisions over the years, and some of the bad ones will haunt me until the day I die. I don't want my decision to destroy you…what was left of you, to keep the barons from feeding off you, to be one of them."

Again, he stared down at the badge. He remembered the first day he had donned the Magistrate armor and strapped the death-dealing Sin Eater to his forearm, and he recollected clearly his sense of pride as he stared at his imposing reflection in the mirror. He couldn't remember anything he had ever seen before shining as brightly and as powerfully as that small red badge had done that day. He couldn't know for sure, but he had always hoped he had made his father proud when he became a full-fledged Mag.

But he hoped his father took far more pride in him now, even when so many things had changed and his whole world had been turned upside down.

He held the badge up toward the Archuleta Mesa, letting the last vestiges of the sun glint off its surface. "To your memory, Dad. To all the Magistrate Kanes."

Kane heaved the badge into the twilight sky, watching it as it arced up, then descended, vanishing into the shadows of twilight. Turning his back on the depression and the Archuleta Mesa, he marched back to the Manta ship. He wasted no time climbing back into the cockpit, sealing the canopy and settling the control helmet over his head.

Closing his hand around the joystick lever, he pulled it back slightly, then pushed it forward. It caught and clicked into position. The hull began to vibrate around him, in tandem with a whine, which grew in pitch. On the inside of his helmet flashed the words: VTOL Launch System Enabled.

With a stomach-sinking swiftness the Manta lifted upward. The humming drone changed in pitch as the aircraft rose as smoothly as if it were being raised on a giant hand made of compressed air. The helmet's HUD displays offered different vantage points of the ascent, and Kane's eyes flicked from one to another. He watched as the monolithic mesa and the barren wasteland surrounding it receded so quickly, they became mere ripples of contrasting texture and color.

The last shimmer of daylight disappeared beneath the horizon. The Manta rotated majestically to the northwest, before lancing across the sky, trailing a sonic boom.

Far below at the edge of the depression in the desert, the eagle took flight, as well. For a moment, it wheeled above a small red badge, half buried in the sand, then it soared high into the sky to search for its evening meal.

Readers won't want to miss
this exciting new title
of the SuperBolan series!

Don Pendleton's Mack Bolan®
Zero Option

Zero Platform is about to become the first
orbiting weapons system operated by human/
machine interface. Its command center has
been razed to the ground, but the person
willing to become the first human prototype
of bio-cybernetic engineering survived the
attack. Now Doug Buchanan is running for his
life, a wanted man on three fronts: by
America's enemies determined to destroy
Zero's capabilities, by traitors inside
Washington plotting a hostile takeover of the
U.S. government and by the only individual who can save
Buchanan—and America—from the unthinkable.

Available July 2004 at your favorite retail outlet.

Or order your copy now by sending your name, address, zip or postal code, along with a
check or money order (please do not send cash) for $6.50 for each book ordered ($7.99 in
Canada), plus 75¢ postage and handling ($1.00 in Canada), payable to Gold Eagle Books, to:

In the U.S.
Gold Eagle Books
3010 Walden Avenue
P.O. Box 9077
Buffalo, NY 14269-9077

In Canada
Gold Eagle Books
P.O. Box 636
Fort Erie, Ontario
L2A 5X3

GOLD
EAGLE®

Please specify book title with your order.
Canadian residents add applicable federal and provincial taxes.

GSB97

DEATH LANDS®

Death Hunt

*Available September 2004
at your favorite retail outlet.*

Ryan's razor-sharp edge has been dulled by the loss of his son Dean—but grief is an emotion he cannot indulge if the band is to escape the chains of sadistic Baron Ethan. Now with the group's armorer, JB Dix, imprisoned and near death, Ryan and the others are forced to join Ethan's hunt—as the hunted. But the perverse and powerful baron has changed the rules. Skilled in mind control, he ensures the warriors will not be tracked by high-paying thrill seekers. Instead, they will hunt each other—to the death.